FINDING *Mr. Purrfect*

ALSO BY CODI GARY

A Cat Café Christmas

FINDING Mr. Purrfect

CODI GARY

FOREVER

NEW YORK BOSTON

This book is a work of fiction. Names, characters, places, and incidents are the product of the author's imagination or are used fictitiously. Any resemblance to actual events, locales, or persons, living or dead, is coincidental.

Forever
Hachette Book Group
1290 Avenue of the Americas, New York, NY 10104
read-forever.com
@readforeverpub

First Edition: January 2024

Forever is an imprint of Grand Central Publishing. The Forever name and logo are trademarks of Hachette Book Group, Inc.

Library of Congress Cataloging-in-Publication Data

Names: Gary, Codi, author.
Title: Finding Mr. Purrfect / Codi Gary.
Description: First Edition. | New York : Forever, 2024. | Series: Cat Cafe
Identifiers: LCCN 2023031134 | ISBN 9781538708187 (trade paperback) |
ISBN 9781538708200 (ebook)
Subjects: LCGFT: Romance fiction. | Novels.
Classification: LCC PS3607.A782976 F56 2024 | DDC 813/.6—dc23/eng/20230711
LC record available at https://lccn.loc.gov/2023031134

ISBNs: 9781538708187 (trade paperback), 9781538708200 (ebook)

Printed in the United States of America

LSC-C

Printing 1, 2023

To my editor, Alex, for her infinite patience and help making this manuscript better.

FINDING
Mr. Purrfect

CHAPTER ONE

Purrfectly Buttery Shortbread Cookies

These deliciously delectable squares come six to a plate and can easily be shared with friends.

Charity Simmons removed her gloves and tossed them into the nearest trash can, surveying the trays of square cookies she'd been prepping all morning. When she'd decided to take a vacation to Mexico for the holidays, Charity pictured days of lounging by the resort pool or even the beach, being served fruity drinks while reading several of the paperbacks she'd brought along. She'd done that every afternoon during her stay—after getting up early and making her way over to the large industrial kitchen to help prepare breakfast pastries and sweet treats for the resort guests.

It was ironic that a baker from the US would go on vacation to relax and recharge, only to offer herself up as tribute like Katniss Everdeen in *The Hunger Games* when she overheard hotel staff talking about losing their pastry chef the day after Christmas. She'd been by the pool at the time, trying to focus on a psychological thriller, and her ears perked up at the mention of baking. Thanks to three years of Spanish in high school and a year in Spain after college, Charity was proficient enough to catch the gist of the rapid-fire conversation between the manager and her assistant. She'd stood up and approached them, offering her assistance during her stay or until they managed to find a replacement. It had taken some convincing, but the manager accepted her help. She hadn't slept in late a single day, but that was what naps were for.

Besides, relaxing wasn't exactly Charity's MO. She liked staying busy, and being in the kitchen gave her an excuse to avoid other people, especially men. Maybe it was the tragic state of her love life or that she would be thirty-three in a month, but hanging out and partying all night with a bunch of strangers didn't sound at all appealing. This trip was supposed to be Charity and her best friend, Kara Ingalls, following the love of Kara's life to Mexico so she could profess her love for him. Instead, Kara and said love, Ben, decided not to go to Mexico, and they headed for Boston to spend the holidays with his family, leaving Charity alone on vacation.

Well, technically not alone. There was Schwartz.

Of course, he was a viable option to hang with. Ben's best friend was in the same boat as her, ditched at the last minute in pursuit of true love and familial reconnection, but while she'd found something productive to do during her vacation, she'd caught glimpses of him swaggering around the resort, and usually not alone. There was something about his Clark Kent vibe that drew the women to him like bees to a flower. He did smell good, and he was funny to boot, but she had no interest in playing third or fourth wheel as he reeled in women left and right.

Not that Charity was interested in Will. Any man using his wiles on unsuspecting females and breaking hearts all over the place didn't sit well with her, especially given her dating history. He was just her type.

When they'd first met, Will had been flirtatious and charming, two characteristics she'd recognized as red flags when it came to men. It had taken her about fifteen years to see it, but from her first date at sixteen, Charity had an annoying habit of being attracted to womanizing, cheating, stealing, lying bums, and even when she thought they might be different, they always proved her wrong. And while many women might say they had the worst taste in men, it was *really* true in Charity's case. Even if the company may have eased her loneliness a bit, the last thing she needed to do was hang with a man Charity knew was bad news.

"Charity, these look delicious!" Loretta Guzman gushed, coming around the table from the lobby's entrance to the kitchen. Her dark hair was pulled back from her face, and her wide smile spread warmth throughout Charity's chest. She loved when people appreciated her work.

"Thank you. The staff can dip one half in chocolate and use the edible sprinkles and glitter for the New Year's Eve party tonight. I make them at home for my café, but I imprint them with a cat's paw." Just the mention of her beloved cat café, Meow and Furever, sent a shot of longing to the pit of her stomach. She was ready to be home with her cat, Robin Hood, and Kara.

"I cannot tell you enough how appreciative we are of you helping out. Not many guests would have given up hours of their time." Loretta linked her arm with Charity's. "And to truly show our appreciation, we have a surprise for you."

Charity started protesting even as Loretta steered her toward the door. "Oh, you don't have to do anything! You already comped my room when you really didn't have to."

"Nonsense. It's because you gave up your time without asking for anything in return that we wanted to do this for you." Loretta took a pathway to the right, her arm still linked with Charity's. "I wanted your last two nights with us to be truly special. Although I'm glad we were able to hire another pastry chef, I will miss you, and I know the staff feels the same way."

Charity could never get enough words of affirmation and beamed at Loretta's praise. "I'll miss you all, too. Especially working in your kitchen. You've given me so many ideas to improve Meow and Furever's setup and create more productivity for the catering side of things."

"I'm happy we've given you inspiration for your business."

Although she and Kara had plans to expand Meow and Furever's bakery to include a full catering service, they'd only managed to raise enough to complete the renovations on the low-cost veterinary clinic Kara would run. They'd almost lost their beloved cat café before Christmas because they didn't have enough money coming in to keep them afloat. Thanks to Ben and Will's marketing skills, they'd pulled off an amazing fundraising event, bringing in enough money to finish the low-cost clinic Kara wanted. Charity could be patient about building a bigger kitchen, but it didn't hurt to get ideas on how best to set it up and what equipment was essential. Especially if Charity was chosen as a contestant for *Bake That*, the number one reality show on television. She'd sent in her audition tape and sample recipes in November, and she should hear within a week or two about whether she was chosen. It was both nerve-racking and exhilarating.

They passed through a gorgeous garden with fragrant flowers and a bubbling fountain that fed into a deep koi pond. The orange-and-white fish wiggled through the water, drawing closer to the edge as if waiting for them to toss food to them.

"I haven't been on this side of the resort."

"It's usually kept private for our guests staying in our bungalow suites." They broke through the gorgeous greenery, and Charity spotted a line of stilt houses backed up against the stone wall of the resort. Each door was painted a brilliant color, and Charity glanced at Loretta when they stopped in front of number four.

"What are we doing here?" Charity asked.

"This will be your home for the next two nights," Loretta said, holding out a key. "I've arranged for someone to help you carry your bags over as soon as you are done packing up your room."

"I—this is too much. I'm fine in my room!"

"It isn't too much. This one had a last-minute cancellation, so no one is booked to stay here until you leave. Please, accept this gesture from your friends at the Grand Mar Resort."

Charity took the key from Loretta, stunned. "I still think this is too much, but my mother always told me it was rude to refuse a gift given graciously."

"Your mother is a wise woman," Loretta said with a smile. "Feel free to inspect your new accommodations, and a staff member will be waiting for your call when you're ready to move." With a nod, Loretta spun on her sensible flats and headed back toward the garden and the way they'd come.

Charity gripped the key in one hand and the wooden banister in the other, climbing the stairs. As she drew closer to the canary-yellow door, she noted the front balcony of the bungalow wrapped all the way around to the back. Instead of heading inside, she followed the wood planks around to find that it overlooked the resort's private beach. Waves crashed against the sand while people sunbathed and played in the water, the view something out of a '60s beach movie. She turned her back to the scene and retrieved her phone from her pocket, snapping a selfie to text Kara.

Wish you were here.

Charity's phone rang instantaneously, and she answered the video call laughing. "Well, hi!"

Kara smiled at her on-screen, Charity's tabby cat, Robin

Hood, on her lap. "Hey! How is Mexico? It looks beautiful, but you're still coming home, right?"

"I am. I was thinking today how I can't wait to be back. Plus, I miss that big guy. Hi, baby."

Robin Hood got so close to the camera that all she saw was his nose, and then it went dark, the loud rumble of muffled purring coming out of her phone speaker. Suddenly, Robin Hood disappeared, and Kara's face came back into view. "Wow, you miss this food-thieving tyrant and not me?"

"Of course, I miss you." Charity settled into one of the yellow deck chairs and asked, "What's going on there?"

"Your mom called me," Kara said.

Charity tensed. "What did you say?"

"That I hadn't had a chance to talk to you."

"I thought you'd tell me something good, like we got a giant, anonymous donation that would pay for a new kitchen."

"Sorry, babes."

Charity released a long, heavy breath. "It's going to be bad, isn't it?"

Kara smiled ruefully. "It won't do any good to worry about it now, will it? You've already missed the holidays with your family, and you have two more nights in paradise. Might as well enjoy them."

Charity knew her bestie was holding back on the extent of her conversation with her mother and could only imagine the tirade Kara had been forced to listen to, but she didn't press her further.

"I want to hear about Boston," Charity said, in an attempt to distract herself, but Kara shook her head on-screen.

"When you get back, we'll have fun catching up. I just wanted to show you proof of life, but Ben is waiting on me. I can't wait for you to get back."

Charity laughed. "So, I can crash all your dates?"

"Absolutely. This is your home."

"I think Ben might have something to say about that, but I love you for it."

"Love you. Safe travels."

She stared out at the waves as they crashed onto the beach, her mind drifting. Instead of canceling the trip when Kara had gone to Boston, Charity decided being alone for the holidays would be more fun than enduring awkward dinners where her parents constantly criticized her, compared her to her older siblings, and attempted to play matchmaker with men they thought were appropriate for her to date. While some of them were nice enough guys, she'd taken on the role as family rebel long ago and wasn't about to conform now.

Had she handled everything with her parents like a child, instead of the adult she was? Perhaps; but if she really thought about her life, she'd been doing the same thing with everyone. Avoiding confrontation. Running away from her problems. She needed to grow up, but not today. Or tomorrow. Charity planned to enjoy Mexico before she headed back to reality and all the crap she was going to get from her parents and siblings.

Her phone beeped, and she checked the notification, wincing when she saw it was a text from her sister, Billie.

You need to call Mom and Dad. They are freaking out. None of us have heard from you since Christmas.

Charity stared at the message for several seconds, debating on how to respond, before she finally took a breath and typed.

I left them a voice mail telling them I was going out of town. They called Kara to interrogate her. I'm constantly posting on social media, and I'll be back the day after tomorrow. So why, exactly, are they freaking out?

Her sister responded instantaneously.

Because you're not talking to them, and they are worried about your mental state.

"Oh, for the love of—" Charity said aloud, tapping the call button. She'd take the international call rate to tell her sister her mental health was just fine.

Billie answered after the first ring. "Hi."

"A bit dramatic, don't you think?"

"Is it? You skip out on the holidays with your family with just a voice mail and no other communication."

"Excuse me for wanting to enjoy my vacation."

"Charity, being an adult means owning your decisions and dealing with the fallout."

Charity clenched her jaw, thinking it was easy for her perfect, married sister to tell Charity to take her medicine. Their dad worshiped Billie, raved about her, whereas he introduced Charity to people as, *"Still figuring things out."*

"I'll deal with the fallout when I'm back in town, but until then, I'm going to enjoy the sunshine and the New Year's Eve party I'm hitting tonight."

"Charity?"

Charity froze when her mother's voice registered, and Charity planned to murder her sister and make it look like a painful accident when she returned.

"Hey, Mom. How's it going?"

"Better if my daughter hadn't taken off to another country in order to avoid spending the holidays with her family."

She counted slowly in her head. "Like I said in my voice mail, it wasn't about you—"

"That is a little hard to believe given the circumstances and that you called your sister, but you can't return one of my or your father's calls?"

Charity gritted her teeth, knowing her mother wasn't wrong, but could she really blame Charity for not wanting a bunch of grief heaped on her?

"I'm sorry, Mom. Kara asked me to go with her, but I'd be lying if I didn't admit the thought of spending the holidays being set up on awkward blind dates by my parents factored into my decision to go."

"I don't think wanting to see you happy with a stable, successful man is something to run away from."

"I'm not running. I'm on vacation."

"Alone! Kara went to Boston instead of going with you, and you still went."

"Yeah, I did."

"Is that all you have to say?" her mother snapped.

"At the moment, yes. If you want to hash this out when I get back, fine, but I've got to go, Mom. This call is going to cost me a fortune."

Her mother's voice softened, twisting the knife of guilt in her chest. "Be safe, sweetheart. I love you."

"I will. I love you, too."

"Sorry, Sis!" Billie hollered.

Charity pressed the end button before she said something to her sister she'd regret. Her stomach knotted with anxiety as she processed the conversation. Her entire childhood, she'd known the score. Her older brother, Anton, was the golden boy with a bright future, following in their father's footsteps. Her sister was an up-and-coming political genius and never stepped a toe out of line.

Charity came along as a surprise and ultimate disappointment in their picture-perfect family.

She climbed out of the chair and went around the front to open the bungalow. While reality was just a plane ride away, Charity wasn't ready to go back there yet. The last eight days had been like living a fantasy life, without any stress or financial obligations.

When she unlocked the door and stepped inside, all the anxiety of what waited for her melted away as she took in the open suite with a soft-looking king-sized bed. To the left was a cloudy glass partisan that she slipped through to find a luxurious bathroom with a deep soaking tub.

Oh, yeah. Reality could definitely wait.

CHAPTER TWO

The Cat's Meow Peanut Butter Cookies

These melt-in-your-mouth cookies pair well with an oat-milk latte and a chubby cat on your lap.

WILL SCHWARTZ STEPPED OFF the elevator, his flip-flops slapping against the short carpet in the hotel hallway as he sucked down the fruity cocktail he'd made during mixology class. He'd booked this vacation with Ben thinking they would drink and have fun and bond, but he didn't begrudge his friend going to see his family at Christmastime.

It had been a busy week of poolside lounging and flirting with gorgeous women, which should sound fun, but it was exhausting. He hated having to put himself out there constantly just so he wouldn't have to be standing around like a friendless loser. While he adapted over the years and acquired the skill to engage people in conversation, it was a learned behavior and not his natural personality.

When Will was an awkward gawky teen, he'd preferred playing Dungeons and Dragons with a few friends to hitting the latest party with a bunch of people who loved to torment him. By the time he was a senior, Will learned that the only way to survive was to make people like him. He changed his personality, his clothes, and he'd put all his favorite things into the dark recesses of his closet. Nowadays, people didn't hide their nerd side quite the way they used to, and he was glad for it. Unfortunately, many still tended to gravitate toward big personalities that were always-on, and being in marketing meant *he* always had to be on, too.

Which was why he'd been seriously considering leaving his job at Kilburn Marketing and starting his own graphic design firm. While he loved working with Ben and creating art for clients, Will hated the marketing side. The schmoozing. The presentations.

Unfortunately, he didn't know how to tell his boss that after ten years, and he didn't want to think about it now. This was his first vacation in over a year, and even without his wingman Ben, he hadn't wasted a minute of it.

And yet he couldn't wait to get back to reality.

Staying in this tropical paradise all alone just made him realize how lonely he was. Granted, he wasn't looking for marriage, but it would be nice to have somebody to go out with on a Friday night. A date to take to a friend's wedding or even just enjoy a quiet night at home with, snuggling, eating bad snacks, and watching a movie.

Unfortunately, every woman Will had gone out with expected an engagement ring, and that was just something he wasn't willing to give. Not because he wasn't capable of commitment. He'd had a few lengthy relationships over the years, but he didn't think a signed contract and a piece of jewelry more expensive than his house payment was necessary to stay true to one person.

Will opened the door to his hotel room with his key and, once he pushed it open, stepped over the threshold and closed it behind him. The room was cool and smelled like fresh linens and ocean, thanks in part to the open window on his fourth-floor balcony. He kicked off his flip-flops and pulled his shirt off, fully intending to hop in the shower. He had plans to go to the New Year's Eve party tonight, alone once again, because hooking up with a stranger on vacation might sound fun but it wasn't his style.

He stepped out onto the balcony and took in his view of the pool and the edge of the garden. A couple strolled through the greenery hand in hand until the man suddenly dropped to one knee in front of the woman. Her hands flew up, covering her face and most likely muffling her cry of joy based on the emphatic "yes" she screamed. Several nearby onlookers clapped and cheered as the couple embraced, kissing without a care in the world.

If Will was the killer of dreams, he could bump into that guy later and show him a financial spreadsheet of all the ways that one romantic gesture would impact his life for however long the marriage lasted. That every decision was now tied to another person, and he no longer had any independence or real choices. His fate was sealed, good or bad.

Will's stomach roiled in panic at the thought. Why couldn't a relationship be two people with completely different names and separate bank accounts choosing to be faithful to each other without having every aspect of their lives tied together?

The two girls he'd been hanging with by the pool briefly were flirting with a couple of beefed-up men with military cuts. While they'd seemed like nice twenty-two-year-old women, he wasn't what they were looking for. Will figured that out within ten minutes when they'd propositioned him to a little adventure, and he'd politely declined.

A familiar form caught his eye, coming out of the garden, and Will recognized Charity practically skipping past the pool area toward the front of the hotel. While he'd seen her around the resort a few times, she'd seemed absent from all the late-night events. Otherwise, he would have noticed her, along with every other man. She was too gorgeous to miss.

From the moment he'd met Charity, Will recognized what an amazing, passionate woman she was. He'd experienced an intense, instant chemistry with her, and briefly, he'd thought maybe there was something between them. Since about mid-December, however, Charity had been chilly, and he didn't understand what had triggered her aversion to him. He'd thought they were at least acquaintances, if not friends, but she'd avoided him since they'd boarded the plane to Mexico.

Charity's cold one-eighty still stung. One minute they were laughing about their friends' obvious attraction to each other and the next, he barely got a hello. He'd tried to give her back the same energy, but it was hard because he genuinely liked Charity, and with their mutual friends in a relationship, they saw a lot of each other. If nothing else, Will wanted to discover whatever he'd done to offend her and bury the hatchet. Maybe he could catch her later and buy her a drink.

Will pushed off the railing, stripping his way to the shower. Vacations were supposed to be about lessening stress and drama, not seeking it out, but sometimes, you had to take the bull by the horns and get it over with.

He finished showering and returned to pull clean boxers from the dresser in his room. Will thought about taking a nap before the party, but he was too wired to sleep. He threw on the board shorts and a fresh T-shirt before picking up his phone from the bedside table where he'd left it charging this morning. Since international calls were so expensive, it didn't make sense to keep it with him. Although, he should video call his mom to wish her a happy New Year's Eve.

Will pressed the video call button and sat on the bed, waiting for her to pick up.

His mom's smiling face filled the screen. "Hi, honey! How is your vacation?"

"Hey, Mom. It's busy. I just got back from a mixology class. I can now make a pretty mean Moscow mule."

"Sounds fancy. I think I'll stick with my mimosas."

Will laughed. Since both his sister and Will had moved

out, they got together every Sunday for brunch and mimosas. They'd sit around for hours, talking about their week. When his dad was alive, he'd usually convince Will to work on the car they'd rebuilt together while his sister and mom gossiped, but he hadn't touched an engine since his dad had been gone. Turned out, he liked mimosas, too.

"Tell me what else you've been doing at that all-inclusive resort. Met any women?"

"Not something I want to talk about with my mom, thanks."

She rolled her eyes. "I just want someone for you to ring in the new year with. I imagine there are a lot of single women there."

"And their relationship status isn't going to change because of me."

"Spoilsport," she muttered.

"Why would you want me to meet a woman on vacation? What if I fall madly in love and she lives in Australia? Then I'm living in Australia, far away from you."

"No, because you would never live in a place where every animal could kill you," she said, making Will laugh. "So, she'd move to California."

"That's a big ask for someone she just met, Mom."

"You don't have a romantic bone in your body."

"You're probably right," he chuckled. "Maybe that's why I'm single."

"You're single because you won't settle down. Look at Theresa! She was perfect for you."

Will snorted. "How can you say that? She set my Xbox on fire!"

"Because you told her you'd rather marry that machine than her."

"That's not actually what I said—" Will sighed, waving a hand in front of the camera screen. "Mom, this isn't something I want to rehash—ever—but especially not when I'm in Mexico and supposed to be having fun. So, I'm going to sign off and head out."

"All right, I'm sorry. I just love you, honey."

"I love you, too. Happy New Year's Eve. See you soon."

Will ended the video call and fell back onto the bed, taking in a deep, soulful breath. He ran both hands over his still-damp hair, staring at the white ceiling, the disappointment in his mom's voice echoing through his mind. He knew that she wanted him married and making the next generation of Schwartzes for her to spoil, but he wasn't ready for that. Not for kids and maybe never for the married part.

Pushing himself up, Will shook his head, speaking aloud in the empty room. "No, we're not doing this. I have a day and a half left before I return to reality, and I'm not wasting a minute of it."

Will climbed off the bed, and after slipping into his flip-flops, he grabbed his wallet and left the room. He whistled his way down the hallway, pushing all the heavy stuff away. Maybe he'd take a walk on the beach, breathing in the scent of the ocean.

He pressed the lobby button on the elevator and watched

the numbers above light up as it descended from the sixth floor. When the metal doors opened, Will hesitated for a moment when his gaze caught Charity's. She was the only person inside, standing in the corner with three suitcases surrounding her.

"Hey," he said, stepping onto the elevator and leaning against the right wall, facing toward her. "What's going on?"

"I'm switching rooms."

He shouldn't respond to that, just escape the elevator and move on with his day, but whether it was curiosity or residual interest in her, he didn't think he could leave it at that. "Why?"

"I won a contest," she responded, her lips twitching like she'd made a joke.

"Congratulations."

"Thank you. I'm excited."

Her friendly tone gave him pause. There had been moments of teasing, of playful banter and charged interactions between them, and he thought... Well, he'd tricked himself into thinking several times that Charity might be into him. Only each time, she'd managed to disappear, and Will figured he'd misread the situation.

His gaze trailed along her tall, curvy frame, and his throat squeezed. Will knew he should bury this attraction to Charity into the deep, dark space inside himself where other impossible hopes go to die, but from the first moment he'd seen her behind the counter of the Meow and Furever Cat Café, it was like being slapped in the face. Her dark, smooth skin stretched over high cheekbones and those thick, fanning lashes obscured her obsidian eyes as they swept over him in warm amusement at his flirting. She'd had her hair out of the way that day, but down here? Her thick hair fell around her shoulders in tousled waves, and if possible, she was even more beautiful.

"I haven't seen you much," he said.

"Really?" she drawled out. "Maybe you weren't looking in the right places."

There was that sharp tongue. Will smirked. "You're hard to miss."

"I'll take that as a compliment," she said, smiling. "You seem to be doing fine without me hanging around."

Will shrugged. "It's nice to see a familiar face. I'm getting tired of introducing myself and having to explain why I'm alone."

"You could be like me and avoid people." The doors opened, and she struggled to gather up all her baggage handles, wheeling them toward the door.

He stretched his arm out, holding the door for her. "You're skipping the party tonight?"

"Probably. New Year's Eve is for individuals who want to party and find someone to kiss at midnight."

"Not necessarily. I'm going because I look dang good in a tux and have few excuses to wear one."

Charity laughed. "I bet you do look good."

The way she said it made his heart pick up speed, and he

wanted to tease her, to ask her to elaborate, but he didn't want to scare her. This was the first easy conversation they'd had in weeks.

Besides, she was already several steps ahead of him before he could collect his thoughts, the littlest suitcase wobbling and twisting on her arm, when she called back, "Have fun tonight."

Will couldn't stand watching her struggle and caught up to her in a few strides. "Do you mind if I help you with those? They look like they're running away from you."

Charity ducked her head. "I was supposed to call down for someone to help me, but I didn't want to bother anyone."

"You're not bothering me at all."

Her dark eyes met his briefly, before she pushed the smallest one his way. "Thanks."

Will snorted and took a hold of the two larger cases, wheeling them away before she could protest. "No problem."

Will heard the rush of her feet behind him and grinned, making his way through the automatic doors. Charity fell into step beside him as two employees came around the corner and their faces lit up as they spotted her.

"Charity, I need your peanut butter cookie recipe. There was a stack in the staff lounge, and we only got one apiece."

Will shot a glance toward Charity, who was beaming. "Of course! I'll make sure I leave it with Loretta."

"Thank you," the younger woman said, casting an interested glance Will's way before she dragged the other woman along with her, giggling behind them.

Charity rolled her eyes. "Do you ever get tired of leaving swooning females in your wake?"

"Don't change the subject. Why does the staff have access to your peanut butter cookies and not me?"

"Because I've been working in the kitchen."

Will almost stumbled in surprise. "What?"

"They lost their pastry chef the day after Christmas, and I offered to help out."

Will wasn't sure what to say at first. "That was awfully altruistic of you."

"To be fair, this upgrade is a thank-you from them," she said, turning down a sidewalk and past a sign that read "Private." "I didn't ask for it, but they insisted."

When Will got a look at the bungalows, his jaw dropped. "Man! Can I stay with you?"

"Not a chance," she said with no real heat. "Thanks for the help."

"Don't you at least want me to carry them up the stairs for you?" he asked, watching her grunt as she lifted the smallest one onto the first step.

"No thanks. I got this."

"Okay, well, have a good night. Maybe you'll change your mind about the party?"

"Probably not," she groaned, launching the suitcase up two steps.

Will had no idea what possessed him, but he called after her, "I'm in room 404 if you change your mind."

CHAPTER THREE

Doughn't Pet Me Bagels

These saltwater bagels are so fluffy and delicious that you'll want to swallow them whole, but watch out for the jalapeño. It has quite the bite.

CHARITY SANK DEEPER INTO the soaking tub, taking a deep, blissful breath as the hot water covered her from the neck down. Her hair was piled above her head so she wouldn't get it wet, and the cheerful melody of "Walking on Sunshine" played from her phone speaker and echoed off the bathroom walls.

This is the life.

After Will had disappeared earlier, she'd regretted refusing his offer of help. By the time she'd managed to drag the last of her bags up the stairs, every muscle in her body hurt. When he'd offered to carry them up the stairs, she was still reeling from the easy way she'd fallen back into playful flirtatiousness with him, and it freaked her out. Especially when he'd started asking about the New Year's Eve party tonight. It almost seemed like he'd been inviting her to be his . . . date.

Which she wouldn't have accepted if he'd asked anyway, because Charity didn't want to give him the wrong impression. Will was a womanizer, and she wouldn't be another one of his conquests.

Without a date, she'd stand out like a sore thumb if she went. Men would think she was after one thing, and it wasn't as if she could just throw herself in with another group of women. That would be really awkward.

Still, in two days, Charity would be headed back to California, and she hadn't done anything but bake in the kitchen, lounge around, and sleep. It could be fun to dress up and go to dinner and do a little dancing, even if it was by herself.

Her eyes popped open as she realized all this arguing within her head was ridiculous. Her first instinct had been the wise decision.

Someone was knocking rapidly on the front door, and Charity sat bolt upright in the tub, water sloshing over the rim a bit. "Just a minute," she shouted, using the side of the tub to stand up and grabbing a towel off the shelf on the wall. She dried off her legs and feet swiftly and wrapped it around her body before padding across the tile floor.

Charity rushed to open the door and found a petite woman holding a basket in one hand and a garment bag over her shoulder with the other.

"Good evening, Ms. Simmons. This basket is compliments of the resort and this"—she held out the garment bag—"is from Mrs. Guzman. She hopes you enjoy yourself at the party tonight."

Charity took the garment bag and stepped back, allowing the woman to enter the room and leave the basket on the table against the wall. She didn't bother telling the woman that she'd opted against attending the party, studying the garment bag curiously. When the woman turned around to face Charity, she clasped her hands in front of her. "Will there be anything else, ma'am?"

"No, thank you, but just one second." Charity hurried into her room to pull a five-dollar bill from her purse and returned, holding it out to the employee.

"Thank you, ma'am. If I may say, you're going to look beautiful tonight." The woman closed the door behind her, and Charity took the garment bag into the bedroom, laying it across the top of her bed. She unzipped it slowly, her breath hitching as she revealed the glittery silver gown inside. Charity picked up a note pinned to the top of the garment bag with a sparkling black masquerade mask and read it, smiling.

Have an enchanted evening. Resort Staff

A warmth spread through Charity's chest as she removed the dress from the garment bag and hung it on the back of the door, checking the tag inside. How did Loretta know her size? She stepped back and admired the deep neckline and mermaid hem, her mind inventorying the jewelry she'd brought and what would go best with the gown, suddenly excited for the party.

Charity dropped the towel to try on the dress. She'd been

sticking to her plans to avoid men for weeks, enjoying her me time and taking the opportunity to reset her priorities. One night out in a gorgeous dress wouldn't jeopardize that.

Once she'd put on a strapless bra and a pair of matching panties, Charity stepped into the dress, sliding it over her body. Once the zipper was all the way up and the dress in place, she moved in front of the full-length mirror in the corner and smiled, feeling like Cinderella before the ball.

Slipping off the gown and hanging it back inside the garment bag, Charity put on a tank top and a pair of lounge shorts. She padded out to the living room to study the contents of the basket. Some fruit, nuts, and cheese and a bottle of champagne and two flutes. There was a bag of jalapeño bagels and a block of cream cheese tucked off to the side, along with a box of gourmet chocolates. She'd mentioned to Loretta that nothing woke her up faster in the morning than a jalapeño bagel, and it warmed Charity's heart that she had remembered.

Charity busted into the basket and prepped a bagel, taking a bite with gusto. She picked up her phone in her other hand and found her Good Mood playlist on Spotify. A little upbeat music and something good to eat put her in the right mindset as she danced around the bungalow to "I Wanna Dance with Somebody," which was serendipitous considering Charity was teetering on the edge of calling Will. Despite her reservations about his behavior with women, he was a fun guy that she knew well enough to trust not to get pushy if she laid out clear rules regarding tonight.

Charity dialed the front desk and asked for room 404.

Will picked up on the second ring. "Hello?"

"Hi, it's Charity."

"Ah, I knew you'd come around."

Charity groaned. "Ugh, I'm hanging up now."

"Wait, wait," he begged between bouts of laughter. "I was kidding. Don't go."

Charity hung on the line without saying anything.

"Hello?" he asked.

"Are you done being cocky?"

"I don't want to lie, so I'm going to say pretty sure."

"Good enough," she said, clearing her throat. "I've been thinking about what you said earlier. About going to the party. I don't really want to go alone and was hoping that maybe you'd be my wingman."

"Like help you meet other men? Ouch."

Charity felt her face burning. "I meant just being my friend. Someone to eat and converse with, maybe dance."

"Could be fun. I've been bummed because I spent this vacation alone. Going to classes alone. Pools. Bars."

Charity snorted. "Please, it's not like you were lonely. I saw you around the resort, and you've gotten plenty of attention."

"You've been watching me, Charity?" he teased.

Her face burned. "I said I saw you. Noticed. Barely glanced in your direction."

"Really? That explains a lot because your assumptions about me are wrong. Yes, I met people. I talked to them. I even danced with a bachelorette party until two in the morning the Saturday after we arrived, but I don't do random hookups with strangers on vacation. And being a single dude on vacation alone? It makes me look like a creep."

Charity chuckled. "I don't know what's worse, your situation or mine."

"What do you mean?"

"A single woman on vacation? Men look at me and think I'm asking for their attention when, really, I just want to finish one book. I've been so busy with the café and catering deliveries and moving and life that I haven't had a chance to just be, you know? I could be wearing a shapeless cover-up and they'd still think I was giving off a *come here, big boy* vibe."

"It could also be that you're a beautiful woman, and they can't understand why you're here alone."

Charity wasn't sure how to respond. People had been telling her how beautiful she was her entire life, but just because someone was attractive didn't mean they couldn't struggle when it came to love. Being with someone long-term had very little to do with outside appearance and everything to do with trust and compatibility. While she'd thought several times over the years that she might have found someone she could stand to spend her life with, it was the trust part that was a continuing problem for her. Either they were insanely jealous and didn't trust her or she discovered their deceptions. Either way, the relationships crashed and burned.

"Sometimes it's just easier to be on my own," she whispered, turning away to look out at the sea.

"Easier than what?" he asked.

Charity let out a huff. "You're like a dog with a bone. Anyone ever tell you that?"

"Not in those words, but something close to it." Will cleared his throat. "Still want to be my plus one tonight?"

Charity swallowed. "You want to go with me?"

"Will you make sure I get back to my room all right? You know, since you won't share your cottage."

"You don't want to stay with me," she said, her stomach fluttering at the thought of Will coming back with her.

Nope, you shouldn't be reacting that way. You're on a break from men, especially players like Will.

"Oh, really? Why is that?"

"I have rules for men who stay at my place and if they break them, they're likely to meet a terrible fate."

"I'm dying to know what these rules are that could leave me bleeding out in a bathtub due to a black-market kidney harvest gone wrong."

"When did I say black-market kidney harvest?"

"It's the worst fate I could think of."

"You obviously don't watch enough ID. I'd make it look like an accident."

"Push me down the stairs?" he queried.

"Too suspicious. Maybe you slip in the shower. Conk your head."

"I don't know how I feel that you've thought about how to kill someone and get away with it."

"Don't you know?"

"Know what."

"Men watch sports for comradery. Women watch true crime together."

"I'm rethinking if I'll be safe with you tonight."

"Now, why would I kill you before you broke a rule?"

Will chuckled. "Because I might say something stupid."

"Hmm, true."

"Hey, all joking aside, whatever I did to upset you before we arrived in Mexico, maybe we could call a truce for tonight?"

Charity didn't bother telling Will it wasn't him, but the type of guy he was, because he had a point. She deserved fun, and Will was fun.

"Maybe we could. As for my rules for guests, it's the common rules women have for men. Put the seat down when you finish and, if you miss, clean it up."

"I wouldn't expect you to clean up, even if I did miss, but to clarify, would you want the lid down, too?"

"No! Absolutely not. If you put the lid down, I will be so enraged, there will be no careful planning to cover up your murder. It will be a crime of passion."

"Okay, dramatic, but at least I know where you stand. I do have one follow-up question."

"All right."

"What is women's obsession with the toilet seat?" he asked.

"I can't speak to all women, but I hate stumbling to the bathroom in the middle of the night to go and fall into the toilet because someone forgot to put it down."

"You don't look before you sit?"

"No, because I'm drowsy, and it's usually dark. I'm not expecting a snake or spider to bite me in the butt."

"Yeah, I still check for spiders. Not a fan." Will cleared his throat. "I mean, I am very manly and not afraid of anything."

"Good to hear." Before she could overthink it, Charity said, "I'll be ready at seven. Should I meet you there?"

"No, I'll come to you. And Charity?"

"Yeah?"

"I'm glad you called."

Her heart lodged in her throat. *This might be a mistake.*

CHAPTER FOUR

Better than Catnip Three-Cheese Panini

This ooey-gooey masterpiece will warm you from the inside out. Pair it with one of our delicious soups for the perfect winter meal.

WILL JOGGED UP THE steps at ten minutes to seven, debating on whether he should hold off knocking. Most of the women he'd dated didn't appreciate him showing up early, but he hated being tardy to anything. Not that this was an *actual* date. It was... He wasn't sure how to describe it. Will couldn't call them friends. Acquaintances who didn't want to be alone?

If he were being honest, Will still couldn't believe she'd called him. If someone had told him he'd be taking Charity Simmons out for New Year's Eve two weeks ago, he wouldn't have believed it. He'd thought about their earlier conversations throughout the day and found himself smiling, anticipating spending the evening with her. Will didn't know what had happened to her here in Mexico, but things between them were lighter than they'd been in weeks. No walking on eggshells or tension today after the initial elevator ride, and it made him look forward to tonight. When they'd first met, Will remembered thinking that, if nothing else happened between them, at least they could have fun together. If they could get back to that, Will would be a happy man.

"Sometimes it's easier to be on my own."

The sad way she'd said it tightened Will's chest with empathy. He couldn't imagine any man treating Charity poorly, but from some of her previous offhanded comments, Will knew her love life hadn't been a basket of kittens. At least for tonight, he could chase away the hurt in her tone with a little dancing and, hopefully, a whole lot of laughter. Charity had a great laugh.

Will took a breath and knocked on the cabana door, shuffling in his squeaky dress shoes. The door opened slowly, revealing Charity, and he forgot to breathe. Her curls were pinned back on one side of her head. Dangling earrings dropped from her earlobes, flashing through her dark curls on the other side. The neckline of the dress dipped, and Will's gaze followed the line of her body to the floor where the hem hid her feet and then back up to her obsidian eyes.

Charity smirked and pointed to the side of her mouth. "You've got a little drool here."

Her joke broke him out of his stunned silence, and he wiped a hand over his mouth before revealing his grin. "Can you blame me?"

"Not at all. I spent a lot of time putting myself together, and that is exactly the reaction I want."

From me? Or every man?

Will didn't dare ask the questions aloud, especially since he had no reason to be jealous. Tonight wasn't about him wooing Charity. His only goal was to have a good time and make sure she did the same.

Her gaze drifted over him, and her smile widened. "Dang it, you do look good in a tux. And no glasses tonight?"

"Contacts."

Charity shrugged. "I think you're handsome either way, but there is something about the Clark Kent look that seems to make all the ladies swoon."

"Except you," he said.

"My knees may wobble a bit."

Was she blushing? Will's chest puffed out a bit at the thought, and he held out his arm for her. "Should we head over and see how many more men we can slay?"

"I'm really not interested in slaying anyone." Charity took his arm, giving it a squeeze. "I want my efforts appreciated, but I'm going to eat, dance, and make merry."

"Sounds like a plan to me." Will helped her down the stairs, and when they reached the bottom, Charity kept a hold of his arm. He couldn't deny loving the warmth of her palm through his tuxedo sleeve, and as they strolled down the quiet pathway, the murmuring of people grew louder.

When they exited the garden, the poolside patio was

crowded with people in formal wear, the sound of music echoing from the open doorway of the ballroom entrance. Two men in suits who Will towered over stood on either side of the doors like sentries, barely flicking a glance their way as Will and Charity crossed over the threshold and into the darkened event. Lights from two circular balls dotted the walls and people inside as they danced, ate, and mingled. It reminded him of his senior prom, the only dance he'd ever attended, minus the crepe paper and tacky photo booth.

"Oh, I want to check out the dessert table," Charity said over the music, tugging on his arm.

"Before dinner?" he teased.

She arched a sculpted eyebrow. "Are you food shaming me?"

"That's not a thing."

"It is a thing. And it's rude."

"I would never. I love food. Show me the goods!"

"That's better," she said, her mouth twitching.

Will allowed her to lead him to the table and studied the array of treats with her. Charity picked up a small pie with fruit on top and took a bite, licking crumbs from her lips. "Hmm, perfect. The trick to a good fruit tart is adding a touch of lemon juice to the custard."

"I prefer chocolate to fruit desserts."

Charity held the dessert out to him. "Try it."

Will didn't hesitate, consuming the rest of the tart. The buttery crust combined with the fruit and sweet custard was definitely tasty, and he nodded approvingly. "Not bad."

"I'm surprised you ate after me."

"Why?"

"Some people are weird about eating after people."

"If I've thought about kissing you—" Will realized what he'd started to say and cleared his throat, avoiding her wide-eyed gaze. "I mean, I've got a hearty immune system. Germs don't scare me."

"Um, that is not what you were going to say. Something about kissing me."

"Yeah, we don't need to go into that."

"We don't? I think avoiding it is just going to make things weird tonight. You should probably come clean."

Will met her twinkling gaze and shook his head with a rueful grin. "I was going to say, if I've thought about kissing you, then I'm not scared of eating after you."

A smile teased her glistening lips. "You've thought about kissing me, huh?"

"Have you seen you? Of course, I have."

Charity laughed. "Normally, I'd call you out for that line, but I'm okay with over-the-top compliments today. I'm all about it so keep 'em coming."

"Your wish is my command." Will took her hand, nodding toward the closest bar. "How about a drink and some real food?"

"Yes, please."

The line for the bar moved incredibly fast considering how many people were in attendance, and once they had their drinks in hand, Will steered Charity toward an empty table at the back of the room. He set his drink down on the table and pulled out her chair, waiting for her to take a seat.

"You're really pulling out all the gentlemanly stops tonight," she said, sitting in the chair he offered and setting her drink to the right on her dinner placement.

"Might as well show off all the spiffy manners my parents instilled in me."

A server rushed over the minute that Will sat down next to her and asked their dinner preferences. They both chose the chicken Alfredo with a Caesar salad, although Will joked about craving a grilled cheese.

"You'd really rather have that over chicken Alfredo?"

"If it was your three-cheese panini, and a cup of red pepper bisque, absolutely. One of the best things I've ever put in my mouth."

Charity straightened in her chair. "Thank you."

Alone again, Will shifted in his seat so he was facing Charity. "Do you regret taking this trip?"

Charity shrugged. "Yes and no. It's nice to get away and forget about reality for a while. I just wish I wasn't alone the whole time."

Will sipped his whiskey thoughtfully. "You could have hung out with me."

Her gaze flicked his way briefly. "I was actually trying to avoid you."

"Oh, I knew that. I'm trying to figure out why, though. Do I offend?" he quoted Duckie from *Pretty in Pink* and sniffed himself.

Charity grabbed his arm with a laugh. "Stop it. No, it's... you might not have been the only one thinking about kissing, and I didn't think it was a good idea."

Will grinned. "You've avoided me for weeks because you didn't think you could resist me?"

"That's not what I said. I just didn't want to give you the wrong impression. I'm not interested in romance, especially the fleeting kind."

"Who said I'm interested in romance?" Will asked.

Charity rolled her eyes. "Exactly."

"Wait, now I'm confused."

She turned in her chair to face him, leaning closer. "You might not have been sleeping your way through the resort, but I don't think you're looking for monogamy, either."

"I'm not looking for anything when it comes to relationships. Those I like to take day by day." Charity took a drink instead of responding and Will had a feeling she'd had a snappy comment on the tip of her tongue, so he pressed her. "Why aren't you interested in romance?"

"Because I have a terrible habit of choosing the wrong guy. I can't trust my libido or my heart." The server came by and filled their water glasses. She waited to continue until he was gone, waving her hand dismissively. "I don't really want to bring down the mood talking about this."

"I get that, but my two cents? Sometimes talking about what's bothering you diminishes the power it holds over you."

Charity hesitated, and he waited. "Every time I'm drawn

to a man, it ends in disaster. I figured my instincts must be broken. Apparently, it's me. I'm broken."

"Why does it end in disaster? Because the relationship doesn't work out? That's life and part of dating. It doesn't make you broken. It makes you human."

"Well, this human wants to meet a steady guy with a kind heart and a great personality, who I share a mutual attraction with, and who is not already seeing someone else, lazy, or a liar."

"That doesn't sound hard to find, especially for someone like you."

Charity arched a brow. "Someone like me?"

"Smart. Gorgeous. Successful."

"Right, I'm so successful. We almost lost the café, and I need more money to keep the catering side up and running. Oh, and I'm back living with my college roommate in her house."

Will took her hand, holding it between his own. "I've never heard you belittle yourself before, and I don't like it. You're going to repeat after me."

"Will—"

"Uh-uh, no arguing. Say, 'I am a catch.' "

"I am a catch," she mumbled.

"Louder."

Charity laughed. "I'm a catch."

"I deserve the best."

"I deserve the best," she echoed, smiling.

"I'm going to take Will out onto the dance floor and challenge him to a dance battle."

When she burst out laughing, Will beamed, his mission accomplished.

"I won't do that," she said, standing with her hand still in his, "but I do think we should get out there and shake off this downer conversation."

Will let her lead him onto the floor, but he didn't think the conversation had been a downer. If anything, it had been enlightening, giving him a better understanding of Charity and her behavior toward him. If she thought he was some jerk who only thought of himself, he was going to prove her wrong.

CHAPTER FIVE

Cattitude Fruit Tart

This sweet dessert will remind you of your favorite calico. Even when they're a little tart, you still want another.

CHARITY'S STOMACH HURT FROM laughing, and it was the best ache. They'd been on the dance floor for twenty minutes, and while they'd had to nearly shout to be heard over the music, their conversation had gone from the depressing state of her love life to his funny anecdotes about his failed relationships. Between his tales of dating misadventures and random wacky dance moves, she'd been dying.

"Wanna grab another fruit tart on our way back to the table?" he asked breathlessly. "The server probably came by with our dinner and wondered where we got off to."

"Aha! I knew you were going to like the fruit tarts. Chocolate schmocolate."

"Hey, I can like other desserts and still believe chocolate is the GOAT."

"Goat?"

"Greatest of all time, or in this case, the *t* stands for treats."

Charity laughed in spite of herself. "You're a nerd."

"I dated a con man who used to call me that."

"Really? I thought you were straight."

Will chuckled. "I meant con woman. I met her on a dating app. She was great at computers, the only thing she didn't lie about, and opened several credit cards in my name before I found out. Luckily, she couldn't completely obliterate my credit. It did make me wary of dating apps."

"Last guy I met on a dating app had a pregnant girlfriend. So yeah, I don't trust those, either."

They stopped at the dessert table, and Will picked up two tarts, handing one to her. "Wow, that sucks. How'd you find out?"

"She showed up at the restaurant where we were eating. Dumped my drink on me and not him."

Will shook his head. "I'll never understand that reaction." He took a bite of the tart, and a smear of cream lingered on his lips for a moment. Charity found herself focused on his mouth until he licked it away. Her face flushed with heat, and her gaze darted around, looking anywhere except his mouth.

"If my girlfriend was out with another man," Will continued, oblivious to her discomfort. "I'd be upset with her, not the dude."

"Girlfriend? I didn't know you had those. You've called them 'women you've dated.'" Charity used her free hand to make quotation marks with her fingers before taking a bite of her tart.

Will grinned, pulling out her chair for her. "Well, when I get one."

"You tend to flirt... a lot," she said, taking her seat.

He didn't answer right away, as if considering whether she may be right. "I guess I do, but I'm a single guy. If I was with someone, that wouldn't happen."

"Could you help it? I think it's second nature to you."

Will frowned as he sat down next to her. "I'm a friendly guy, but there is a difference between being nice and flirting. I'd never do anything to make my partner uncomfortable, and I'd make sure she knew I was fully committed to her."

Why did the deepening in his voice kick her heart rate up a notch?

A man and a woman who appeared around their age approached the table, stopping behind two of the empty chairs across from them.

"Do you mind if we join you?" the woman asked.

"Not at all," Will said, waving to the seats.

"Please," Charity responded at the same time, grateful for the distraction. Being with Will was exactly what she needed tonight, if not for those pesky moments when he did or said something that made her lose her mind and imagine kissing him.

"Thank you so much," the woman said, sitting down. She wore a purple iridescent sleeveless gown, her long brown hair falling around her shoulders. "I'm Maribelle, and this is my husband, Tom. We're from Texas."

"Hello," Tom said, smoothing his shirt down the front of his stocky frame. His dark hair was threaded with strands of gray, and his eyes were heavy lidded, as if he'd already had a couple of drinks.

"I'm Charity, and this is Will. We're from California."

"Very nice to meet you," Maribelle said.

"How long have you been married?" Charity asked after spotting the gorgeous diamond on her ring finger.

"Ten years," Tom replied, placing his arm along the back of his wife's chair. "How about the two of you?"

"Oh, we're not together."

Charity didn't love how quickly Will blurted that out, even if it was the truth, but took it in stride. "We're just friends."

Charity noticed Will turned her way and wondered if he was thinking that they weren't, but obviously she didn't have a better explanation for being out with him tonight. It wasn't a date, so what else was she supposed to say?

"Really? You look comfortable, like you've been a couple for years," Maribelle piped in, her bright blue eyes shifting between them before placing a hand on her husband's arm. "Tom and I met in college. Two kids and a mortgage later, here we are."

The two of them kissed with a touch more enthusiasm than was appropriate for a public event, and Charity glanced over at Will, sharing an awkward smile with him.

"Sorry," Tom said, releasing Maribelle with a sheepish grin. "It's been amazing getting away from the kids and reconnecting as a couple again. You get so busy with everything, sometimes you neglect each other without meaning to."

"Forgive us for doing all the talking." Maribelle waved a hand toward Charity and Will. "What do the two of you do?"

They looked at each other momentarily before Charity piped in. "Will is a marketing genius and design guru. He completely rebranded the business I created with my best friend, and it saved us."

Will beamed at her, and Charity realized she may have sounded as if she were gushing about him, but it was his work, not him personally.

"What business do you own?" Maribelle asked.

Will jumped in. "Charity and her partner own a cat café. She handles the café side and creates amazing, mouthwatering food and desserts."

Charity warmed at his praise and brushed her hand against the back of his before she realized what she was doing. She tried to casually reach past his hand for her water glass and took a sip, her brain screaming at her. They weren't actually on a date, and no matter how comfortable they may seem to other people, he wasn't right for her.

Are you so sure he's the womanizing jerk you assumed he was?

No, but even if Charity had doubts about Will's character being shady, how could she trust it, given her history?

"Oh, I wish I wasn't allergic to cats!" Maribelle bemoaned,

drawing Charity out of her thoughts. "Tom is actually a better cook, and he likes doing it, so I don't mind letting him. It frees me up to take the kids to activities and..."

Maribelle continued talking as the server returned with Charity and Will's salads, her stomach rumbling. She hated to be rude and eat in front of these strangers, but the two fruit tarts had done nothing to take the edge off her hunger. The server took Maribelle and Tom's order while Charity nearly polished off her salad and caught Will watching her, his fork resting on his plate.

"Good?" he asked, clearly amused.

"Yeah. Why? Do I have food all over my face?" she asked.

"No, I just like your enthusiasm. It matches mine."

"I noticed," Charity said, taking another drink of her water. "Telling me how good my food tastes is one of the things I like about you."

"Oh, so you like me now?" he teased.

Charity gave him a small smile. "Maybe a little." She caught Maribelle and Tom watching them curiously and cleared her throat. "Sorry for eating in front of you two."

"Oh, you're fine. We had a late lunch, but I've got to ask, are you sure y'all are just friends? Because I have this sixth sense about people, and I just know when they're really into each other. And you two are definitely feeling something."

Neither one of them responded right away, and then Will said, "Unfortunately, no. We are just here to have a good time."

Charity's face burned as she went back to her salad,

listening to Tom chide Maribelle with half an ear, wondering what Will's *"unfortunately"* meant. Did he want something to be going on? He'd said kissing her had crossed his mind, but that had just been flirtatious teasing, right?

The server came back to the table with salads for Tom and Maribelle and dinner for Charity and Will. The conversation stalled as the four of them ate, and when another couple joined them from Arizona, Tom and Maribelle turned their attention to the newcomers.

"Charity!" Will whispered loudly, startling her. She swung his way, and he glanced at their companions and back to her. "You about ready for another drink?"

Charity nodded. "Yeah."

"All right, I'll grab it." He leaned in closer and spoke a little softer, "I'm having a great time."

Charity's shoulders relaxed slightly. "Me too."

Will pushed back his chair and climbed to his feet. "I'll be back, and then we'll eat, drink, and dance our way to midnight. Deal?"

"Deal."

The server came back with the other couples' food, but they didn't try to include her in the conversation, which was fine with her. She was too busy watching Will shrug out of his tuxedo jacket and lay it over the back of his chair, shooting her a wink. "In case some guy thinks you're alone, he'll see this, know you're with someone, and keep moving."

"Oh, so all that talk about being my wingman and slaying men was just bull?"

"You're the one who said tonight was about fun, and I plan to give you more than you can handle."

Charity's stomach dropped out, and she watched him walk away with a definite swagger in his gait, and she couldn't help thinking how sexy it was.

Dang it, no! This is about fun, not feelings.

She'd thought any and all attraction to Will had been quashed, but then he'd shown up on her doorstep looking dapper and staring at her as if she was everything he'd been searching for. Ever since, her body had been in a perpetual loop of stomach flutters and warmth flushing through her. They still had almost four hours until midnight, and she was already this hot and bothered with him?

Isn't there a rule about things that happen on vacation? They stay there?

Was she thinking about taking this step with Will? A day ago, she'd thought the worst of him, but maybe she'd misjudged him.

Will leaned on the bar, waiting for the drinks, and Charity watched a woman approach him from the right, her black halter dress short and hugging every curve. Whatever the woman said to Will, he shrugged her off and pointed to Charity. She held her breath as the woman turned toward her and caught Charity's gaze briefly before she ducked away, obviously embarrassed. Charity bit back a smile, wondering what in the heck he'd said to her.

Will returned with two drinks and handed her the mojito. "Here you go. The food is probably cold."

"It's still good." Charity took a sip of her drink and set it on the table beside her. "What did you say to the woman at the bar?"

"That I was with you," he said in a matter-of-fact tone.

"But you're not. I mean, not really. This is a pity date."

Will snorted, sitting down in his chair. "Charity, no man would take you out because of pity. I wanted to make you smile because you've got a great one. Contagious. Makes the moon shine a little brighter."

"Dang," Charity murmured, taking another drink, trying to cure the sudden dryness in her mouth. "You really brought the charm tonight."

"I always bring it. I just don't usually get a chance to show you because you've been avoiding me." He swirled some pasta onto his fork and nudged her with his arm. "Or giving me the cold shoulder."

"I'm not—" She stopped her denial because that was exactly what she'd been doing. "It's not personal. I've been keeping my distance from all the men I'm attracted to."

Will visibly perked up, his fork stalling a few inches from his mouth. "You're scared you won't be able to resist me?"

"That is not what I said!"

"I can read between the lines." Will finished his bite and swallowed, pulling a napkin from his pocket and wiping his mouth. He set his plate aside and leaned his elbows on his thighs, smirking. "You know how to get over simmering sexual chemistry?"

"Watch them eat fettuccini?" she deadpanned.

"Give in. Get it out of your system and move on."

Charity's jaw dropped. "Are you suggesting I go to bed with you?"

"I would not be mad if you wanted to take advantage of me," he murmured, his gaze sweeping over her face. "I'd welcome it."

Charity warmed, thinking of the last time she'd been intimate with a man. It had been months, and she'd thought that he'd been serious about all the promises he'd been making to her. Turned out, he'd been making those same promises to his wife, and Charity hadn't had a clue he was married.

"What happened with the last girl you were dating?" she asked.

"Things were moving too fast. She wanted a commitment that would eventually lead to marriage, and I needed to take a step back."

"You're a commitment-phobe? Shocker."

"No, I'd be happy to commit to someone as long as marriage was off the table."

That took her aback, and she snapped her mouth shut when she realized it was hanging open. "Why?"

"Why what?"

"Why are you opposed to marriage?" she asked.

Will shrugged. "I just don't see why a paper is the definitive symbol for love. Why can't people just be together, sharing their lives without having to give up everything they've worked for?"

Charity cleared her throat, reaching for her drink. "I'm still not following. What are they giving up?"

"Financial independence, for one," he said, reaching for his drink. "Once the ink dries, that person is entitled to half of everything I own. What if they're financially irresponsible and we divorce? Why should they get my money?"

Charity scoffed. "You've heard of a prenup, right?"

"If I ask a woman I love and plan to marry to sign a prenup, I'm basically telling her I don't trust her. If I feel the need to go to those lengths, that's just another reason to avoid marriage altogether."

She'd suspected that Will might not be ready for marriage, but sharing a bank account hadn't crossed her mind as a possible reason for it. Charity wondered why this was such a dealbreaker for him, but it wasn't her business to ask. Especially since it didn't affect her; she didn't want to even *date* Will.

"I don't have an issue with marriage," she said cautiously, wondering if he regretted saying anything to her. His jaw was tight, and his shoulders looked tense. "Finding someone I want to get to that point with has been a struggle for me, though."

"I find it hard to believe men aren't lining up for you. You can cook. You're smart. Witty. And a lot of guys dig mean girls—ow!" Charity had whacked him with her napkin on the arm.

"Whoa, what's going on over there?" Tom asked playfully, and Charity realized she'd forgotten about the other couples at their table.

"Nothing," she muttered, glaring at Will. "I'm not mean."

He clutched his arm dramatically. "Says the woman who just smacked me."

"Oh please, I barely touched you."

"Despite what you may have heard," he said, blue eyes twinkling, "I'm not into pain, thanks."

"Oh, really? Then what are you into?" She nearly slapped a hand over her mouth. What had possessed her to ask him that?

Will cocked his head to the side. "Are you asking for a real answer?"

"I mean, I don't want you to lie."

"But are you asking because you're interested or curious?"

Interested. "Curious," she answered firmly, ignoring the little voice in her head.

"Hmm." Will went back to eating without giving her an answer, and Charity joined him, chewing her food. Could they cross that line, go home, and have no residual awkwardness? Their respective best friends were a couple, which meant they'd have to see each other on a regular basis. She hadn't had a fling since college, and if she was being honest, Charity hadn't realized she'd been casually involved until he gave her the goodbye speech. If she said yes to Will tonight, she'd be going into this with her eyes open, knowing the score.

"What does *hmm* mean?"

Will set his fork down and turned her way with a saucy grin. "It means, I think you're reconsidering your aversion to me and I'm here for it."

"Maybe I am and maybe I'm not," she said, taking a bite of her pasta with relish.

"Well, when you make up your mind, I'll be waiting. At least until midnight."

Charity laughed. "You're putting a time limit on me?"

"Don't you know? I'm like Cinderella, baby," he said, sipping his whiskey without breaking eye contact and setting it on the table with a smile. "If you want me, you're going to have to chase me."

CHAPTER SIX

Meowcktail

For our after-hours crowd, try one of our signature Meowcktails, a great way to unwind and still get home safe to your feline friends.

HOURS LATER, WILL WAS still having a wonderful time. Charity had grabbed the next round of drinks after dinner, and they hadn't left the dance floor. Although their dancing had been crashed by the bachelorette party he'd hung out with the previous Saturday, they'd been paying more attention to Charity than him. Right now, they were jumping up and down, screaming the lyrics to "Love Shack." Charity held her long skirt in her hands, her face split into a wide, happy grin, and he was mesmerized by the sight.

"Will!" The bride to be, Mia, hollered to be heard above the music. "Charity is amazing! How did you meet?"

"Our friends are dating, and they were supposed to come here with us, but they went home to visit family instead."

"You should totally lock that down!" Mia said, her bride tiara wobbling precariously on top of her head.

"It's not like that. She's not interested in me."

"She said that?" Mia asked.

"Pretty much."

Mia patted his shoulder. "Well, that is too bad. I think the two of you could be awesome. Like Jake and me!"

Will had heard so much about Mia's fiancé Jake that he felt like he knew him. "Hey, we're just out here to have a good time. I'm going to the bar. You want something?"

"No, thanks. I'm good."

Will nodded and excused himself, working his way closer to Charity. He'd chugged a glass of water for every whiskey, and while he had a good buzz going, he wasn't drunk. When he reached her side, she turned to him with a gleeful expression. "This is so much fun!"

Will chuckled. "I'm going to get a drink. You want something?"

"Yes, please! Mojito and water!"

"I'm on it. I'll grab a table. Watch for me."

"Okay!"

He weaved around the masses of bodies to the crowded bar in the corner, stopping behind a couple engaging in some serious PDA. Will turned away slightly, keeping an eye on the line movement while still watching Charity dance. Despite catching a few men checking her out, she hadn't been approached by any of them, but it was only ten minutes to midnight and the place was packed with tipsy single people.

Will could imagine that, if they were waiting to make a move, that countdown to midnight would be their opening, and a sharp pang of jealousy settled in the pit of his stomach.

While Will knew he had no right to feel that way, it didn't change the fact that he was interested in Charity, and the thought of her meeting someone else didn't sit well with him. But as her escort, Will would make sure Charity made it back to the bungalow safely, no matter if she found someone else to kiss at midnight.

The line shortened by two people, and PDA couple broke apart long enough to take a step forward, and Will moved along with them. The music switched up to "I Gotta Feeling," and he lost sight of Charity for a moment as more people surged onto the dance floor. His phone vibrated, and he checked the message. His sister, Sarah, had sent him a text.

I miss you. Be safe!

You too, he responded, slipping the phone back into his pocket. Will adored his sister. Granted, she'd been a stubborn pain in his tuchus most of his life, but she was still his go-to support when he needed someone to talk to. With his dad gone, it was his mom, Sarah, and Will against the world.

Finally, he made it to the bar, and after paying for their drinks, he carefully carried them back toward the edge of the dance floor. He searched the dancing crowd and finally spotted Charity, still dancing with the bachelorette party, but on the edge of their group, a couple of guys lingered. One of them, a tall, muscular man with a shaved head and sharp cheekbones, was watching Charity. Will found an unoccupied table and set the drinks down, debating on what his next move would be. Charity was so wrapped up in the music that she wasn't looking for him, and he didn't want to leave their drinks unattended.

The DJ's booming voice broke through the music. "All right, folks, we're down to the final minute to midnight. Are we ready to ring in the New Year?" The crowd cheered, and Charity turned his way, spotting him. He picked up her drink and held it in the air like a toast. She nodded, speaking earnestly to the woman she'd been dancing with, who threw her arms around her. They hugged briefly, and Charity headed toward Will.

Cheekbones followed behind her, and when she was nearly at the end of the dance floor, the guy jumped ahead of her, his back to Will. Charity pulled up short, her gaze flicking over the man's shoulder to Will.

"Twenty seconds!" the DJ called out.

Will didn't want to overstep, but when Charity shook her head and tried to step around the man, he blocked her path.

Abandoning the drinks, Will closed the distance, and as the DJ started counting down from ten, Will clasped the man on the shoulder. He jumped under Will's hand, and when he swung Will's way a little unsteadily, he knew the guy was drunk.

"Hey, babe," Will said, moving to Charity's side and placing his arm around her waist. "Ready to ring in the New Year?"

The relief on Charity's face was evidence enough that his rescue was timely. "Absolutely."

Will ignored the drunk guy and cradled the back of Charity's head with his other hand, dropping his mouth to cover hers as the DJ yelled, "One! Happy New Year!"

Charity's lips parted under his, and Will pulled her closer, his heart thundering in his ears, drowning out "Auld Lang Syne." Charity's hands rested on his waist, the warmth of her palms burning through the fabric of his button-down dress shirt. The scent of vanilla surrounded him, and he deepened the kiss, sinking into the heady taste of mint and Charity.

Charity's fingers dug into his side, and he felt her lean into him, kissing him back enthusiastically.

"Whoooo, go Will!"

"Get it, boy!"

An array of obnoxious cheering broke through the moment, and Will pulled back, breathing hard. Charity stared up at him with a dazed expression, her lips still parted.

"What..." She swallowed, as if trying to find her voice. "Was that?"

Will chuckled. "I think most people call that a kiss."

"Some kiss," she murmured.

"I'd say."

"Kiss her again!" Will recognized Mia's voice and found her a few feet away, clapping enthusiastically with the rest of her friends. The man who'd accosted Charity was nowhere in sight.

Charity followed his gaze, and when she saw them watching, she laughed. "Is it me or are they being total creepers?"

"It's not just you." Will brushed his fingers over her cheek, stroking down her neck with his thumb. "Do you want to get out of here and away from our cheerleaders?"

"Yes, please."

Will slipped his arm around her shoulders, excitement flipping through his stomach when she snuggled into his body. He gave the women a goodbye wave over his shoulder as he led her back to where he'd left his tuxedo jacket. The couples from earlier were nowhere to be seen when they reached the table. Will didn't let Charity go, picking up the jacket with his other hand and holding it over his shoulder.

"I'm sorry about our drinks," Charity said as they passed by the four glasses on their way to the exit.

"Don't be. It was worth it."

"Yeah?" she asked.

"I mean, I didn't want to overstep, but I can't say I didn't thoroughly enjoy that kiss."

"Me too," Charity murmured. "I mean, I liked it. Great timing."

"I wish I could say I planned it, but it was all instinct." They passed through the doors and outside onto the sidewalk, the air still heavy with humidity. "It's still hot enough to take a dip in the pool."

"By the sound of the splashing and laughing, I think everyone else thought the same thing," Charity said, pointing to the crowded pool as they passed by.

"Great minds, I guess." Will was keenly aware that she

hadn't shrugged off his arm and wasn't ready to say good night. "I'd say let's go for a walk on the beach, but they closed it tonight for security reasons."

"We could go back to the bungalow and sit out on my balcony."

Yes. "Sounds good to me."

They walked in silence for several minutes until they passed into the garden, the sounds of the music and laughter growing quieter.

"Will?"

"Yeah?" he asked.

She slowed to a stop and turned toward him, her palm resting on his chest. "I—can you kiss me again?"

Will's pulse kicked into high gear as he brought his hands up, cradling the back of her neck. The urgency of the first kiss was replaced by a slow, savoring passion that sparked to life the minute their lips touched again. Will tilted his head, and her lips opened for him, allowing him a thorough exploration with his tongue. The buzz he'd had going had faded and been replaced by a high he'd never experienced. Kissing Charity was a consuming, intense eruption of heat and adrenaline that made him want to kiss her harder, but he didn't want to scare her off.

Charity moaned against his mouth, her breathing ragged as she whispered, "Not a fluke."

"What's that?"

"Nothing." She gripped the back of his head and brought

his mouth back to hers. Will's hands slid down her neck and shoulders, settling on her hips. When he gripped her thighs and lifted her against him, she broke the kiss with a gasp.

"Wanna skip the balcony and just come inside?" Charity asked.

Did she even have to ask?

"Abso-friggin-lutely."

CHAPTER SEVEN

Catpawccino

Not into sweet drinks? Try a Catpawccino for a foamy, espresso pick-me-up that will have you doing zoomies with your furry pal all day long.

CHARITY BLINKED HER EYES open, staring at the empty space in the bed. The bedspread was rumpled with the evidence that Will spent the night, but when she reached out a hand to run it over the white cotton sheet, it was cool to the touch. Charity sat up in the bed, pulling the sheet with her and wrapping it around her body.

"Will?" she called, padding out to the back door of the bungalow, and peeking her head out. Nothing.

Charity frowned, her mind swirling with possibilities and not all of them were good.

He wouldn't just take off. The last thing he wants is to create bad blood or make things awkward.

Besides, the night had been too amazing to end with a

morning-after ghosting. Right? What if he'd thought sneaking out would be easier than having to explain to her the reality that last night was a one-time—correction, *two-time*—thing and it wouldn't be going any further than that?

Wasn't that the point? You wanted to try your hand at a fling with eyes wide open? What happens in Mexico stays there?

That was her thought process until the moment Will kissed her, officially putting every other kiss in her past to shame. At first, Charity thought maybe it was the excitement of New Year's Eve mixed with one too many mojitos, but the heat, the tingles, none of it had faded in the middle of the night when he'd woken her with a deep, passionate kiss and his hands doing amazing things to her body. Buzzed or sober, being with Will was different than anything she'd ever experienced before, and Charity wasn't sure she wanted Mexico to be the end of it.

Charity heard faint whistling and peeked outside, spotting Will coming up the stairs, carrying a decanter with a coffee logo in the crook of his arm, the handles of two mugs threaded through his fingers, and a basket with pastries, cream, and sugar in his other hand. In a flurry, she rushed into the bathroom and checked her reflection in the mirror. Black makeup circled her eyes like a raccoon, and she winced. "Let's get you cleaned up."

After she washed her face and used the facilities, Charity traded out the sheet for her robe, tying the belt around her waist as she left the bathroom. Charity saw Will on the back balcony, pacing back and forth with his phone pressed to his ear. Brushing her hair back over her shoulder, Charity pulled back the drapes on the back window and watched him. It was beautiful outside with the sun shining down on Will, who held a mug in his free hand.

"How was Boston?" she heard him ask, his voice muffled through the glass of the window. She knew it was his friend Ben on the other end by that question alone and stepped back to give him privacy as he continued, "Mexico is beautiful and unexpected. Right now, I'm watching the waves crash on the beach." Several beats went by before Will spoke again, his voice light and teasing, "It would have been better if my friend hadn't ditched me at the last minute."

Charity rolled her eyes. Why did he insist on giving Ben a hard time when Will had told her himself that he didn't blame Ben for going to Boston?

"I've seen her around. Why?" Will asked, and Charity's ears perked up. Were they taking about her? Will wouldn't say anything about last night, would he? They hadn't talked about keeping it between them, but—

"I do not have a thing for Charity!" Will's voice was firm, and when what he'd said sank in, Charity stiffened. "No, I'm not being defensive, I was just telling *you* because you keep suggesting I'm carrying some torch for her."

Charity's stomach twisted into knots until nausea climbed up the back of her throat. Even if he was protecting their privacy, did he have to sound so disgusted? As if it was absurd for him to want her?

"I'll see you tomorrow, then. Are you grabbing me from the airport?" Another pause. "Sounds good. See you then."

Will slipped his phone into the pocket of his shorts and settled into one of the chairs, his back to Charity. As he sipped his coffee, Charity dropped the drape, a lump of misery lodging in her throat.

Stupid woman. What are you getting emotional about? You got what you wanted! A vacation fling with no strings attached. Get it together.

The door opened, and Charity jumped, too late to run to the bedroom. Will gave her a once-over, smiling. "Hey. How long have you been standing there?"

Did he sound guilty or was that just her imagination?

What should she tell him? The truth? *I was coming out to join you and heard you emphatically telling someone on the phone you do not have a thing for me. Good to know.*

No, because he hadn't done anything wrong. He hadn't made her any promises. They'd had fun, and just because he wasn't interested in anything more than that didn't make him a bad guy. That was exactly what she'd expected from him, and just because she'd somehow convinced herself that last night might mean something more, Will hadn't gotten the memo.

"A moment or two. I didn't want to interrupt your phone call."

"It was just Ben." Will took a step in her direction, reaching for her. "I have pastries and coffee on the balcony, if you want to join me."

Charity sidestepped his reach, shaking her head. "Actually,

I was going to head back to bed. My head is hammering this morning. I just wanted to make sure we were good."

"Good?" he asked, his expression befuddled. "You don't want me to stay?"

"Oh, no. It's your last day. I'm sure you've got something fun you're dying to try."

"Actually, I thought we could do a little tourist shopping together," he said, his crooked grin tugging at her heart-strings. "I still need to find something for my mom and sister."

His words rushed over her like a bucket of ice water. "Excuse me?"

"What? I wanted to spend the day with you."

What was he doing? Why was Will dragging this out, when he'd been very clear with Ben about having no interest in her at all? "Why?"

"Because I had fun with you," he said slowly, like the reasons were obvious.

"I'm sorry. I should have been honest, but I had no idea you were going to prolong this. I heard you tell Ben vehemently that you have no interest in me at all. If that is true, why would you invite me to help you pick out gifts for your family, and if it isn't true, why did you say it?"

Will's expression was unreadable as he stood stock-still, as if afraid to make any sudden movements. "I feel like anything I say right now is a trap."

Charity shook her head. "That wasn't my intention. I just wanted to have a good time and part on a high note."

"Okay, well, this conversation has taken a series of turns, and we've ended up in the land of misunderstanding. I *am* interested in you. I just didn't want to reveal our personal business to Ben because we hadn't had a conversation about what this was. I didn't think there was any point in involving our friends until we'd hashed that out."

"You don't have to work out anything because this"—she gestured between them, her robe flowing like a wing—"is nothing. It was a great night in Mexico that has now turned into a dramatically awkward morn—" she checked the clock on the wall "—afternoon, and I think you should probably head back to your room and forget this ever happened."

Will stood there, blinking at her, and her shoulders drooped slightly. "Listen," she said, her tone softening, "it was wonderful. Really. But last night I got caught up in your charm and how good you looked in your tux, and I forgot that we're not a good match. We'd both agreed to one night to begin with, and nothing more."

After several silent beats, he nodded. "I'll see myself out then. Trying to change your mind about spending the day with me seems counterintuitive at this point."

Charity didn't know what to say. She'd ripped the Band-Aid off for both of them by telling the truth. No sense in dragging this out. Having amazing chemistry with someone wasn't a good enough reason to get more deeply involved when it's going to end sooner rather than later.

Pausing with his hand on the door, Will turned toward her, his expression blank. "Just so we're clear, you talk about men being dogs and treating you terribly, but this whole scene? You were the villain, not me."

Charity sucked in a breath, and before she could respond, he was out the door. It clicked shut behind him, and she stared at the yellow wood, her jaw clenched in frustration. How could he say she was the bad guy? Because she'd tried to protect herself? He should be happy she'd let him off the hook without some dramatic blowout.

Maybe she'd bruised his ego by cutting the cord. Charity didn't think Will was that type of guy, but even so, he would get over this and see she'd done them both a favor. By this time tomorrow, they'd be headed home and they'd laugh about this.

CHAPTER EIGHT

Whiskers and Whipped Cream Puffs

Delightfully light pastry puffs filled with sweet cream and topped with adorable cat faces in milk chocolate. Savor or devour; there is no wrong way to eat these babies!

CHARITY WAS DEFINITELY NOT laughing as she descended the escalator, watching the back of Will's head with annoyance. He was several steps down from her, carrying on a conversation with a couple of women in crop tops and yoga pants. She couldn't hear what they were talking about, but every time Will laughed, the sound set her teeth on edge.

What did you expect? You weren't the best version of yourself yesterday.

The little voice didn't need to pile on to the guilt she'd been wrestling with since he'd left her room, and she didn't have an excuse or a reason—except panic. While falling into bed with Will had seemed like the best way to end her vacation with a bang, in her foggy, day-after brain, she'd played their awkward return to the States over in her mind before she'd even opened her eyes. Despite Will's promise of discretion, guys talked, and if he told Ben, then Ben would share it with Kara, and her best friend would skin her alive for not divulging every last detail to her.

Could she have been a tad more tactful? Absolutely, but at the time, she wasn't functioning at full mental capacity. Especially when she'd heard him telling Ben how emphatically uninterested in her he was, which hurt more than she'd liked to admit. And despite his backpedaling when he'd discovered she'd heard every word, Charity hadn't planned on making their encounter a regular thing.

No matter how good he looked out of those board shorts.

Yes, she may have ogled him a bit. She was human, and the warring emotions raging inside her had been fighting between inviting him back to bed or kicking him out. Their night together had been wonderful—playful and fun, sensual and illuminating—but Charity knew it only ended one way. Heartache for her the longer it dragged on. And while she'd put this weekend in the bank as one of those amazing nights she'd think about when she was alone and lonely, that was all it could be.

Why was he taking offense that she'd stuck to her principles and pretending she didn't exist now? She could have dealt with the aftermath with more tact, but it didn't warrant the silent treatment. Or that little dig at the end that she was somehow a villain because she didn't want to spend the day snuggling and repeating what was meant to be a single event.

The man was a hypocrite, talking to his friend about the lack of interest he held for her and then playing the victim when she let him off the hook.

Which had left Charity spending her last day in Mexico alone in her bungalow, reading and enjoying room service. It wasn't like the thought of tracking Will down hadn't crossed her mind, but she'd figured he'd get over whatever hurt feelings he'd had by the following day.

No such luck.

Will got off the escalator and headed for the baggage claim ahead of her, his groupies following along and completely engrossed in whatever story he was regaling them with. Although they'd shared a taxi to the airport, he hadn't said more than three words to her the entire ride, mostly offering *hmms* and grunts of affirmation to whatever question she'd asked. She'd finally stopped trying to engage him, stewing in her frustration. It wouldn't have been that hard to apologize, but the words wouldn't come out, especially after he'd carried her bags into the airport and ditched her in the baggage line.

"Char!" A cheerful voice called out, and Charity spotted Kara Ingalls waving enthusiastically. She had on a robin's-egg-blue peacoat and khakis, a wide smile on her round face.

Charity stepped off the escalator, and in a few feet, she was engulfed in Kara's tight embrace. She returned the hug, realizing how much she'd missed seeing her friend every day.

Kara pulled away, her hazel eyes sparkling. "Let's get your

bags and collect Schwartz. Ben is circling the place so we don't have to park."

Charity bit back a groan. Would her suffering never end? Being stuck in a vehicle again with Will?

"What's wrong?" Kara asked.

"Nothing some cream puffs and a hot bath won't fix."

"Come on, I can tell there's something. Talk to me, Goose."

It was there, resting on the edge of her tongue, but she'd be breaking the code of Mexico if she told Kara what happened. And after her reaction to Will's conversation with Ben, she could imagine the field day Will would have if she spilled the dirt to Kara. "I'm tired. I might need a day to recover from my vacation."

"I get that. I slept in yesterday, and I'm still dragging my rear around after a week in Boston."

"I bet. I'll be fine once we get home and wash the travel grime off. Then I'll be awake enough to regale you with all of my adventures." *Except for the one that involves your boyfriend's best friend.*

"I can't wait to hear it all. How was your New Year's Eve?"

"It was uneventful," Charity lied, her face burning.

"Did you go to the party or stay in?"

"I went to the party for a little while, then went back to the bungalow."

"Alone?" Kara teased.

"Yes, all by my lonesome." Charity rubbed her temple. "I have a headache."

Kara linked her arm through Charity's and squeezed. "You definitely need a nap and some one-on-one time with me."

"That sounds awesome. You mean I won't have to fight Ben to get you to myself?"

"Nope, he is dropping us at home, and I am all yours. Oh, there's Schwartz!" Kara waved, and Charity followed the direction of her gaze to where Will was dragging his single duffel behind him.

"I'm going to get my bags," Charity muttered, releasing Kara and passing Will on her way to the rotating conveyor belt. Lifting the first bag off the belt, she reached for the second at the same time a male hand moved past hers and gripped the handle of her larger bag. She glanced up at Will as he heaved her bag onto the ground next to her other one.

"Thanks."

"No problem. Kara thought you could use the help."

They were far enough away from Kara to not be overheard, so Charity said, "Listen, about yesterday. I didn't mean it to come off like New Year's Eve wasn't wonderful. It was. We just can't—"

"Don't worry about it. It's already forgotten." He lifted her last bag off the belt with a grunt and set it on the ground.

His cool tone rankled her. "Okay, well, I'm sorry she put you out about the bags."

"It's fine. Do you have it from here?"

"Actually, could you take that one? The wheels spin, but it's hard to maneuver both."

He snorted. "Maybe next time don't pack so much if you can't handle it."

"Excuse me?" she snapped.

"Nothing, not my business."

"You're the one who came over here like a gentleman, offering to help. Excuse me for thinking you were sincere, but forget about it. I'm a big girl who can handle herself."

"No, I walked all the way over here—" Will reached for the bag and clutched the handle, but Charity grabbed it too, jerking it back toward her.

"I've got it, thanks," she said, trying to yank it away, but he was too strong.

"I insist," he ground out, pulling so hard she was afraid he would rip the handle off the luggage, and without considering the consequences, she let go. Before Charity could call out a warning, Will stumbled back and connected with a guy dragging a bright yellow duffel. He tumbled over it, dropping her bag handle and managing to catch himself on a pillar. Will's wide eyes met hers before his face snapped into a furious scowl.

Charity covered her mouth with her free hand, muffling the horrified laugh that escaped her.

Kara ran over, hauling Will's bag behind her, and retrieved Charity's bag from the ground before addressing Will. "Are you all right?"

Will straightened, rotating his arms and wincing. "I'm fine. That will teach me to watch where I'm going." He rubbed his shin, shooting Charity a dark look, and she glared back.

"I told you I had it."

"Next time I'll listen."

Kara glanced between them. "What's up with you two? You're even more hostile than when you left."

"Nothing," they said unanimously and not at all suspiciously.

Before Kara could question them any more, Charity grabbed her bag from Kara's hand and motored toward the door, gritting her teeth as her smallest bag wobbled a bit on its wheels. It was annoying, and she planned on replacing it before she went anywhere ever again. "We better hurry before Ben has to make another lap."

Charity heard the grind of Will's duffel behind her and Kara exchanging pleasantries with Will.

"Did you have fun in Mexico?" Kara asked.

"For the most part."

"Uh-oh! What happened?"

"I had something that didn't agree with me. Left a sour taste in my mouth."

Did he really just go there?

"Oh, that's awful. Were you sick on the plane?"

"No, the feeling went away for a little while and suddenly came back."

"I've heard food poisoning is like that and can linger for days."

"Thankfully, I don't plan on ever eating that particular dish again."

Passive-aggressive much?

Charity tuned them out as they waited on the curb for Ben because one more subtext from Will and she might accidentally push him into oncoming traffic.

"What was that?" Kara asked.

Charity realized she was talking to her. "What?"

"You said something about traffic."

Crap, she'd said that out loud? "Um, I was just saying the traffic is bad. It might take him a while to get back."

"Uh-huh," Will said, his lips curved in a smirk.

Oh God, he'd heard her.

"There's Ben! I'll ride in the back with Char so we can catch up," Kara said.

Thank goodness for small favors.

Ben pulled his SUV into the empty spot in front of them, and when he hopped out, the first thing he did was take Will's hand and give him a couple of hard slaps on the shoulder.

"Good to have you back in one piece."

"Same to you."

"Let's get all your luggage loaded so we can get out of here. The traffic is rough, and people are getting impatient." Ben smiled at Charity, reaching for her bags. "Hey, Charity, did you have a nice flight?"

"It was uneventful, thanks. I appreciate the help."

"No problem. Hop on in."

Charity did as he asked and shut the door behind her as Kara got into the other side.

"Are you going to explain why there's an extreme amount of tension with Schwartz or do I need to come to my own conclusions?"

Charity leaned her head back with a groan. "Can I just plead the fifth and leave it at that?"

"For now."

So much for leaving what happens in Mexico there. Why did she have to engage? Kara was like a dog with a bone. She'd never let it go.

Ben opened the driver's-side door and started the SUV. When the passenger door opened and Will looked over the seat at her as he climbed inside, she scowled.

He returned it with a curled lip.

Kara leaned over as Will took his seat, eyes wide. "You didn't."

Charity groaned and sank down. It was going to be a long ride home.

CHAPTER NINE

Avo-gato Toast

An excellent, health-conscious way to start your day; and don't fret, no cats were harmed in the making of this dish.

WILL MUST HAVE STILL been running on vacation time because it was a struggle getting out of bed the next morning. He slept through his backup alarm and didn't bother taking the time to shave or eat breakfast before he raced out the door. He was getting out of his car when his boss called.

"Hey, Roy," Will said, tucking the phone between his cheek and shoulder as he shrugged into his jacket. "I'll be there in a minute."

"Actually, can you swing by the café down the street and pick up our breakfast order for the meeting first? It's under my name."

"Which café?"

"Meow and Furever? The one Ben's girlfriend runs."

Will put his boss on mute and rested his forehead against

the top of his car with a groan. After yesterday's awkward car ride, he thought he'd be able to avoid Charity for a few weeks at least.

Hopefully, Michelle was running the front today, and Charity was out delivering orders.

"Schwartz? Hello?"

He unmuted his boss and said, "Yeah, sorry, I can do that."

"Thanks. I'd send an intern, but they were all miraculously sick today. I'll see you when you get here."

Will didn't even get a goodbye out before his boss hung up, but he didn't take it personally. Roy was brusque with everyone.

Heading down the stairs of the parking garage, Will gave himself a pep talk about why it didn't matter if he had to interact with Charity. He'd politely make small talk, grab the order, and go. He was an adult, and although he'd let his snarkiness get the best of him yesterday, Will was determined to put aside any animosity for Charity. New year, fresh start, and he'd act like Mexico never happened.

He opened the front door to Meow and Furever and took one step into the line, grimacing when he spotted Charity's smiling face, which dimmed a little when she caught his eye.

"Welcome to Meow and Furever," she called. "We'll be right with you."

Will wasn't sure exactly how pickup worked if the order was called in, so he stayed where he was, his gaze flicking around the lobby. Sparkling snowflakes dangled from the ceiling, and along the top of the clear wall separating the social area from the café, the thick glass had been frosted to look like snow. Sitting on top of a cat tower, a fluffy black-and-white cat watched them, his thick tail flicking.

The line moved, and he took a step forward, his gaze still on the intense cat. It was better than accidentally meeting Charity's gaze and giving her the impression he was uncomfortable being here, because he wasn't.

Suddenly, a large paper bag was being thrust toward him, and he turned, doing exactly what he'd been trying to avoid and looking into Charity's dark, thickly lashed eyes.

"I put the avo-gato toast containers on top so they wouldn't get smushed. I'll get the drinks and help you carry the order over to your office. I need to speak to your boss."

Great.

He took the handle of the large bag, and before he could respond, she was headed back around the counter. He couldn't hear what she said to Kara and Michelle, but both women glanced his way, lingering on him for several moments before they went back to helping people.

Had she told them about what happened? She'd made such a big deal about them never speaking of it again, but there was no way Kara hadn't picked up on their tension yesterday. Especially after Charity muttered something about pushing him into traffic.

He'd snickered, and he could tell by her shocked expression she hadn't meant to say it out loud, but he'd prefer her honesty than ice-cold silence.

Isn't that what you were doing to her?

Touché, voice inside my head.

As Charity came back toward him with two trays of drinks, the swinging door that created a barrier between the front and back of the café swung open, and a young Latina woman called out, "Charity, is it fifteen minutes for the muffins or fifty?"

Charity closed her eyes, her mouth moving silently, and he realized she was counting. Finally, she called over her shoulder. "Twenty-five, and let them cool on the rack for fifteen. It's in the recipe I left on the counter."

"Oh, I totally missed that! Sorry! Thanks!"

The girl disappeared, and Will grabbed the door for Charity. "New baker?"

"Assistant baker," Charity muttered.

"She seems nice."

"She is very sweet, but she's already burned my cookies and mixed up the salt and sugar quantities in my brownies this morning, so I'm behind."

"Then why didn't you send her to help me carry things and fix her mistakes?"

"I told you, I want to talk to your boss about something. Why?"

He glanced over at her, noting the slight narrowing of her eyes. "Why what?"

"Why did you suggest I send her? Because you can't be around me for a five-minute walk?"

"Whoa, time-out. I asked because you just said that you were behind. It makes sense to delegate something like this."

"I have a business proposition for Roy, and those are things I like to handle in person."

"Gotcha," he said, his gaze flicking over her purple sweater dress, black tights, and tall boots. It was cold today, and while it wasn't raining now, he wouldn't be surprised if she got caught in something on her way back. The clouds above looked ominous.

"Do you want to run back and grab your jacket?" he asked.

"I'm good."

They walked along the sidewalk, her boots tapping across the cement. He eyed the two trays of drinks in her hands and reached out. "I can take one of those and free up your hands."

"I've got it."

"It looks weird for me to be carrying one bag and you loaded down with heavy trays."

She laughed. "Is this a masculinity thing? Me carrying more than you makes you feel like less of a man?"

Will stiffened. "Never mind, I'll open the door."

He moved a few steps ahead of her, humiliation burning beneath his skin. Why did he keep trying to make things less awkward between them? It only created more friction.

"Will!" she called after him. "I'm sorry! It was a bad joke."

Will grabbed the door and held it as he turned to face her. "You know I'm not a bad guy, right?"

That pulled her up short, and her eyes lowered to the ground. "I know that," she said quietly.

"Then why do you act like I'm a jerk? You crack jokes at

my expense. You treat me like I'm some guy who uses women and tosses them aside—"

"Hey, you were the one who told me you don't do commitment!"

"No, I said I don't want to get married. I would fully commit myself to a woman if marriage was off the table, but every woman I date knows my views by the second date, and that's probably why I don't get a lot of third dates. I'm not the dog you think I am."

"I never called you a dog. I said you don't do commitment, and you flirt with every woman you meet."

"Why do you care, Charity?" he asked, wishing he could call back the words, but it was too late now.

Several beats passed before she walked through the door ahead of him and to the elevator. He figured she wasn't going to answer him, but after the doors opened and they stepped inside, she said, "I think my current feelings regarding men have skewed my views on any man who comes within my purview. I'm not making an excuse, but I apologize. It isn't you personally."

"Sure feels that way," he said, pressing the button for the office floor, and the doors closed. "But this isn't all on you. I reacted poorly at the airport, and I was a tad—"

"Passive-aggressive?" she said sweetly.

"Hey, hey," he laughed. "I don't need your help apologizing."

"Is that what you're doing?"

"I'm trying to," he said, pressing the stop-service button, "if you'd stop interrupting."

"Will! They are going to think there is something wrong!"

"Then let me get this out."

Charity nodded. "Please, continue."

"I'm sorry I was a jerk and didn't handle it the way a grown-up should have."

"I accept. Are you willing to forgive me for being a bit—"

"Tactless?" He grinned.

"Fine. Yes, tactless."

"I'm willing to let it go if..." Will thought for a moment, his lips twitching.

Charity's gaze narrowed. "If what?"

"If you hand over one of those trays of coffee before we get off on my work floor."

Charity released a cough that sounded a lot like a stifled laugh and held out the tray to him. "Knock yourself out. Now, press the button. Lord knows what they think is going on in here."

"Nefarious things, indeed." Will took it with a grin. "Thanks for saving my fragile male ego. Can we be friends now?"

"You just told me I make you feel bad. Why on earth would you want to be friends with me?"

"It seems safer to be your friend than your enemy."

"You're not wrong." The doors opened with a ding. "Is it too early to ask a friendly favor?"

"What's that?"

They fell into step as he rounded the cubicles toward the conference room. "I'm about to ask your boss if he'll allow

Meow and Furever to cater your company meetings exclusively for the next three months. Will you tell him how amazing and professional we are?"

Will opened the conference room door with his butt. "Sure, I'll lie for you."

"Hey," she chided with a laugh, "I thought we were going to be friends?"

"That's what friends do."

CHAPTER TEN

Pawp-Tarts

In a hurry? No worries. We got you with our delicious Pawp-Tarts, tasty enough to make your whiskers twitch! Strawberry Nutella is our favorite!

Charity pulled up to her parents' six-bedroom home in El Dorado Hills and considered driving around the block one more time. She'd been home from Mexico for five days and had spoken to her mom long enough to get half a tirade before she made up a cake emergency and was able to end the call. Her mom sent her a text immediately that ordered her to attend family dinner on Saturday night. No excuses.

"You cannot avoid them forever," Kara said from the passenger seat, holding a large casserole dish in her lap. Charity had recruited Kara as her buffer during dinner. And when her bestie balked, Charity resorted to bribery. One extreme-chocolate lava cake. Kara had tried to finagle the whole story about Will and Mexico with no edits, but Charity had put her foot down. As far as Kara knew, they'd hung out, argued, and now had agreed to a tentative truce. Unlike her family, who were waiting inside to pounce.

"No, but what's one more week?"

Kara scoffed. "Come on, Char. You knew that there would be heat after you bailed on the holidays. The longer you wait, the worse it will be."

"But if I come another day when it's just my parents, I won't have to listen to my brother and sister pipe in." She'd spotted her brother's black BMW in the driveway and her sister's powder-blue Prius parked next to it. Their spouses would be with them, which brought the total up to six perfect people judging her tonight.

Actually, that wasn't fair. Her sister-in-law, Elena, would silently support her, but there was no way she'd speak up against Charity's parents. She was the favorite in-law for a reason.

"If the lecture lasts longer than five minutes, I'll suddenly come down with stomach discomfort, and we can bounce. Deal?"

Charity put the car in park with a grumbled, "Fine."

"Good. Come on." Kara opened her door and climbed out of the car, leaving Charity to gather her nerve. Confrontation didn't bother her under normal circumstances, but her parents had the power to render her tongue-tied against their grievances, which were usually lengthy. And although she loved them, having a break from their disappointment had been nice.

Since coming back from Mexico, the world had been coming up Charity. Roy had agreed to a one-month trial period of the café supplying breakfast and lunch to Kilburn Marketing three times a week for a flat fee. The mechanic shop had called about the catering van she'd picked up for a steal last month and said it would be ready Monday. And any day, she should hear whether or not she'd be one of ten contestants on *Bake That*.

Even with the hefty donations they'd received before Christmas, Charity knew Meow and Furever could use the money if she won the reality baking show, especially if she wanted to expand the kitchen into the small space next door. She wanted the catering side of the café to take off, and that meant she needed more equipment to run simultaneously to fulfill orders. And there was no way she could ask her parents for a loan. They'd been perfectly clear that she'd made a mistake going to school for business rather than applying to law school and that rejecting every eligible man they'd thrown at her was juvenile. She'd been disappointing her parents for nearly thirty-three years. Why stop now?

Fine, maybe she was behaving childishly when it came to their matchmaking attempts. All the men they'd introduced her to had the same qualities. Successful. Stable. Intelligent.

If he wasn't so against marriage, Will would have been a catch in her parents' eyes.

Now, why the heck did I think that?

Maybe because he'd been on her mind a lot lately. Hanging with Will had been the best night of the entire trip, even before they'd taken things to the next level, and now that they weren't at each other's throats, memories of their time together kept invading her subconscious at the most inopportune times. She'd almost burned an entire batch of pawp-tarts yesterday thinking about the way his lips—

"Charity? Let's go. Your mom has already looked out the window and waved at me."

She sighed, grateful for the interruption. Unbidden thoughts of Will were throwing Charity off her game and putting her at a disadvantage for battle. And she needed her wits about her to deal with her family.

It didn't take them long to reach the front door of her childhood home, and before she could ring the bell, the blue door swung open, revealing Iris Simmons's tastefully made-up face scrunched into a scowl. Her dark hair was swept up in a simple clip, the shiny waves falling down her back. The teal of her top brought out the green of her eyes, and Charity swallowed, waiting for the first zinger to land.

"For a moment there, I thought you might drive off."

Snap!

"Of course not," Charity said, kissing her mother's cheek before stepping over the threshold. "I was just answering a text."

"I see. Hello, Kara. It's nice to see you."

"Thank you, Mrs. Simmons. I appreciate the invitation." Kara held up the casserole dish. "We brought assorted pastries."

"Thank you. You're always welcome, although I was hoping to have a moment to speak to Charity alone. Would you mind taking those into the kitchen and excusing us? There are drinks and hors d'oeuvres in the family room."

Charity reached out discreetly to grab Kara's hand, even as her friend eluded her grasp and said, "Of course, Mrs. Simmons."

Silent curses rushed through her mind as her mother took her arm and Kara mouthed *I'm sorry* before disappearing into the other room.

"Your father and I have been waiting for you to arrive."

"Lucky me," Charity deadpanned.

"You're very lucky, Charity. You have no idea what we've been feeling and thinking the last few weeks."

The emotion in Iris's voice was unfamiliar, and an uncomfortable knot formed in Charity's throat. "I'm sorry I upset you both, but—"

"You might as well wait and tell it to the both of us." Iris led her toward her father's study. She knocked twice, and when her dad's deep voice called, "Come in," her mother pushed the door open, and Charity's stomach dropped out, taking her back to being an errant teen in deep with her parents.

"Look who's here."

Royce Simmons slipped his phone into his pocket, dark eyes taking her in. Even with silver threading his black hair, her dad didn't look his age and had passed along his good genes to his kids. Although Charity had her mom's nose and mouth, those eyes were the same shade as hers. The simple, expensive line of his suit jacket highlighted the wide shoulders that had served him well playing defensive line in college.

"Hi, Dad."

"Charity," he rumbled as he came around the desk, kissing her cheek. "I'm happy you could join us. I feel as though I haven't seen you in over a month."

Guilt trips and sarcasm created a powerful combination and her shoulders slumped. "I was gone for less than two weeks and attended Isabelle's Christmas concert the weekend before I flew out."

"Yes, you came to your niece's event and then left us a voice mail at four in the morning on Christmas Eve, letting me know you were going out of town for the holidays. Incredibly considerate, don't you think, dear?"

"Absolutely," her mother agreed.

Charity would have laughed at their perfectly executed front if it wasn't directed at her. "It was a spur of the moment thing, which I can enjoy since I'm a single adult."

"Adult decisions come with adult consequences, and your actions not only upset and hurt your mother, but they disappointed me. We had a guest staying with us during the holidays. I was hoping you would show him around the area, and instead, I had to take off work to do it."

"I'm sorry I couldn't be here for your guest, but like I said, it was a last-minute opportunity I couldn't pass up."

"Going to Mexico is hardly an opportunity," her mother scoffed. "You would rather spend the holidays alone in another country than with your family?"

Her mother's eyes shimmered, as if Iris was holding back

tears, but Charity was used to the tactic. If guilt didn't work, deploy the tears of shame. She knew when that happened that they weren't even listening to her, and in reality, there was no good way to excuse her decision, so Charity went for the truth.

"Yes, I would rather spend the holidays alone, so I know I won't have to suffer through awkward blind dates set up by my parents or listen to the two of you tell me why my whole life and career are meaningless."

"Do not raise your voice to your mother," her dad growled.

Charity threw up her hands. "I don't understand why you want me here anyway, unless it makes you feel better to have someone around to belittle."

"That's enough," Royce snapped. "Yes, we wanted a different path for you, but as you said, you're an adult and need to take responsibility for your actions. Your behavior showed a lack of consideration and regard for your mother and me—"

"I apologized for hurting Mom's feelings, but that doesn't change the fact that your treatment of me played a part in my decision to go away, rather than stay here to absorb all of your disappointment and criticism."

"Stop, both of you," Iris said, wiping her eyes discreetly. "Let's just sit down for a nice dinner before someone says something they can't take back." Her mother took a step toward her, gripping her shoulders in her hands. "I forgive you, and we won't speak of it anymore. All right?"

Charity glanced at her father for confirmation, and he nodded his assent. "Fine."

"Good. Now, why don't you do something with your hair before you join us?"

My hair is done, she thought, running a hand over her loose curls. She'd had it up in a bun most of the day while she baked and prepared catering orders, but there was no embarrassing hair-tie kink in it. When she'd stopped blowing her hair out every morning and embraced her curls, it was actually a relief to go natural. And gentler on her bank account.

Iris left the room ahead of Charity without waiting for a response, and she gritted her teeth. The pressure of her father's hand on her back propelled her out the door after her mother, and she let him lead her into the family room.

She recognized everyone in the room except one. He was tall and built, wearing a navy sports coat over a gray T-shirt that showed off impressive pecs. His dark hair was brushed back off his forehead, and his smile was even, white, and expensive. Her brother, Anton, was speaking to him in the animated way he did with everyone, his hands waving excitedly while his five-year-old daughter, Isabelle, hung off his left arm, her legs dragging across the floor.

Her father stepped around her to join them, picking up Isabelle, removing her from her dad's arm, and setting her back on her feet with a few stern words. The little girl curled in on herself, and it took every ounce of Charity's self-control not to go to her niece and comfort her, but that would only escalate things with her and her father again. Isabelle ran to her grandmother and threw herself into Iris's arms. Charity watched her mother exit the room with the little girl, catching the unmistakable scowl Iris cast in Royce's direction. Although her father hadn't seen it, Charity's mind raced.

Isabelle is her granddaughter. She'd react to anyone scolding her that way.

Charity made her way farther into the room and searched for a friendly face. Kara was deep in conversation with Charity's sister, Billie, but thankfully, her sister-in-law, Elena, spotted her and hurried across the shiny wood floor to greet her. Elena's dark hair was braided intricately into a gorgeous hairstyle and fell into a fountain of curls down her back. She'd been a cosmetologist working on her psychology degree when she'd met Anton, and although her parents had had reservations initially, Elena had dropped everything to be at Iris's side when she'd been diagnosed with breast cancer. After a double mastectomy, she'd been cancer-free for seven years, and ever since, Elena and Iris had developed a close bond, solidified even more when she'd married Anton and given birth to the first grandchild.

Although there were times Charity envied their relationship, it was hard not to adore her sister-in-law.

Elena stopped next to her, her gaze locked on the door her mother had disappeared through. "I swear, your father has gloves of steel when it comes to Isabelle, and it makes me want to kick him right in his behind."

Charity smothered a laugh. "I'd love to see that."

"I don't know how you and my husband came from that man."

"But with Billie, you can see it?" Charity teased.

Elena smirked above her wineglass, motioning to Billie, who was ducking out of the room. "She does not have your soft side."

"Speaking of soft sides, where is my sister's doting hubby?"

Elena grimaced. "I think he's still upstairs. I thought I heard raised voices, and when I got to the top of the stairs, I heard them arguing."

Billie and her hubby were perfect together, or so it seemed. She'd obviously missed a lot the last couple weeks.

"Who's the tall guy?"

Elena smirked. "That's Christopher Varton, officially here as the newest district attorney, but unofficially, I overheard Royce telling him about you."

"What about me?" Charity whispered.

"That you're beautiful, smart, and driven."

"And leaving out that I'm a stubborn law school deserter and a constant disappointment?"

Elena frowned. "I think your dad just wants you to find someone to make you happy."

Charity almost snorted. Her entire life, she'd been told her parents only wanted what was best for her, but as a teen, she'd realized what was best didn't ever take her desires into account. Neither a weeklong vacation nor her being honest had gotten through to them that she could handle her own life. What she needed to do was to find an opportunity to take herself out of the dating equation, and then maybe they'd finally lose interest in constantly manipulating her.

"If he sat down and had an actual conversation with me, he'd know that I met someone." Charity didn't know how the lie flowed so easily off her tongue, but she was satisfied when her sister-in-law's eyes widened.

"You did? When?"

Charity headed for the wet bar with Elena hot on her heels and poured herself a glass of wine as her mind raced. "In Mexico."

"What happened in Mexico?" Kara asked, coming up alongside her.

Crap. If she made up a random man, Kara would have questions, but that only left—

"Remember that guy I was telling you about? The marketing executive I met in Mexico?"

Kara's brow wrinkled. "Schwartz?"

"Yes, Will Schwartz." Charity took a long, healthy drink from her glass, praying her best friend would play along. "I'm dating him."

Kara slowly started nodding, even as her eyes silently seemed to be screaming, *What are you talking about?*

"Tell me more about him. Is he handsome?" Elena asked.

"Is who handsome?"

Charity almost groaned aloud but turned to smile at her mom, who had come back sans Isabelle. "Where's my adorable niece?"

"Getting a cookie in the kitchen. Who are we talking about?"

"Charity's new boyfriend," Elena offered, taking a sip of her wine with her lips curved above it. "She met him in Mexico while she was on vacation."

Her mother frowned. "You didn't tell me you had a boyfriend."

"You didn't ask. And I said we were dating. It's too early to call him that."

"But who is he? What does he do?" Iris asked.

"He works with Kara's boyfriend, Ben, at Kilburn Marketing. We were surprised to bump into each other, but one thing led to another."

"Ah, Charity," Royce called, approaching them with Christopher Varton and her brother in tow, cutting off whatever follow-up questions her mother had. "I want you to meet someone. Chris, this is my daughter. She runs a nonprofit in Roseville."

"Hi. I've heard a lot about you." Chris flashed that perfect smile, and Charity took his outstretched hand.

"Sorry I can't say the same, Chris, but I'm afraid my father is exaggerating. This is my partner, Kara. We run a cat café together."

"It's nice to meet you, Kara." He shook her hand, his gaze still trained on her. "What exactly is a cat café?"

"It's a cat rescue, but with a café attached. Charity creates all the delicious goodies, and I keep the cats alive since I'm a veterinarian."

"We make a great team." Charity caught her dad's compressed lips and almost laughed. What did he expect her to do? Throw Kara under the bus like Charity could do any of it without her bestie?

"That's great," Chris said. "I've actually been thinking of getting a companion animal. Do you have a card?"

Charity hadn't been expecting that, and thank goodness Kara jumped in. "I do, in my purse. I'll go grab it from the car. Charity? Can I have the keys?"

Charity pulled them out of her dress pocket and held them out to her friend. "I can go with you—"

"No, I'm fine. It's just right outside." Kara gave her a thumbs-up behind Chris's back and mouthed, *He's cute.*

Charity rolled her eyes.

"Why don't we go in to dinner?" Iris suggested, taking her husband's arm.

Chris fell into step beside her and leaned in close, whispering, "What was the eye roll for?"

Charity could feel her face burning. "Nothing, private joke."

"Hmm, okay."

Her parents led the way into the dining room, and it was convenient that Chris ended up on one side of her while she saved the other chair for Kara when she returned.

Billie came into the room, smoothing her long, sleek ponytail and giving Charity a little wave. "Hi. Sorry. Jean will be down in a moment. He got a work call."

While her father was busy asking her sister questions,

Chris leaned over and said, "Your father seemed to think the two of us might hit it off."

"Did he now?" Charity's tone was cool, arching her brow at him.

"He did, but it's a little hard to tell with your entire family around. We might have to set up a time to meet for lunch."

Charity hadn't expected a suit like Chris to have charm, and she caught herself before she returned his smile. "I don't know what my father told you, but I'm seeing someone."

"Is it serious?" he asked.

"That matters how?"

He shrugged. "If you aren't exclusive, there's no harm in meeting me for a meal."

"Except I don't go out with men my father sets me up with."

"I see." He leaned away from her, the slight tilt of his lips transforming into a full-on cocky grin. "I guess I'm going to have to figure out a way around that rule."

Kara returned at that moment, saving Charity from almost falling for his game.

"Like I said, I'm seeing someone."

"Well, I can't wait to meet him. I bet he's one heck of a guy."

CHAPTER ELEVEN

Chocolate Meowcarons

These sweet treats are light, decadent, and hard to resist. Just like our adorable, adoptable cats. Grab a plate and sit a spell.

The Sunday after Will's return from Mexico was cool and crisp as he climbed the porch steps to his mom's house, pulling his jacket up around his neck. Although it was hardly freezing at fifty-five degrees, compared to the sunny, tropical atmosphere he'd left behind a little over a week ago, it felt like the frozen tundra outside.

He knocked on the door, noticing the peeling exterior paint around the doors and windows. Growing up, he'd never wanted for anything, but his parents hadn't made a lot of money, either. And what they did bring in didn't go to home repairs unless they couldn't put it off another month. When his mother told him they *couldn't afford that right now*, Will knew they'd gotten behind on one bill or another because his dad hadn't been paid for an architectural project yet, but the minute the money came in, whatever he wanted would show up on his bed, and before too long, they'd be waiting on the next check.

After Will's dad passed away, his life insurance went to bills and paying off the house, so his mother's salary could take care of the month-to-month expenses. Obviously, they should have created an upkeep account.

The door flew open, and his sister stood in the doorway with an open bottle of champagne and a wicked smile on her face.

"Hello, brother dear."

"Uh-oh. It's never good when you call me that."

"I'm just excited to see you," Sarah said, stepping back so he could come inside. His sister's willowy frame didn't take up a lot of space, and he easily slipped by her into the entryway.

"Why? Is Mom asking when you're going to marry and give her grandchildren?"

Sarah tossed her dark hair, which fell below her chin in a neat, silky bob. "No, I think at this point, she'd be happy if I just inseminated myself sans matrimony. Or if you found someone to—"

"Nope, I'm skipping brunch," he joked, pretending to head back out the door, but his sister grabbed him by the back of his jacket and yanked him inside. She was three years younger than him, but if he hadn't hit his growth spurt, she'd have stayed taller than him at five foot eleven inches.

"Absolutely not. I need your trip to distract her."

"All right, but if this bites me in the rear, you're on my list," he muttered, hanging up his coat and rubbing his neck dramatically. "Any marks?"

"Not yet, but I can change that," she said, her blue eyes twinkling.

"No wonder you can't find a—ow!" He yelped when she grabbed his hair and gave it a yank. "Okay, I apologize!"

"What's going on out here?" Anna Schwartz called, and his sister released him seconds before his mother came through the doorway of the kitchen, her sharp gaze passing from one to the other. Her dark hair was smoothed back from her face and twisted into a tight bun on top of her head, her shoulders thin and stooped from always trying to appear shorter. "What happened to your hair? It's all over the place."

Sarah snickered as he ran a hand over it. "It's a new style I'm trying."

"I like your old style, but it's not my hair." She held out her arms, and he went in for the hug, squeezing her tight. He noticed her stiffen and loosened his grip.

"You okay?"

"A little sore lately." When she pulled back, his mom cupped his face with her hands, studying him. "You're tan. I hope you wore sunscreen. The last thing you need is to get dark spots all over your face from too much sun."

"I did, Mom."

She released him with a swift shake of her head. "Did your sister tell you that two of my fellow teachers had grandbabies born over the break?"

"No, she didn't. Mazel tov to them."

"One of them was Gretchen Olsen! You remember her daughter, Hannah? I tried to introduce you, but you had to leave the barbeque early for a so-called work emergency." His mother used her fingers to make air quotes on the last two words, and his sister snickered.

Will remembered Hannah Olsen had been overly assertive and had a dreamy twinkle in her eye, as if she'd already been planning their wedding. Whether the second was true or not, he'd gotten the heck out of there and avoided all future events where his mother invited her fellow teachers or their kids.

"Seems it worked out for the best. Hannah found someone great, and now they've got a baby—"

"Actually, she's a single mother living with Gretchen. Maybe..." His mother trailed off when her blue eyes glanced at his face and what he suspected was the look of abject horror on it. "Never mind. I better go check on the eggs."

The minute she left the room, Will snatched the champagne bottle from his sister and took a swig before passing it back. "She really is on a tear today."

"I told you. She woke up and chose violence."

He chuckled. "Then bite the bullet and give her what she wants so she'll leave me alone."

"Are you crazy? You're the oldest. It should be you taking that plunge."

"My biological clock isn't ticking yet, whereas—" Will stopped talking when his sister took a threatening step toward him. "Never mind, I'm kidding!"

"Seriously, dude, you need a girlfriend to teach you a little sensitivity. When's the last time you had anyone in your life last more than a few months?"

"Hey, now, you're not Mom. I don't get up in your business, so you stay out of mine."

His sister held up her hands. "Fine, I'm sorry. I'll pick a less personal topic. How's the job going?"

"It's fine." Glancing toward the kitchen, he leaned closer to his sister, lowering his voice. "We landed a big account a few weeks ago, and even with the vacation, I finally have enough saved to strike out on my own. When I'm ready, that is."

"Will, that's amazing!" When he shushed her, Sarah continued with a whisper, "You've been talking about freelance graphic design since you graduated college. Why you went into marketing is beyond me, but hey, if it helped get you closer to your dream, then it was worth it."

"I'm not sure when it will happen, but knowing I could..."

"Why wouldn't you just take the plunge?"

Will didn't want to voice his fears aloud, especially when his mother could be listening. Despite dreaming of starting his own graphic design studio, the thought of being self-employed scared the crap out of him. With everything his parents dealt with when his dad had lean years in the architectural business, saying goodbye to a steady paycheck was something he wasn't ready for. At least not yet.

"I want to have all my ducks in a row and finish out this last account. Then I'll be ready."

"What are you two doing out there? Come in here and include me in your conversations. And bring that bottle! Your mother might like to have a mimosa."

Sarah took another drink from the champagne bottle before handing it to him. "Into the lion's den we go."

Will led the way into the small kitchen and dining room. Same oak table and chairs, the seats covered in blue cushions and a table runner of the same color stretched across the center of it. His mom was bent over with her head in the oven, removing a pie pan from inside.

"Smells good, Mom."

"Thank you," Anna said, setting the pie pan on a hot pad on the table. "Your sister helped me prepare it."

"Please, I cut up the vegetables while she cooked the meat. It wasn't much." Sarah grabbed the orange juice from the fridge and set it on the table. "Mom, do you want a mimosa?"

"With the way you were drinking the champagne, I didn't think there'd be any left."

Sarah grabbed three flutes from the cupboard, and when Will caught a glimpse of her expression, he suppressed a laugh. "Are you saying I'm a drunken spinster, Mom?"

"I just made an observation that my daughter seems to need a drink or two to visit me."

"Only when you talk about harvesting my eggs."

Will coughed.

"I did not! I was just telling you about an article I read detailing how women with careers are freezing their eggs to use later. I can't help it if you read into everything I say."

"Will," his sister said abruptly, taking the champagne bottle from him and setting it on the table, "Tell us about Mexico and in great detail. Please."

"Sure. It was warm. Sunny. Good food. Drinks."

"Did you meet any women?" Anna asked.

"A few," Will said, Charity springing to mind, but he wasn't going to share his intimate interactions with his mother and sister.

"How about the resort? I was thinking about arranging a girls' trip with some of my friends," Sarah said.

"The resort was nice, but if you do go with a group of women, stay together and report any inappropriate behavior," he said.

Sarah set the fruit salad she'd grabbed from the fridge on the table, rolling her eyes. "I'm old enough to know how some men operate, and I've handled them fine. Thanks for the tip, though."

"Can we sit down and have a nice breakfast without you two one-upping each other?" Anna asked, taking her seat closest to the window.

"We have to hone our skills on each other because no one can keep up with us," Sarah quipped, taking the seat next to their mother.

"I did meet someone who can. Well, I knew her before Mexico, but she's pretty snark-tastic. You'd like her, Sarah."

"What's her name? How do you know her?" Anna asked.

"She's friends with Ben's girlfriend. They run the café down the street from Kilburn together. Everything she creates is magic, including these chocolate macarons that melt in your mouth."

"Is she pretty?" his mom asked, cutting into the quiche.

Will held his plate out to his mom, his gaze narrowing. "Mom, just because I talk about a woman doesn't mean I'm interested in her, or vice versa."

"That means yes," Sarah said, scooping some fruit salad onto her plate. "But she won't give him the time of day."

"Then she isn't very smart because your brother is the whole package. With his father's good looks and my brains, any woman would be lucky to have him."

Sarah pretended to gag. "Gross. How come when I tell you someone dumps me, you ask what I did?"

"Because you got your father's brains and my good looks. He was a brilliant man, and he knew it, and you are the same way."

Sarah grinned. "Guilty."

"She's saying you're the cocky one, and I'm the levelheaded sibling."

"All I heard was brilliant," Sarah said.

Anna laughed. "You both got his selective hearing." She suddenly sobered, her gaze flicking to his empty chair.

Even though it had been three years, Will knew his mom had been struggling without his dad. The heart attack had hit him in the car on the way to a client's house, and by the time the EMTs had arrived on the scene, Nathan Schwartz was gone. At least now they could talk about him without his mother bursting into tears.

"I also got his sense of humor," Will said.

Sarah groaned. "Which consisted of bad dad jokes."

"The jokes aren't rated on a good or bad scale, but a stinky-cheese scale."

"You're ridiculous," Sarah said, but he watched his mom's melancholy slip away in lieu of laughter, and Will didn't mind his sister's analysis. Will hated to see his mother in pain and would do anything to make her smile.

"And you get to say you're related to me," he said, taking a bite of his quiche with a grin. "Lucky you."

Sarah stuck her tongue out at Will while Anna ignored their childishness. "Well, I hope you find someone who makes you as happy as your father did me."

Except for when he wouldn't take a job that gave him a steady paycheck. Will remembered overhearing that particular argument when he was nine. His dad had been offered a position with a large architectural firm but declined to take it. His mother had called him selfish, and he had stormed out of the house and didn't come back until the morning. When Will woke up, he found his parents embracing in the kitchen, but his dad still hadn't taken the job.

Maybe if he had, his dad wouldn't have been as stressed all the time. Wouldn't have died young.

"Relying on other people to make you happy puts undue pressure on the relationship. I'm better off finding my own bliss and then inviting someone to join me," Will said.

"Wow, that's very profound, honey," Anna said.

"Thanks. I saw it on an Instagram meme."

His mother and sister laughed, changing the subject to Anna's students while Will ate his food in silence, a strange melancholy settling over him. He didn't like to think about his dad negatively, but how he had stressed over work was part of Will's fear about going out on his own. He had a good job, health insurance, and loved aspects of his work. If all he had to focus on was the artwork and not the pitching, staying at Kilburn would make him incredibly happy, but he was too afraid to ask. Roy was a good boss, but he liked things his way. It was his company after all, and Will didn't want to come across as a whiner.

"Will? Where did you go?" Sarah asked.

"Sorry, the minute you two started talking about snotty children, I lost interest."

His mother reached out and gave his arm a light pinch, and he comically cried out, "Ow, Mom."

"You were once one of those snotty kids, and I have the pictures to prove it."

"So?" he asked.

"So, pay attention when your mother's talking, and while you're at it, pour me a mimosa!"

"Yes, ma'am."

CHAPTER TWELVE

Meowcchiato

Our Meowcchiatos are sure to satisfy your need for flavor and pep in your step! Grab yourself a Tuxedo Biscotti for dipping! I recommend starting with the tail!

CHARITY READ THROUGH THE email one more time to make sure she fully comprehended its contents before she let out an earsplitting scream and jumped off her bed. Robin Hood, who'd been sleeping soundly, sprang up and scrambled after her, his claws scraping along the floor.

Charity raced down the hall and burst into Kara's room with a squeal, flying through the air to land on the bed, something hard connecting with her shins, but she was too excited to care. "Kara, they picked me!"

Kara sat up with a jolt, blinking rapidly. "Who picked what?"

"Ow," a male voice grumbled from under the comforter,

and Charity's face burned when realized she'd landed on Ben's legs.

"Sorry, Ben. I forgot you were sleeping over."

"Charity, what are you talking about?" Kara prodded, rubbing a hand over her eyes.

"*Bake That*, that reality show I applied for months ago? They picked me as one of the contestants!"

Kara's face split into a wide smile. "Oh my goodness, what?" Kara threw back the blankets, revealing a pair of blue sleep shorts with matching shirt, little white cats spaced out all over them, and flew across the bed to hug Charity, both jumping up and down on their knees. "This is amazing!"

"Kara!" Ben shouted, flipping the comforter down, revealing a bare chest and grumpy expression. "You're bouncing on my legs!"

"Sorry!" Both women scrambled over to Kara's side of the bed and continued their excited hopping.

"I don't know why I'm surprised!" Kara hollered. "They'd be crazy not to pick you."

"While I appreciate your confidence, I had my doubts. I'm sure they got thousands of applicants."

"But how many of them opened a cat café with their best friend and are doing amazing things?" Ben cleared his throat, and Kara rolled her eyes. "With the help of a very creative boyfriend."

"I can't take all the credit," Ben said with a grin. "Schwartz helped with the logo design."

"Speaking of Schwartz," Kara started, but Charity pinched

her underarm sharply. "Ouch! What? I wasn't going to tell him *that*."

"Tell me what?" Ben asked.

"Nothing!" Charity said quickly.

Ben frowned. "I don't believe you. What happened with Schwartz?"

"I was going to say that he stopped by the café and said he's thinking about adopting a cat."

Charity almost blew out a sigh of relief at Kara's quick thinking. She didn't want Ben to know she'd used his best friend as her fake boyfriend. The dinner with her family had become an inquisition as each person found out about her new man. She'd thought they'd asked every question under the sun until the news made it to her dad.

"When do we get to meet him?"

Charity had promptly excused herself to go to the bathroom and come back using Kara's upset-stomach excuse to get the heck out of there before she did something crazy like admit she'd been lying through her teeth!

"I wonder why Schwartz came to that conclusion, especially after all the grief Chaos gave him."

"Maybe seeing how happy Chaos makes *you* inspired him?" Kara said, her tone teasing.

Ben snorted. "Yes, I love finding kitten-size claw marks in my brand-new blackout window shades."

"Hello, can we get back to me and my good news?" Charity asked.

"You mean amazing news," Kara said, hugging her tight.

"I need to hop in the shower, so I'll leave you ladies to discuss." Ben leaned over and kissed Kara before getting out of bed. "Thanks for the wake-up call, Charity."

"You're welcome," she sang after him.

"Congratulations on the show. I know you're going to kick butt."

"Then you're a very smart man," she quipped. When he disappeared into the bathroom, Charity grinned. "I really like Ben. Not many men would be as chill about me bolting in here and waking them up."

"Yeah, he's pretty great," Kara mused, and Charity's stomach clenched with jealousy. She loved that Kara had found someone who realized how amazing she was, but when Kara had invited Charity to move in with her, she'd imagined nonstop girls' nights like when they'd roomed in college. Instead, five out of the ten days since Charity arrived home, Kara had either been sleeping over at Ben's or he'd been here. It made her realize how lonely she was.

"So, when do you leave for filming?" Kara asked, dragging Charity out of her head.

"They said they'll be in touch, but gave me a tentative timeline. They'll come here first to do some background on me. Then I head down to LA for filming in February. I'll be gone a couple weeks—or less if I get eliminated."

Kara squeezed her hand. "That's not going to happen, but we're going to need someone who can handle the baking and catering side. I'll be useless in your kitchen."

"Amen," Charity joked, earning a shove from Kara. "I'm

hoping Marcela catches on, but I'm afraid to leave her alone in my kitchen."

"Not everyone is born with your talents. But she'll catch on." Kara clapped. "This calls for a celebration, but we've already got your birthday party planned for Saturday."

Charity groaned. "Please tell me you didn't invite my family."

"It's your birthday, Char. Of course I did."

"But this should be a friends-only thing. They can torture me at the next family dinner."

"You're just worried that Ben is going to invite Schwartz to the party, and they're going to jump to conclusions when he has no idea what they're talking about." Kara paused, as if waiting for Charity to agree with her, but when she stayed silent, Kara powered on. "What possessed you to say the two of you were dating? I know you said nothing happened except a kiss on New Year's, but why didn't you make up a boyfriend in Canada or something?"

"I panicked, all right?" Charity didn't feel bad that she'd downplayed her night with Will because if he wasn't going to share details, she wouldn't, either. "I needed it to sound believable enough to buy me some time. I was already in the doghouse after bailing on Christmas. At least if they think I got a successful, handsome boyfriend out of it, they won't ride me about it anymore."

"And what happens when this super-amazing boyfriend never comes to dinner?"

"I'll worry about that when the time comes."

Kara studied her for several seconds, and by the pensive expression on her face, Charity knew she wasn't going to like what her bestie was going to say. "You know, Chris seems like a nice guy, and he called the café to set up a time to come by and meet the cats. Maybe your parents weren't so far off with their matchmaking."

Charity groaned. "Judas."

Kara laughed. "I'm not! I am just pointing out that he's still interested, even after you made up a fake boyfriend to throw him off. Maybe you should give him a chance."

She shook her head. While Chris seemed charming and was definitely attractive, he had a serious strike against him. He was her father's choice, and while that might seem like an immature way of looking at it, even when he'd taken her hand later on to say goodbye, there was no spark. No warming of her skin or tingle where their palms touched.

Not that chemistry should be a leading factor in choosing someone to get involved with, considering her track record, but if she was going to start a relationship with someone, it should at least be a man who intrigued her. Excited her.

"When you and Ben first met, were you attracted to him?" Charity asked.

"Well, yes, but you'll remember I kind of forgot about that for a bit because I thought he was an animal-hating jerk."

"But once you got over your disgruntlement and realized how awesome he was, you two had some pretty electrifying chemistry. I didn't have that with Chris."

"And what about Schwartz?"

Charity's cheeks burned, flashes of their night together racing through her mind. But even before that, when Will had come into the café for the first time, his blue eyes had connected with hers, and she'd experienced a bolt of attraction unlike anything she'd felt before.

She knew marriage didn't have to be the be-all and end-all. There were people in this world who stayed together for decades without a signed document, but it was what her family did. It was the expected outcome of any relationship built to last, in her opinion, and the one thing that she and her parents agreed on. And while Charity liked Will's flirtatious nature, his banter, and the way he looked at her, what was the point of falling for him knowing that it wouldn't lead anywhere?

"Schwartz is a snack, something tasty to keep you going until dinner. He isn't the guy."

"And yet he was the first cover you thought of to get your parents off your back. Why is that?"

"Because I couldn't think of a complete lie on the spot. I sprinkled enough truth to make it believable."

Kara opened her mouth, but Charity stopped her by adding, "What if, for today only, maybe we make a couple meowcchiatos and celebrate this amazing opportunity I've been offered. We can worry about my family and Schwartz later?"

Kara huffed. "Fine, but you know what my grandma used to say about lying? Oh, what tangled webs we weave, when first we practice to deceive."

Charity heard her phone blare to life and huffed. "Maybe so, but I've weaved my web too well to fall apart."

"Uh-huh."

Charity rushed out of the room to answer her phone without waiting for her bestie to throw any more doubt her way. She snatched the phone and hit the green phone icon a second before she realized it was her mother calling.

Dang it.

"Hi, Mom," she greeted breathlessly.

"What were you doing?"

"I was in Kara's room and left my phone in mine, so I ran."

"Oh, I see. Speaking of Kara, she invited us to your birthday party on Saturday night."

"Yes, she told me."

"Why didn't you extend the invite? Don't you want us there?"

Charity glanced to the ceiling, quietly asking for strength. "I figured we'd be doing a family birthday party on Sunday or something, since you mentioned a charity dinner on Saturday night. I just assumed you wouldn't want to hang out with a bunch of my friends."

"Well, we do have dinner plans, but I'd like to pick you up Saturday morning and go shopping for your birthday meal and cake for Sunday. Will your new boyfriend be at your birthday party?"

"I told you, Mom, it's too early to call him that, and I'm not sure. He said something about working on a new pitch."

"I don't like that, honey. A man should make his woman the number one priority in his life."

"You're right. I'm sure he'll be there."

"Good. Then your father and I will swing by on our way to dinner. We'd like to meet this young man."

"Great." She'd been on such a high about being accepted to the show that it made sense the universe would come along and burst her bubble. "What time do you want to go grocery shopping?"

"I'll pick you up at around nine."

"All right, but I can't be long. I've got deliveries to make."

"You know, if you went back to school, you wouldn't have to work weekends. Or better yet, give a man like Chris a chance. He asked your father about you."

"Mom, I love what I do, and honestly, I don't need a man to take care of me. Especially one sniffing after a woman already seeing another man."

Silence stretched on the other end of the phone before her mother said, "I'm glad I raised such strong, self-sufficient daughters."

Charity knew her mother had taken offense by the tone of her voice, but she hadn't meant it as an insult to Iris. Her mom had stayed home with each of them until they started school and taken a part-time job at their school to stay on their schedule, but her father was the breadwinner. Her mother has deferred to him for everything, even when Charity thought she should have told him to stuff it.

Charity softened her tone. "I meant that I don't want to give up something I've worked for and love. And I think a man who truly cares about me will understand that."

"I hope you're right, darling. I'll see you Saturday morning."

"Bye, Mom."

CHAPTER THIRTEEN

Russian Blue-Berry Muffins

Baked fresh daily, these muffins are moist, buttery goodness and almost better than a headbutt from your favorite feline. Buy a basket to share with friends!

"Let me push the cart. It helps me walk. I don't know why, but I've been stiffer than a poker the last few months."

Will let his mom take the cart from him, ambling along beside her to match her hitching gait. He'd been in the middle of a titillating dream earlier that morning when his mom's ringtone had blasted through his subconscious. When he'd groggily answered the phone and she'd asked him to take her grocery shopping because it hurt too much to drive, he couldn't say no. His mom had been back and forth to the doctor several times, but they hadn't come to any definite conclusions about what was going on with her. She'd assured him the tests they did this week would give them a cause of her pain, but the mystery of it left him feeling uneasy. He wouldn't share that with her, though, and preferred doing things with her that would take her mind off her worries.

"What else do you have on your list?" he asked, grabbing a package of cookies, and tossing it into the cart.

"I need some fruit and so do you. I've seen what you keep in that cupboard of yours."

"That's because I eat out more than I eat at home. Or use an app to get something delivered."

"You should pack your lunch. Eating out is expensive."

"I budget for it so I don't have to meal prep. I don't have the patience for it."

"I used to make all the fixings for our lunches on Sunday so you could just grab and pack your lunches before school. Do you remember?"

"Of course I do. I had to balance out what I brought to school because, if it was too good, the other kids would try to take stuff out of it. But if there was too much healthy stuff, nobody wanted to eat it, including me."

His mom chuckled. "I miss taking care of you kids. Being in that house on my own gets lonely sometimes."

Will swallowed down the lump of guilt at the back of his throat. When his dad passed away, he and Sarah had alternated days with her, so Mom wasn't ever left alone for too long, but after a while, she'd told them to find something else to do with their time rather than hover over her. They'd settled on Sunday morning brunch and had kept it a standing family meal, plus popping in to visit or help when she needed it.

"I noticed the outside paint's seen better days. You want me to look into finding someone to spruce it up a bit?" Will asked.

"No point in doing that just yet."

"What do you mean?"

"I don't have the money to retire, let alone paint my house, Will."

Will put his hand on the cart handle, stalling his mom's movements. "What are you talking about? You've got retirement through your job at the school."

"Which I can't access yet; same with Social Security."

"What about the funds left from Dad's life insurance?" Will asked, lowering his voice. "I know there wasn't much, but you told me you were going to put it in some stocks—"

"I did, but it turns out I backed the wrong companies. I took a loss and with the pain I've been in, I don't know how I'm going to keep teaching." She patted his hand until he lifted it off the bar and she started walking again. "I don't want you to worry, though. Everything will work out. It always does."

Will dragged a hand down his face, his chest tightening as the full weight of her predicament sank in. She was only fifty-eight. What if her pain became unbearable and she really couldn't continue teaching? He'd seen her power and water bills, and even with insurance, the countless doctor's visits were adding up. Her positive attitude wasn't going to chase away the realities of the world.

The familiar scent of vanilla and sugar distracted him from

his heavy thoughts, and his heart picked up the pace as he looked around, spotting Charity standing a few feet away in the produce section. Her face was scrunched with annoyance as an older woman next to her appeared to be reading the back of a package of blueberry muffins aloud.

"Hey, Schwartz!" Kara called out to him, dropping a bag of chips in the cart that Charity was pushing.

Charity's head whipped around, her eyes widening when she caught his gaze. Decked out in a white sweater and gray slacks, she looked classy and put together, while he'd thrown on a pair of sweats and a gray hoodie. He waved a hand but made no move to go over to them, especially when the older woman looked up from the box and her eyes raked over him.

"Who is that?" his mom asked.

"Ben's girlfriend, Kara, and her roommate, Charity. I don't know who the other woman is."

"Oh, which one is the girlfriend?"

"The redhead."

"She's lovely. Her roommate is beautiful, too. That's the one who was in Mexico with you?"

"She wasn't with me, Mom," he mumbled. "She was just there at the same time."

"You know what I meant. If you want to go say hi—"

"I don't, Mom. I'll see them later tonight. It's Charity's birthday, and they're having a party."

"She invited you?" Her tone was way too excited for Will's comfort.

"No, Ben did."

"Oh. What did you get her?"

"It's not a gift-giving thing, Mom."

"William, I raised you better. You should at least pick her out a nice bouquet or a box of chocolates."

Will scoffed. "I'm not bringing her flowers and chocolates!"

"Why not?"

"Because she's not my girlfriend." Will noticed all three women approaching them and nearly groaned aloud.

"Hey, Will," Kara said, turning to his mom with a wide smile. "Hi, I'm Kara." She held her hand out to his mom, who took it into both of hers.

"I'm Anna Schwartz, this one's mom." Anna released Charity's hand and tapped the back of her hand to Will's arm to emphasize their connection.

"It's very nice to meet you," Kara said, slipping her arm through Charity's. "This is my best friend, Charity, and her mother, Iris, who graciously allowed me to crash their shopping trip."

"I told you it was fine, Kara." Iris took first his mother's hand and then his. "How do you do?" Her eyes were a deep green, and although Charity shared her mouth and nose, their similarities ended there. Iris was several inches shorter than her daughter with olive skin and straight hair pulled back into a sleek ponytail. Her forehead suddenly wrinkled, and her eyes narrowed on him. "Will Schwartz?"

"Yes, that's me."

Iris's green eyes brightened. "I've heard a lot about you. You're in marketing, I understand?"

Will shot Charity a quick glance, wondering why she'd been discussing him with her mother. "Yes, I work at Kilburn down the way from Meow and Furever."

"Meow and Furever?" his mom asked, jumping into the conversation.

"It's our cat café," Kara offered. "We offer pastries and espresso drinks and quality time with adoptable kitties."

"Oh! I had no idea we had one of those! Will just called it a café, so I assumed it was a regular coffee shop. I'll have to come see it some time. I love cats, but when our last old man died, I didn't have the heart to adopt another."

"Well, maybe you can at least come by for a coffee and scone and get your kitty fix," Charity said, finally engaging with them.

"That sounds lovely."

"I had a different picture in my mind from what Charity described of you, Will," Iris said, bringing his focus back to her.

Will was sure he heard Charity grumble, "Dang it, Mom," and his curiosity was piqued.

"How did she describe me?"

"I believe snazzy dresser was the term she used."

Will glanced down at his Hey Dudes and sweats. He probably looked like he'd just rolled out of bed and thrown something on, which was a little too close to the truth.

"I can assure you, William usually looks like a million bucks," his mom said, coming to his defense, "but I've been struggling health wise the last few months and called him early this morning to take me grocery shopping. So we call this casual Saturday chic."

Will watched Charity share a warm smile with his mom and hated how the sight of it sped up his pulse. "I tried going for that look but was ordered to go change."

Her mother huffed. "Yoga pants are for working out, not the grocery store."

"Your daughter is lovely enough to leave the house in a trash bag and turn heads," Will's mom quipped, and Charity's whole face lit up like a hundred-watt bulb.

"Thank you," Iris responded, waving her hand. "Would you and your mother like to join us for dinner tomorrow night? We've heard so much about your Will, it will be nice to compare the myth with the man."

"I—" Will started, but his mom responded faster. "We'd love that."

"Perfect. Charity will give you the address. Dress is business casual, and please let her know of any dietary restrictions. We'd stay for a longer chat, but I special-ordered her birthday cake, and it needs to be picked up in twenty minutes."

"Of course. Happy birthday, young lady," his mom said.

"Thank you, Mrs. Schwartz."

"We'll see you tomorrow," Iris said, pushing the cart away. When the threesome disappeared toward the front of the store, his mom turned to him with a puzzled expression on her face.

"I thought you weren't seeing anyone?"

"I'm not."

"Then what was that about?"

Will's gaze followed Charity's retreating back, his mind racing. "I have no idea, but I intend to find out."

CHAPTER FOURTEEN

Mousetrap Snack Tray

A beautifully arranged assortment of fresh fruit, cheese, and crackers. So good there won't be a crumb left for even the tiniest mouse.

CHARITY STOOD IN FRONT of her bedroom mirror, giving her eyelashes one last sweep with the mascara wand. The party wouldn't start for a few more hours, but Charity was too keyed up to relax. She'd spent hours on finger food prep and snack trays with Kara's help after grocery shopping this morning, so there wasn't anything left for her to do except get ready. Kara had gone with Ben to the store to grab a few last-minute things they'd forgotten this morning, telling Charity to take a bath and relax. Even though Kara hadn't come right out and said it, Charity knew her bestie had picked up on the tension between Charity and her mom. Despite Iris inviting Kara to come along, she'd obviously been put out when Kara accepted, and Charity had held back on calling her out on it.

After the run-in with Will, Charity and Iris had gotten into a heated discussion on the way to pick up the cake while Kara had sunk into the back seat, texting furiously on her phone. Charity found out later that she was texting Ben, jokingly asking him to come save her, and Charity couldn't blame her. If she'd been able to safely escape without escalating things, she would have.

Charity sighed, studying her handiwork in the mirror before twisting the lid back onto the mascara. The argument in the car had kicked off because Iris had made a comment about Will's clothes. Charity couldn't remember exactly what was said, but the gist was that Will looked like a low-class slob, and she'd immediately jumped to his defense. It was the weekend, and he was helping his mom.

Charity didn't want to dwell too much on why she was ready to go to the mattresses with her mother over Will. She'd watched his confusion bleed into slowly dawning shock and wished she could melt into the tile floor of the supermarket. Thank goodness his mother had been there. It must have been killing him not to ask what was going on but Charity figured he wouldn't want to cause a scene in front of his mom. She'd been mentally preparing for him to show up tonight with Ben and demand answers. Just what she wanted for her birthday, humble pie with a scoop of humiliation.

Someone pounded on the door, and Charity's heart leaped in her chest. It was too early for most guests, but maybe Kara had her arms full and was signaling Charity for help. She skidded down the hallway in slipper socks and her party dress, laughing when Robin Hood puffed up and scrambled out of her way. Apparently, he was still holding a grudge after her excited reaction to discovering she was going to be a contestant on *Bake That*.

"I'm coming," she called two seconds before she pulled the door open and found Will on her doorstep.

Ah, crap.

He was no longer in a hoodie and jeans but sported a pair of khakis, a navy-blue T-shirt, and a plaid button-up shirt open over it.

"Hi," he said.

Charity had hoped to pull him aside during the party when there were people around in case he got upset. Prior to Kara opening her big mouth and waving him down at the store, Will had seemed to be avoiding her, which she'd been fine to continue. When her mother brought up Will in the car, Charity had almost come clean about her fake boyfriend, but she couldn't bring herself to open herself up to ridicule, especially on her birthday. She'd already been a bit mopey about turning thirty-three, and having the bickering with her mother turn into a full-fledged blowup would be the icing on the cake, so to speak.

"Hi," Charity said, breathing hard. "You're a little early for the party."

Will crossed his arms over his chest, blue eyes narrowing on her like lasers. "You know why I'm here. What was that this morning?"

"You mean my mother inviting you to dinner tomorrow?" Charity asked sweetly. "She was being nice."

"But why? And what has she heard about me?"

Charity stepped to the side, waving her hand. "You might as well come in for this conversation."

"Gracious of you," he muttered.

"Sarcasm. That's original." She shut the door with a heavy sigh and leaned against it, bracing herself for his reaction. "Last weekend, my parents were giving me hell about ditching them over Christmas and ambushed me with a blind date at family dinner. I just wanted a little peace, and suddenly, I was gushing about this marketing executive I met in Mexico and your name kind of spilled out because it sounded less like a lie—"

"What the heck, Charity?"

"I know!"

"No, seriously, after how strongly you were against what happened between us carrying over when we got back home, why would you use me as your fake boyfriend?"

"I told you! I suck at lying, and at least I know enough about you to give them snippets of accurate information. If I had to make up every detail, I'd be a stuttering, stammering mess, and I never in a million years thought that they would ever meet you! Especially since we've hardly said two words to each other in over a week."

"Well, now you've got my mom asking questions about all this!" Robin Hood started weaving between his legs, and Will leaned over to stroke the cat's back. "She thinks I'm holding out on her."

"Maybe that's not such a bad thing?" she said hesitantly.

"What are you talking about?"

"If your mom already suspects we're dating and my parents think it, why not let them continue—"

"Are you out of your mind?" he exploded. "I don't want to fake date you."

All right, that stung a little, but she couldn't blame him. "If this is about Mexico, I thought we'd both apologized and agreed to put it behind us?"

"That was before you offered me to your parents as a sacrificial boyfriend." He'd started to pace the length of the entryway, Robin Hood following him with rapt fascination.

"Do you want to take this to the kitchen or continue to wear a line in the floor?"

"I'm too keyed up to sit," Will said, finally coming to a halt in front of her. "I guess my real burning question is, why am I good enough to date but not sleep with?"

"Oh, for the love of—you were fantastic in bed, all right? You were a stud. I would have climbed back under those sheets in a second if I'd thought there was any kind of future between us. Do you feel better now? Have I praised your prowess and inflated your fragile male ego enough?"

Will's expression darkened. "You are not winning any points for your case right now."

"Look, I'm not in the market for a friend with benefits, which is why I turned down round two in the first place—"

"It was round three if we're being honest."

"How can you go from furious to joking?!" she asked.

"It's a gift, and my *fragile male ego* prefers accuracy."

Charity would have rolled her eyes at the absurdity of his argument, but she needed his help and being snarky wasn't going to get it. "You've told me that you don't have any issues with women, so why are you so hung up on the fact that I didn't want to sleep with you again?"

"Because now you're looking for a boyfriend without benefits, in which case, I'm not interested. Like you said, I don't have any trouble with women, and if I wanted a girlfriend, I could get one like that."

He snapped his fingers, and her temper flared. "Yes, I know, you're so hot with your bright blue eyes and charm!"

"Was that supposed to be a compliment? Because your tone makes me think you meant it as an insult."

Charity threw her hands in the air. "What do you want from me? Do you want me to tell my parents the truth tonight, at my birthday party, and get berated once again for being the disappointment of the family?" Charity hated that her voice broke, disgusted with the show of emotional weakness. "I didn't go to law school like my dad while my brother is following in my father's footsteps as a prosecutor and my sister is on her way to being the best political kingmaker in the state. Instead, I chose to open a nonprofit with my best friend, and some months I eat way too much ramen to stay under my budget. I'm thirty-three with a roommate and a cat, who lied about a boyfriend like I'm the awkward girl at summer camp again. So, sure, let me lay it all bare for them at my birthday party, in front of all my friends. Because that would be on-brand for how my life is going."

Will didn't respond for several beats, his tone lighter than before. "Your mother didn't seem too impressed with me, so it would probably be a relief if you said we broke up."

"It's not you. My mother doesn't leave the house without being decked out to the nines with a full face of makeup, and she expects everyone around her to always look ready for a photo op."

Will's gaze swept over her, pausing on her socks. "Glad you're not that high-maintenance."

"Har-har! My point is when you're dressed for work, or like now, you look sharp. Someone put together. She sees you like this, and you charm the pants off my dad, and I get a break from their disappointment."

"And what do I get out of it?"

"My undying gratitude?" she asked.

"Nice try, but no. If I'm involving my mother in these shenanigans, then we're going all-out for both sides."

Charity arched an eyebrow. "You were previously upset that your mother thought we were dating, and now you want her to think we're together? What changed?"

"I had a moment of self-reflection during the pacing and realized you're not the only one disappointing their parent."

The tension in her shoulders eased, a rush of empathy tightening her chest. "I'm sure that's not true. Your mom clearly adores you."

"I know she does, that's not the issue. My lack of urgency to give her a daughter-in-law and grandchildren are the cause of her discontent with me."

"Ah, and given your views on marriage..."

"Exactly," he said.

"Where's your dad in all of this?"

Will swallowed. "He died three years ago."

Charity winced. "I'm so sorry."

"Thanks."

She held out her hand to him, and he slowly took it, his big hand wrapping around hers. It was the first time they'd touched in weeks, and her face burned, remembering how much she'd enjoyed having his undivided attention.

Clearing her throat, she asked, "Then we have an accord?"

His lips twisted into a smirk that made her stomach flip-flop. "For now."

Charity released the breath she'd been holding. "Thank God. I am not ready to go back to random men being thrown at me every weekend."

Will chuckled. "At least you're not regaled with how many grandchildren your mother's friends and coworkers have."

"Thankfully, my parents have one grandchild from my brother, and Isabelle keeps my mother busy."

"Lucky. I keep trying to get my sister to give my mom what she wants, but Sarah says I'm the oldest, so it's on me."

"She's not wrong."

"Hey, if you're going to be my fake girlfriend, I expect you to take my side."

Charity grimaced. "And tick off your sister? No, that is the wrong move for any girlfriend to make, real or fake." She patted his chest. "Don't worry, my dude. Your family is going to love me."

He seemed to sober, his expression thoughtful. "Do I really want them to? What happens when we break up? They'll be devastated."

"No, because we'll tell them it was my fault so you look like the wounded party, and I'll tell my family, when the time comes, that you were the issue, which they won't believe because—never mind." She didn't want to come off like a whiny victim.

"And when will this breakup go down?" Will asked, bringing her back to the matter at hand.

"When it's convenient for both of us?" Charity rolled her eyes when he gave her an arch look. "Okay, fine. How about we keep this going until either one of us meets someone we're interested in getting serious with? Or we're just sick of being around each other? Until then, we're available for all important family events."

"Fine. Is this something we shake on or does it require something more personal, like a kiss?"

Charity grabbed him by his nose gently, bringing him down until they were eye level. "Unless we're performing for family, don't even try it."

"Yes, ma'am," he said, nasally. She released his nose, and he sniffed. "I'll see you tonight, birthday girl."

Before Will could open the door, Charity called after him, "Hey, Will?"

"Yeah," he said, looking over his shoulder at her.

"Thanks for doing this."

"No problem, but fair warning. This is going to be fun… for me," he said, waggling his brows.

"What does that mean, Will? Will!"

Too late; he'd already escaped out the door.

What have I gotten myself into?

CHAPTER FIFTEEN

Breakfast Purrito

You'll be feline fine when you imbibe this Breakfast Purrito with scrambled eggs, cheese, bacon, sausage, and pico-de-gato salsa! Spicier than a calico on catnip!

WILL PULLED UP TO Kara and Charity's house two hours later, parking next to Ben's SUV. His friend was on the porch talking to a group of guys, but when he spotted Will, he headed down the stairs and across the yard swiftly.

Will exited his car with a wave. "Hey, buddy. What's happening?"

"A little birdy told me that you've been keeping a secret."

Will paused, cocking his head to the side. "You'll have to be more specific. I am, after all, a man of mystery."

"That you're dating Charity?"

"Oh, that."

"Yeah, that. I'm just curious how this whole dating my

girlfriend's best friend came about, because when I asked you about your trip, you never mentioned hooking up with her."

"We weren't sure whether we wanted to take this thing between us to the next level. You know how it is. Swift passion can burn out just as fast—"

"Come off it and tell me the truth," Ben said, his Boston accent more pronounced.

Considering the hooking-up part was the truth, he found the command rather ironic. "No, we didn't hook up. I agreed to go along with being her pretend boyfriend, and in exchange, maybe it will give my mother a little peace of mind about her perpetually single son."

"Seriously?" Ben asked, his eyebrows hiking up his forehead. "While it might ease things up in one department, it seems like you're making your life overall more chaotic."

"It's complicated and between the two of us, so while I appreciate the concern, worry less about my shenanigans. I got this."

Ben shook his head. "I just hope you know what you're getting into. Meeting a girl's parents is stressful under the best circumstances, without lying."

"Oh, that reminds me." Will reached into his back seat and brought out two bouquets. "One for the birthday girl and the other for her mom."

"Never mind," Ben said with a smirk. "Seems you have the situation well in hand."

"I'm glad you noticed. Are her parents here yet?"

"I haven't seen them."

Will gave the guys on the porch a little salute and followed Ben into the house, heading straight for the kitchen. Charity was setting a tray of bacon-wrapped wieners on the table next to an array of finger foods and dips. Her eyes widened when she saw him, drifting down to his designer shoes and back up over his tailored gray suit. He'd worn a blue collared dress shirt without the tie, because he knew the color made his eyes pop.

"Wow. You look great."

"My girl said dress to impress." He held out one of the arrangements to her. "Happy birthday."

She took it hesitantly, her forehead furrowed. "Thank you. Who is the other one for..." She trailed off, her eyes widening. "Wait, did you buy flowers for my mother?"

"Of course I did," he said, pushing his glasses back up onto the bridge of his nose. Most of the time he wore contacts, but he'd thought they completed the distinguished look tonight. "I'm going to be the best fake boyfriend you've ever had."

Charity grinned. "I don't know. It's hard to compete with Joey Trenton from Austin, Texas. He sent me flowers and chocolates at school for Valentine's Day in seventh grade."

"Joey Trenton's a boy. I'm a man," Will said, deepening his voice.

Ben glanced between them and threw up his hands. "You two are freaking me out! I'm going to find Kara."

Will watched his friend escape and chuckled. "Ben is terrible at subterfuge."

"I'm not much better. I have this weird tick where I click my tongue when I'm lying and can't seem to stop fidgeting."

"Don't do that." He set the other bouquet on the kitchen counter and leaned over her.

Charity arched away from him. "What are you doing?"

"If they're going to believe we're together, you need to relax and pretend that you want to be around me."

"I'll be able to pretend once they get here. It's the waiting that is getting to me. I just want to get this over with."

"Ouch."

"You know what I mean. It's them, not you."

"I guess I should be grateful it's not the pretending to like me that's got you on edge. Maybe we should practice before they arrive."

Her dark eyes narrowed. "Practice what?"

"Being a couple. Hugging. Touching. Natural inclinations every real couple has. Well, the ones that still like each other, that is."

"Is this a ploy to be close to me?"

"Would I take advantage of being your fake boyfriend to hold an attractive woman in my arms? Absolutely not."

Charity laughed and set her flowers down next to the other bouquet before stepping closer to him. She wrapped her arms around his waist, her body melting into his. "Like this?"

Will cleared his throat, trying not to think about how good she felt pressed against him. "Better, but I'm an affectionate guy. Are you all right with that?"

"What kind of affections?" she asked, suspicion laced through her tone.

Will dipped his head, breathing her in. "A random kiss on the cheek."

"Acceptable," she murmured, and he brushed his mouth against her skin. Her eyelashes fluttered, and he wondered if his proximity was affecting her, because being this close to her had a serious hold on him.

"Hand-holding."

"Yes."

"What about the mouth?" He watched her gaze drop to his lips, and he gripped the counter hard, resisting the urge to close the distance.

"What about my mouth?"

"I know you said nothing when our parents aren't around, but we don't want kissing to be awkward, do we? If we've been dating for weeks, it should be effortless."

"We kissed when we spent the night together."

"It's been a few weeks. Maybe I forgot," he teased.

"Oh, really?" To his surprise, Charity pressed her chest to his without commenting and covered his mouth with hers. His hand came up to rest on her hip, but other than that, he let her take the lead. Even though Will knew it wasn't real, he found himself getting caught up in it.

Charity broke the kiss with a gasp, dropping back onto her heels. "Trigger any memories?"

Will tried not to focus on her husky whisper and cleared his throat. "It's all coming back to me now."

"Great," she said, completely disengaging from him with

a smirk. "We shouldn't have to do that too often. My mother isn't big on PDA. She thinks it's tacky."

"Good to know." How could she go from breathless to cool in a matter of moments? He was still trying to rein in the urge to haul her back in for another kiss and grabbed a wiener from the tray to keep his hands busy. He popped it into his mouth, and once he'd finished chewing it, he said, "Hopefully, you find my performance satisfactory tonight."

"I'm sure it will be fine," she said, her gaze on his fingers, and he almost grinned. Whatever Charity tried to tell herself, she wasn't as immune to him as she pretended to be.

The doorbell rang, and after several seconds, Kara called out, "Charity, your parents are here."

Charity ran a hand over her curls before licking her lips. "I guess it's showtime."

Will went to wash his hands in the sink, collecting himself even as his heart threatened to explode from his chest. He heard heavy footsteps across hardwood floors and turned in time to find a tall Black man in a navy suit cross the threshold, Iris holding on to his arm.

"Mom, Dad, I'm glad you could make it," Charity said, kissing her mother's cheek and then her father's.

"We can't stay long. We have a dinner party to get to," her father said, and Will stiffened at his brusque tone. Why wouldn't he rather be here celebrating his daughter?

"Yes, I know." Even though Will could see her smiling profile, he'd noticed the tightening by her mouth.

"Your mother insisted we come here to meet the man you're seeing."

"That would be me." Will grabbed the flowers off the counter and crossed to Charity's side, holding them out to Iris with one hand while slipping his arm around Charity's waist. "Mrs. Simmons, it's a pleasure to see you again."

Her mother's eyes brightened as she took the flowers, and the smile she flashed him seemed genuine. "Thank you, Will. You cleaned up nice."

"I told you he did," Charity muttered.

"Thank you, ma'am."

"Please, call me Iris."

"Royce Simmons," her father said, holding his hand out to Will.

"It's good to meet you, sir." Will took Royce's hand and squeezed it. "I'm a big fan of your daughter and her culinary talents. Although I should probably lay off eating her breakfast purritos, but they're addicting," Will said, patting his flat stomach.

Royce seemed to be sizing him up, as if he didn't fully believe him. "Charity mentioned you're in marketing."

"Yes, sir. I work for Kilburn here in town. My partner and I are the top-performing team."

Charity's father seemed to nod in approval. "There's good money in marketing, I hear."

"I do quite well. Helps that I live simply, so my car's paid off, no credit card balances."

"Do you rent or own?" Royce asked.

"I own a two-bedroom condo." Why did he feel like he was being interviewed?

"Crap!" someone yelled from across the house. "Charity! Your cat is out of your room!"

"Oh no! Robin Hood!" Charity rushed around her parents and squatted in the door like a football lineman, diving for the orange tabby as he rushed between her legs and into the kitchen. Charity tried scrambling to her feet and hollered, "Will, don't let him get the food!"

Will had no idea how he pulled it off, but he caught the cat in midair before he managed to land in the middle of the food platters, holding him against his chest. The big cat purred, rubbing his face against Will's chin.

"I guess I should add cat wrangler to my résumé?" he joked.

Royce shot a glance of disdain at Robin Hood, but his affect warmed toward Will. "Nice reflexes. Did you play football at all?"

Charity nodded *yes* behind her parents, but Will shook his head. "Tennis, actually."

"No wonder you're quick on your feet. Would you like to hand off my daughter's cat and join me for a drink?"

Winning parents over? Check.

"Absolutely. Lead the way."

CHAPTER SIXTEEN

Shiny Coats, Steel-Cut Oats

The perfect hearty breakfast to make your fur shine. Add in a pinch of brown sugar and maple or fresh fruit for flavor.

"I HAVE TO SAY, honey, I was skeptical at first, but I think you really scored a winner with this one. Your dad wanted to be out of here fifteen minutes ago, and they're still talking."

Charity shot her mom a scowl, her mother's complete inability to read the room rankling her. They were standing just outside the kitchen while her father and Will were in the living room, talking animatedly with each other.

"Am I supposed to feel good that he couldn't wait to bail on his daughter's birthday?"

Her mother released an exasperated huff. "Honestly, Charity, what do you expect? These are your friends. Besides, you didn't invite us or seem too keen on us being here tonight anyway. So why are you upset?"

For the life of her, Charity couldn't figure that out. Maybe showing her parents how full her life was, how many friends cared about her and thought she was doing good work in the world, might change their mind about her choices. Instead, they'd been counting down the minutes until they could leave for whatever function would advance her father's career.

Well, her mother was. Her father was currently throwing back his head and laughing at whatever Will had said.

"You're right," Charity said, sipping from her glass of wine. "I appreciate you coming, and I'm glad you both like Will."

"He's a sight better than the last man you brought home. The man who rebuilt dirt bikes. So crass."

"I wasn't dating Trent for his etiquette, Mom," Charity said, smirking.

It took Iris a moment for her meaning to click, and she let out a horrified gasp. "Charity, I swear, sometimes I don't understand your behavior." Her mother set aside her own glass on the kitchen counter. "I'm going to use the ladies' room, and when I return, I'll gather your father so you can have fun without your parents hovering."

Charity took a large gulp from her wineglass, watching her dad let out another robust laugh. A flash of jealousy lit through her, and she fought to suppress it. Only, she couldn't remember the last time her dad had even chuckled at something she said.

Maybe if you didn't make everything a battle with them, they might relax enough to enjoy your company.

Charity didn't know what it was like to not fight with her parents. From the moment she lost her second-grade spelling bee, it seemed like she'd done nothing but disappoint them, no matter how hard she tried. She'd even done a slew of beauty pageants like her sister, Billie, hoping to bond with her mother, but finally Charity realized she'd spent so much effort trying to make them happy that she was miserable. Once she let go of the hope of gaining their approval, she'd found herself. Her love of baking. Friends who accepted her, flaws and all.

Will caught her gaze from across the room and shot her a wink. This Will was nothing like Schwartz when he'd first walked into the café two months ago, flirting outrageously and making her laugh. This guy was sophisticated and knew how to work a crowd.

This was a man her parents approved of, and Charity had mixed feelings about it.

Her mother returned, her purse and coat in hand. "Honey, you should really think about limiting the pastries and maybe switching to some steel-cut oats in the morning. I really hope you don't eat all of those foods you make. All of that processed, fatty food is not good for you. Now don't get angry, I'm just trying to help. You don't want to end up like your friend Kara."

Charity's head whipped around, her temper flaring. "What are you talking about? Kara is gorgeous in every way."

"I think Kara is a beautiful girl, but it isn't healthy to be that... big."

Iris opened her purse, obviously searching for something inside, and Charity stared at the top of her head, rage twisting inside her like a turning screw. Charity knew her mother worked hard to stay fit and had even mentioned Charity's weight going up and down over the years, but never had she said something so cruel. Charity could roll her eyes and ignore those comments being pointedly made about her, but not Kara. She wouldn't tolerate anyone, even her mother, disparaging the one person who'd stood by her no matter what.

"I think you need to leave," Charity said, her voice low and icy.

Her mother paused, the lipstick she'd finally found in hand, and narrowed her eyes at Charity. "Excuse me?"

"You heard me. I'll never repeat what you just said to Kara, but that was uncalled for, and you should be ashamed of yourself."

Her mother's face flushed. "Who do you think you're talking to?"

"Everything all right?" Will asked, his arm slipping around her waist and squeezing her to him.

She forced a smile. "Sure. Mom was just saying they were going to be late for their dinner."

Charity watched her mother compose herself and nod as her husband approached. She held her coat out to Charity's dad, and he helped her into it.

"Will, it was so nice to see you again," Iris said. "We look forward to your parents joining us for dinner."

"It's just my mom, my sister, and me. My dad passed away three years ago."

"I'm very sorry," her father said, shaking Will's hand.

"Please bring your mother and sister tomorrow. Our other children and their families will be there, and Iris always makes more food than we can eat."

Charity almost corrected him because her mom didn't make anything, their cook did, but she just wanted them to leave.

"I'll extend the invitation. Thank you."

"Happy birthday, honey." Her mom kissed her cheek stiffly, and her dad gave her a hug. "We'll see you tomorrow. Enjoy your party."

"Thanks."

Will opened the door for them, and once it closed, Charity swallowed the lump in her throat to mumble, "Excuse me."

Charity brushed past him to her bedroom, and shut the door, ignoring Robin Hood's angry cries when she foiled his attempt to escape the room. She sat down on the edge of the bed and brushed back tears. Someone knocked, and assuming it was Kara, she called out, "Come in."

Will poked his head and his boot in, blocking Robin Hood. "Hey."

Charity wiped at her eyes and sniffed. "I'll be out in a minute."

"Unfortunately, I can't wait that long to find out what the heck happened," he said, slipping inside and picking up her cat on his way to the bed. He sat down beside her, rubbing Robin Hood's ears. "I thought things went great."

"For you," Charity sniffled, wiping her wet eyes. "They both thought you were fantastic. This was such a stupid idea.

I don't know why I thought that if I presented a great guy to them, maybe they'd back off me for once. Instead, my mother just found other flaws to focus on."

"Like what?"

"Like I'm going to get fat eating all the food I make."

"So?"

Charity stopped sniffling and glanced at him. "What do you mean, so?"

"I mean, so, it's your body. If you want to enjoy food and skip workouts, that's your choice, and as long as you're happy in your own skin, who gives a crap?"

"Apparently, my mother."

Will shrugged. "Well, I'm sorry for her, because a person's worth isn't measured by their weight or muscles or the size of their bank account, but by their heart."

"The heart is a muscle."

Will brushed her cheek with his thumb. "You know what I mean. Being authentic to who you are is sexy, in my humble opinion. If you're happy, and not hurting anyone, then anyone who doesn't like it can take a hike."

Charity stared at him for several minutes, her mind racing. "Why are you single?"

He burst out laughing. "Why do you ask?"

"I used to think that maybe you're just a player or maybe a love 'em and leave 'em sort, but here you are, helping me out despite some of our more disastrous encounters. It just got me thinking, if you are this great guy with a job, decent income, good looks, and your personality doesn't blow, why hasn't some girl snatched you up despite your aversion to marriage?"

"I guess it comes down to me not wanting them to? There have been women in the past I thought were great, but I wasn't ready for a relationship. Or when I was, I couldn't give them what they wanted." He held up his left hand, pointing to the ring finger.

"Many people live together and don't get married. Look at Kurt Russell and Goldie Hawn. I can't believe there isn't one woman with similar beliefs about marriage."

"I guess I'm looking in the wrong places, because every woman I've ever dated has said their goal is to find someone to love and get married."

"So, Ebenezer Scrooge, are you really worried about marrying a gold digger? Or is that just an excuse you use?" she asked.

Will chuckled. "You do realize there is a birthday party for you happening out there and we're talking about why my love life is a train wreck?"

"I'm not quite ready to join the fun."

He studied her until she squirmed under his gaze. "What did she say to you?"

"Nothing that bears repeating. So, can we talk about you or are you bent on putting me back into a foul mood?"

"We wouldn't want that," he said in mock horror. "I appreciate that you no longer think I'm a womanizing jerk, but the truth is fairly simple. My parents were never good with money. Whatever they got went right back out, and most of my life we lived paycheck to paycheck. I've managed to be mostly debt free my adult life and I'm financially sound, but the thought of sharing my money with a wife sends me into an irrational panic."

"You have heard of separate bank accounts, right?"

"Yes, and when I suggested that to a few women I was dating, they had very strong feelings about it. Turns out one of them was twenty-grand in credit card debt, so I dodged a bullet there."

She gave his shoulder a nudge. "So you're worried about marrying a shopaholic who is going to ruin your perfect credit score and spend all your money?"

"You can laugh, but what I'm really saying is, I don't think I'll ever be ready. Being married means compromising and trusting the other person to be responsible, and you add kids into that mix? It's just peaceful only having to worry about myself."

"And I suppose you don't get lonely?"

"Not really. I have friends and my mother and sister. I date. I was thinking about getting a cat, though."

"Kara mentioned that."

"Maybe I'll do that this week, now that the holidays are over. I could swing by the café before work or on my lunch break and find me a new buddy. My mom would probably like a cat, too."

"You're really close with your family," Charity said.

"Yes, I am."

"I can tell from our brief encounter your mom thinks the world of you."

Will's blue eyes met hers. "You don't think your parents love you?"

"I'm sure they do, but it's not how I imagine loving my kids, when I have them."

A soft knock preceded Kara poking her head into the room, frowning when she spotted Charity's tearstained face. "Are you okay?"

"Yeah, you know my parents."

"Oh, honey." Kara stepped into the room and cupped Charity's cheek, smoothing away some tears. "We're all waiting for you to cut the cake, if you're up for it."

"Sure, we'll be out shortly," Charity said.

Kara closed the door, and Will started to rise to his feet. "Do you want me to leave you alone for a minute?"

"No, I'm ready to get back out there. Although next year, Kara is dead to me if she invites my parents."

Will slipped his arm around her shoulders and pulled her close. "I'll help you hide the body."

Charity laughed. "Best fake boyfriend ever."

CHAPTER SEVENTEEN

Soup of the Day

Try one of our delicious soups to warm up the cool winter days, Clawstrike Clam Chowder and Better-than-Catnip Tomato Bisque.
Today's special is Meownestrone with a sliced baguette.

WILL RACED UP THE stairs and burst into his mom's house without ceremony, his heart hammering in his chest. He stopped in the kitchen first where he found his sister sitting at the table with a stack of papers in front of her. She stared at him with open annoyance, waving toward the back of the house. "She's sleeping, you idiot."

Will didn't take offense because she'd called him worse over the years. "All you tell me is brunch is canceled because Mom is sick with no further explanation, and I'm the idiot?"

"I thought sick was the explanation."

"With everything that's been going on with her, you could have elaborated. Is it a cold? The flu? Whatever pain she's been in suddenly got worse?"

"You could have texted me for details instead of crashing in here like the Hulk! Why are you so dramatic?"

"You know I'm worried about her, too, Sarah. You could have given me more than the simplest explanation like I'm some cousin we haven't seen in years."

Sarah nodded. "You're right. I'm sorry I worried you."

"Is she in a lot of pain?"

"Yes, but it's everywhere. Her hands. Her back. Her knees."

"Maybe we should take her to the ER."

"I already tried, and she told me to get out of the room and let her rest. I gave her some pain meds, and she promised she'd call her doctor in the morning. Unless you plan on storming in there and waking her up to force her into your car, keep your voice down."

Even if he was resolved to carry her into the hospital, his mom wouldn't appreciate him treating her like a child. With an exasperated huff, Will took a seat, picking up one of the papers in front of Sarah. "What's all this?"

"Mom's bills. I was going to pay what I could from her account and then do a few on my own."

Will's eyes widened as he took in the stack. "That's one month of bills?"

"No," she said, pointing to the shorter, second stack. "Those are from this month. This stack is all the past due."

"What the..." Will read over the one in his hand. "This is a failure to pay summons." He set the paper down and ran a hand over his face. "Mom is being sued?"

"Yes, some shady law firm buys up medical debt, and apparently, this one slipped through the cracks when Dad died."

"They're coming after her for a three-year-old debt? Wouldn't the hospital have written it off by now?"

"I don't know, but I'm going to call them on Monday and pay them off so there will be no court proceedings." She ran a hand through her dark hair with a sigh. "I don't know how she's going to catch up on all of this if she has to stop working."

"Did her doctor call?"

"No, but there is *something* wrong with her. If the news is really bad and she has to retire, I don't want her stuck with a ton of bills she can't pay."

Will's stomach bottomed out as his sister's words sank in. If their mom couldn't work and neither Social Security nor retirement payments would kick in anytime soon, she would need help. Either she moved in with one of them or they moved in here, but there was no way he could support two households and start up a business.

How did what's going on with Mom become about me? God, I sound like a selfish jerk, even in my own head.

Guilt rushing through him, he gathered up the rest of the past-due stack, leafing through it and running the totals in his head. "How much does she have in the bank?"

"A couple thousand. The funeral and medical bills took up

most of Dad's life insurance money, and she's been supplementing with what was left when she needed it."

"But the house is paid for. What does she have that could possibly put her this far behind?"

"Power? Water and sewer. Cell phone. When her car broke down in September? When she had to call out a plumber last spring or the roofer the year before? You own your place. You know what it costs to fix things when they break, especially in an older home. Plus she had to call out quite a bit the last few months because she's in too much pain to get out of bed. Not to mention every doctor's visit and test is another bill she has to pay, even with insurance. She and Dad have been playing catch-up their entire lives, and now it's just her catching up on everything they had, on her own without any income from him."

"I wish I had known it was this bad."

"I didn't want to tell you because I know you're scared about striking out on your own. I was afraid that you would use this as an excuse to blow your savings helping Mom."

"It's not blowing my savings if Mom is in so deep she's being sued, Sarah." Will started sorting the bills by how far they were overdue, and when he had them in an order he liked, he pulled out his wallet.

"What are you doing?" Sarah asked.

"Same thing you are. Paying off some bills."

"Will, you don't have to do that. I can set up payment arrangements—"

"You have your own bills to pay, too. Your apartment is

well over fifty percent of your income, and it's not fair for you to take on all this, too, when I can help." He glared at her. "I'm your big brother, so don't argue with me."

Sarah snorted. "Being my brother means we should always argue."

"You're exhausting," he muttered with very little heat.

"I prefer to label it persistent. So, are you going to tell me about the woman from the market or am I going to have to exhaust you some more?"

"What?"

"Mom said you introduced her while you were grocery shopping yesterday, and her family invited all of us over for dinner."

Will cursed. "I'll have to call and cancel that."

"Why?"

"Because Mom isn't going to feel up to spending the night chatting with a bunch of strangers. I can go out and pick up some minestrone soup or something."

"Then I'll stay home with Mom, and you go celebrate your girlfriend's birthday. That's what it is, right?"

Despite what he'd told Charity about throwing his mom off his tail and bugging him about dating, he didn't like lying to his family. "Yes, but she's not my girlfriend."

"Dating, then. You should still go." Sarah waggled her brows. "Mom said she's gorgeous, and you're... you."

"You mean awesome, attractive, brilliant, successful—"

"Humble?" she interjected sweetly.

"That was next on my list of attributes."

Sarah laughed. "How did my nerdy brother turn into this cocky pain in my tuchus?"

"You just won the big-brother lottery." Now that he had a better look at his mom's past dues, it wasn't so bad. It would take a little bit off the top of his savings, but he'd saved an extra five thousand in emergency money. "I can take care of her past-due bills and still be good to branch out. What about your pile of monthly bills? Anything that's going to sit on the back burner?"

"No, I think we're going to be okay, but if you've got her caught up, I'm going to make a spreadsheet of her monthly bills so she knows how much she has to make to be able to breathe. Hopefully, it won't be too hard on her, at least until we figure out what's wrong." She looked up at him with a smile. "Thanks, Will."

"We're family. If we don't take care of each other, who will?"

"I have no idea. I haven't been on a date in months because the thought of getting off work and having to put hours into hair and makeup for a fifty-fifty chance I swiped on a dud sounds like too much work for the reward."

"You don't have to do your hair and makeup. Guys don't care about that."

"It's not for them. It's for me."

Will tossed up his hands in surrender. "Then die alone! We can grow old together and live out a creepy horror-film ending."

"That's it. I'm hitting Ulta on the way home tonight for

more primer and brushes. Are you going to let your girlfriend know we aren't coming?"

Will rolled his eyes. "Not a girlfriend, but yes. I'll tell her it's only me."

"It's probably better that way. Don't want her getting scared off by meeting the family too soon."

"Yet you're not worried about me meeting hers?"

Sarah laughed. "Mom called your future mother-in-law 'hoity toity,' which I took as rich and dressed to the nines. I'm sure they're less of a mess than we are."

"I prefer to call our family quirky."

Sarah laughed. "I like that. I'm going to put that in my dating profile."

"That will definitely get the guys' attention."

His sister struck a pose, waving a hand over her from her head to the top of the table. "All of this draws them in. The profile is just to show them my funny side."

"You have a funny side?"

"Shut up."

Will's phone buzzed with a text, and when he picked it up, he saw Charity's name flash across the top of his screen. He opened up his messages and read, Don't worry about coming over tonight. The party has been canceled.

Will tapped back, Are you all right?

She gave him a thumbs-up, and he set his phone off to the side. "Looks like I'm off the hook."

"Why?"

"She just texted that the dinner is canceled."

"That's weird."

"I don't know. I think her relationship with her family is tense, and they got into it last night."

"Huh. Maybe the more money you've got, the bigger the drama."

"I think you might be right."

CHAPTER EIGHTEEN

Hot Chocolate à la Kitty

Need something hot and sweet? Get yourself a cup of our steaming hot cocoa with three inches of whipped cream, your choice of flavored syrup, and a tasty cat's paw cookie perched on the side of the cup. Guaranteed to put a smile on your face.

"How did we run out of flour?" Charity tried to keep her voice low and calm when asking Marcela, but nothing seemed to be going right for her, personally or professionally. After her disastrous encounter with her mom Saturday, she'd canceled Charity's birthday dinner because she was getting sick and didn't want to infect anyone. Her siblings and their spouses responded to the group text with words of sympathy and GIFs of *Get Well Soon*, but Charity wasn't oblivious. Her mom canceled because she was still angry about Charity kicking her out, but the cancellation was a blessing as far as

Charity was concerned. At least she didn't have to be the bad guy and cancel on them.

Her Monday should have been fantastic, considering, but instead, there had been one hiccup after another, putting her further behind on her day and for her afternoon phone call with the producers for *Bake That*. And now they were out of the one thing she needed to make just about everything on their menu.

"I told you on Friday before you went to Costco," Marcela said hesitantly. "You said, 'Got it,' and walked out the door, so I thought you'd remember it."

Charity gritted her teeth. Charity remembered the exchange, and she'd forgotten the flour. She'd gotten into her car, headed to Costco, and completely forgotten to write it down.

When Charity mentioned to Kara and Michelle that she'd need an assistant to run the kitchen, Michelle had recommended Marcela because Marcela had grown up working in her family's bakery. While Marcela was sweet, she'd set her back more than a few times since she started, but despite her frustrations with Marcela, it wasn't Marcela who'd messed up this time. It was Charity's fault they were in this fix.

"I didn't, and now I have nothing. I have things in the oven, and we need flour—"

"Charity?" Kara called from the doorway of the space. "Chris is here to see you?"

"Who?"

"Chris from your parents' house. He says he's looking for a cat, but he asked about you."

"Crapcrudmonkeypoo!" Charity hollered, stomping her feet.

Kara glanced over at Marcela with wide eyes. "Is she okay?"

"We're out of flour."

"Oh!" Kara swung her attention to Charity. "Didn't you go to Costco—"

"I forgot, I know."

"It's okay, breathe. I'll ask Ben if he can grab some over his lunch hour, and we can go to Costco together after work. Your assistant can handle the ovens, and you can take a break to talk to a very attractive man who wants to adopt one of our adorable felines."

"Kara, I really don't think I'm in the best mood to help him."

"Helping one of the cats get adopted should put you in a fantastic mood. Let's go!" Kara said, clapping her hands.

Charity grumbled the whole way out the door of the adjacent space and into the back of the main building. In order to get to the front of the café, she had to pass through a hallway they intended to gut and turn into a waiting area for the low-cost clinic they planned on opening. When she rounded the corner, the hallway opened up into the exam area. Cupboards, cages, a sink, and a small exam table made up the L-shaped room before Charity passed through the closed door separating the café from the clinic. Charity stopped when she spotted Chris in jeans and a T-shirt, smiling at Lucifer through the glass wall separating him from the social room.

Charity smiled involuntarily as she took a step toward him.

"Have fun," Kara sang softly, and Charity rolled her eyes.

She could appreciate a man who liked cats without being interested in him.

"Hi Chris," she said.

He turned her way, flashing that perfect smile. "Hey, stranger. I was disappointed your birthday dinner got canceled."

"You were coming?"

"I was invited. Why? You didn't want me there?"

"I didn't say that, but my boyfriend would have been there, too."

"I can't wait to meet him. He must be quite a guy to rope you in."

"He is. Shouldn't you be at work, putting the bad guys away?"

"Actually, I took the day off."

"To adopt a cat?"

"Close. It's my birthday."

"Oh! Happy birthday. You know you get a free hot chocolate today only, right?"

"Thanks, I'll order that on my way out. Happy belated birthday to you."

"Thank you. So, what else do you have planned besides finding a new fur buddy?"

"I also have plans to meet some of my friends for dinner and drinks tonight. Maybe you'd like to join us. With your boyfriend, of course."

Charity shook her head. "Unfortunately, I had a kerfuffle in my kitchen and have to make an impromptu Costco run later."

"Another time then."

"What I can do is introduce you to our cats."

"Lead the way," he said, holding the door for her. She stepped into the room, where nearly half a dozen tables were set up, with cat towers, houses, and trees stationed between and along the edges. In the windowsill, a white sled was positioned with a blue bed inside.

"You've already met Lucifer," she said, waving her hand toward the fluffy black-and-white cat watching them with half-closed eyes, his tail swishing below the platform of the cat tower.

"Why do you call him Lucifer?"

"Because he looks exactly like the cat from the Cinderella cartoon."

"Not because he's evil?"

"No, he's a sweetheart," she said, reaching out to rub the cat's ears. Lucifer leaned into her touch and flopped to his side, purring loudly.

Chris laughed. "I can see that." He reached out and stroked Lucifer down the back of his head. "Hey, big guy." Lucifer turned swiftly and wrapped his arms around Chris's forearm before raking his tongue across Chris's palm.

Charity laughed. "I think he likes you."

"Is that right?" Chris picked up Lucifer and held him against his chest, rubbing his chin. The cat melted into his touch, and for a moment, Charity reconsidered her earlier protests. Maybe she was being stubborn, ignoring a nice guy like—

"Charity!"

Charity whirled around to find Will coming into the social room, his white shirt crisp beneath his navy suit jacket and gray-and-blue striped tie.

"Hi! What are you doing here?"

"Hey, Kara texted Ben, who sent me on a Costco run, but I wanted to know—"

She gently took his lapels and stood on her tiptoes, cutting off his words with a brief kiss. "Sorry, I'm just happy to see you." He blinked at her, but before he could blow their cover, she wrapped her arm around his waist and introduced him to Chris. "This is Chris, a friend of my dad's. This is my boyfriend, Will Schwartz."

Chris held his hand out, still holding Lucifer against his chest. "Nice to meet you."

Will took his hand with a grin. "Great to meet you, too. You've been over to the Simmonses' for dinner?"

"Yes, the week before last."

"Ah, I haven't had the pleasure yet. New romance, you know."

"Okay, Chris, I'll be right back if you want to get to know the other cats—"

"I'm good. I think Lucifer and I are going to be excellent together."

"Are you sure you want that one?" Will asked, his eyes narrowed at Lucifer, and Charity noticed the cat watched Schwartz with his ears pinned back.

"Hey, every cat picks their person, and he chose Chris, so let's go out here and talk about why you came by." She gave him a gentle shove toward the door and smiled back at Chris. "Someone will be in with paperwork and his adoption kit. I hope you have a great birthday."

"Thanks; I'll see you around. It was nice to meet you."

"Same here," Will said before Charity closed the door and took his hand, leading him through the door to the clinic in the back of the café. "He seems nice."

Charity caught his smirk. "He is."

"Then why did you tell him I was your boyfriend?"

"Because he was there when I told my family I was dating you, and besides, just because he is nice doesn't mean I want to date him. Now, what were you saying about Kara and Ben?"

"Costco run. I'm making one now, and they said you need flour. Well, hello, cuties." Will walked over to the cage where Sausage and Bacon were currently flipping over each other to reach their paws through the bars. Will took each of their paws like a handshake. "I'm Will. What's up with your ears? Are you deformed?"

"He's a Scottish fold mix. They're brothers."

"Are you sure? They don't have the same colors or ears."

"They each have an *o* mark on the side of their bodies."

"Regardless of whether I buy that they're brothers, he's a cute kitten. They both are."

"Agreed. Now," she cut in before he opened his mouth and distracted her with any more kitten talk. "I need flour. Several large bags if you can. I can give you our credit card to buy it."

Charity went into Kara's office and grabbed her purse, rummaging for her wallet as she walked back into the exam area of the clinic. She retrieved the card and held it out to him. "Here you go."

"Thanks. I'll get it back to you when I return."

"I appreciate you," Charity said.

"Not even going to kiss me goodbye?"

Charity rolled her eyes. "No, and I don't have time to put on a show, so how about going out the back?"

"Wow! You use me for your own pleasure and gain, and then you send me out the back as though you're ashamed of me?" He covered his chest with his hands. "You wound me."

"If you don't get moving out that door, I'm going to wound you for real!"

Will pulled out his wallet and slipped her credit card inside. "I come over here to save the day, and all I get is threats of violence."

"Hey," Charity said, wrapping her fingers around his arm. "You are saving the day. Thank you."

Will winked. "Now that's more like it." Before she could react, he'd kissed her cheek, his soft lips pressing warmly against her skin, his breath rushing out as he whispered, "I'll see you later, baby."

He was gone before she could come up with a cutting remark, leaving her with the lingering sensation of his kiss and an unexpected fluttering in her lower belly.

Her phone blared in her pocket, and she brought it to her ear, still in a daze. "Hello?"

"Hi, Charity?" a deep, booming voice said.

"Yes, this is she."

"This is Dan Gage with *Bake That*. How are you?"

Charity gripped the phone tighter, her heart jumping nervously. "I'm doing great, thanks for asking. You?"

"Oh, just trying to get these preproduction interviews scheduled. Do you have a few minutes to sit down and finalize things?"

Charity heard pots and pans banging next door but put her concern for Marcela out of her mind. This was her moment, and if she was going to get that new kitchen, she needed to focus. Not on Will or Chris, or Marcela possibly burning down her kitchen. With a deep breath, she went into Kara's office and shut the door.

"Of course. I've got all the time in the world."

CHAPTER NINETEEN

Turkish Angora Latte

This flavored latte proves that two different things can blend together perfectly, like one yellow eye and one blue! Our favorite combos are vanilla and caramel or chocolate and hazelnut.

"WILL, CAN YOU COME into my office please?"

Will stopped typing, but Roy didn't even slow down. Just delivered that brusque request as he passed by the open door of Will's office and disappeared.

Will got up from his desk, heading down the hall and turning left into Roy's office.

"You wanted to see me?"

Roy took a gulp of his coffee and stood up. "Yes, you did a great job on those graphics for Choco Vino." He picked up two folders on his desk and held them out to him. "These are two clients that would like to rebrand, and I told them I'd get my best guy on it."

Roy wasn't much for high praise, especially not toward Will in all the years he'd worked for him. "I'm your best guy?"

"You are. Now, I want rough mock-ups next Monday for both."

"Absolutely, sir," Will said, leaving the office in a daze. He'd been working for Kilburn since he graduated from college, and he'd flown under the radar. Done his job, let whomever he was partnered with present their pitch, his art on full display, but he didn't think Roy paid attention to that.

"Hey!" Ben came up alongside him, following him into his office. "What did Roy say?"

"He asked me to make up a couple of rebranding portfolios for two new clients."

"That is wicked awesome, bro. Congratulations. Who are they?"

Will opened the first folder, scanning the contents. "Hot Spot Spas and..." He set the folder down and picked up the other, frowning, "Cat's Meow Coffee."

Ben shook his head. "I hope that's not a cat café."

Will sat down at his desk, reading through the description. "No, looks like a Bay Area coffee chain that wants to branch out. They've got their eye on a space—" Will met Ben's gaze. "The next street over."

"That'll hurt Meow and Furever," Ben said, frowning.

Even though the thought crossed Will's mind, too, he said, "They'll be fine. Meow and Furever has cats, and nobody makes a better pastry than Charity."

"It doesn't matter. We've seen it a hundred times. Something new comes in, and the prior business never recovers." Ben crossed his arms over his chest. "We can't let this happen."

"What am I supposed to do?" Will asked.

"Walk in there and tell Roy there's a conflict. That your girlfriend owns a café that will end up being a street over from the client, and you won't help a company that could potentially put her out of business."

Will's mouth went dry. "I can't do that."

"Why not? You're trying to go out on your own anyway, right? To strictly focus on graphic design?"

"Yeah, but until then, I can't lose this job."

Ben's face drooped with disappointment. "Protecting your friend's place of business isn't worth standing up to your boss?"

Guilt twisted Will's guts into knots. He didn't like disappointing Ben, but more than that, he would never want to be involved with something that directly hurt Charity. He just didn't know how to do the right thing without getting fired.

"Let me figure out a way to do this without costing me everything, all right?"

"Sure, man."

Ben left his office, and Will sat down at his computer. He put in a search for commercial property listings, tapping out a text message to his sister while he scrolled through.

Hey, I need you to look up the price and specs for this address and find me a dozen similar properties.

The little bubbles flashed below and then, Okay, why?

I'm trying to help a friend without losing my job.

Would this be a beautiful friend you're dating?

If I say yes, does that make you work faster?

On it like Sonic.

Lame.

You should be nicer to the sister with real estate hook ups.

Apologies. And thanks, Sarah.

NP. More to come.

Will dived into the spa place rebrand, pulling up his design space, and the business logo he'd created for his potential graphic design company caught his eye. It was a bright red phoenix with flames behind it, the words Epic Graphic Design in a black, smoky font. It had taken him years to perfect, but if he didn't get the guts to try, it would be one more thing he made that wouldn't see the light of day.

Refusing to delve deep into the pity party of his own making, he got to work, playing with a few designs.

His phone beeped a few hours later, and Will checked his messages.

I emailed you a list. Hope this helps your "friend."

Will shot his sister a "thanks." He printed out the properties and flipped through them, trying to slow his breathing. While Ben and Will had brought in several large accounts, that didn't mean Roy wouldn't fire Will if he lost a client over a personal conflict.

He headed back down the hallway with his proposal sketches for the spa company and the printed properties, his stomach churning like a washing machine. Will stopped in the doorway and knocked.

"Come in."

Will walked inside and held out the folder. "Some rough designs for the spa company."

Roy slowly took them from him with a frown. "I said you had until Monday."

"I realize that, but I've learned delivering good news with bad is always the best approach."

"What do you mean?" Roy asked.

"If you'd please take a look at them first."

Roy opened the folder, and his face stretched into a grin, flipping to the next page. "This is good stuff, Will."

Will released a breath he didn't realize he'd been holding. "Thanks."

"I like that you gave them choices, and you did it fast. If I'm ever in a time crunch to wow a client, I know who I'm going to turn to." Roy closed the folder and set it on his desk. "And the bad news?"

"Cat's Meow is looking at space the next street over from Meow and Furever."

"So?"

Will swallowed past the lump in his throat and forged on.

"So, I feel it is a conflict of interest to help them since I'm seeing the co-owner of Meow and Furever."

Roy frowned. "I thought Ben... Oh!" Roy leaned back in his chair, a slow smile spreading across his face as he nodded. "You're seeing Charity? The baker... or is it baketress?"

"Yes, I am, and I'm sure it's baker."

"Good for you. She's a smart businesswoman who goes after what she wants. I can respect that." Roy lost his smile. "If you're refusing to work on their rebrand, then what is there to talk about?"

Will held out the stack of papers, and Roy took them, leafing through. "Properties. I said, at this time it would be a conflict because being nearly directly behind them is bound to impact Meow and Furever's business. However, if they were to choose one of these other locations for their store, I'd be more than happy to create an impressive rebrand they'll be more than happy with."

"So you want me to go back to my client and tell them if they don't go with the space they're looking at, we'll give them whatever they want?"

"Yes."

Roy crossed his arms over his chest. "I could just ask Zane to create some mock-ups."

"You could, but Zane doesn't have my eye or experience."

"Is that a fact?" Roy deadpanned.

Despite the years of self-doubt screaming at him to turn back, Will was in too deep to tuck tail and run. "It is."

Roy stood up and came around the desk. Will braced

himself for Roy to kick him out, but he held out the properties to him. "I tell you what. You write up a pitch for the location change and send it to me. I'll forward it to them, and if they agree, then I'll get them in here for you to show them your designs."

His heavy exhale was embarrassing, but Will was too busy wanting to pump his fist in the air to care. "I won't let you down, Roy." Will held his hand out, and Roy took it, squeezing it a little too hard.

"You've got guts, Schwartz, but if you don't wow them after all this trouble, this will be the last time I go out on a limb for you. Do we understand each other?"

Will nodded. "Understood."

Roy released him. "Now, get the heck out of my office. I want that email within the hour."

Will stopped off in Ben's office on the way back to his desk and gave him a little salute. "Step one in the plan is a go. Now I'm off to save the day. Hopefully."

"What did you do?"

"Worked out a deal with Roy. Good news is, he thinks I have guts, but if I blow this, I'm pretty sure he'll fire me."

Ben snorted. "Are you kidding me? When I first started, he told me he was partnering me with the best graphic designer he'd ever seen. That you were a creative genius."

Will's jaw fell open. "He did not."

"Actually, he did. Everything you create is gold, Schwartz. I don't know how you can want to go out on your own but not believe people when they hype up your talent."

"Shh," Will said, looking over his shoulder, "keep it down on that stuff here."

"Sorry, but here is how I see it. If you bomb this, and Roy fires you, it gives you the kick in the rear to do what you've been saving up for. But if you kill it, maybe you ask him what it's worth to keep you."

Will stood, stunned. "Thanks, Ben. You're a good friend."

Ben rounded the desk and slapped him on the shoulder. "I learned from the best. Proud of you, man. You did the right thing."

"With some encouragement."

Ben shrugged. "We all need a little push sometimes. Now, go be a hero. I'm going to get a caffeination recharge from the café and get back to work. Do you want to come get a coffee with me?"

Will shook his head. The last thing he wanted to do was see Charity with this threat to her livelihood hanging over his head and no solution in place. "No, thanks. I've got a lot to do here."

CHAPTER TWENTY

Clawbb Salad

A delicious blend of fresh greens, ham, turkey, egg, avocado, and bacon, sprinkled with blue cheese crumbles, to keep you full until you get home to feed your cat. Just add one of our house-made dressings and enjoy.

The little bistro Charity's dad chose was on the newer side of town by the Galleria, and when she walked inside, he was already seated by a window. Her stomach had been a tight ball of knots ever since she had gotten his text asking her to meet him for lunch. Whether it was to talk about the fight with her mom at her party or to list all the ways she'd disappointed him, this would not end well.

The hostess approached with a wide smile. "How many?"

"I'm actually meeting someone, and I see him right over there," Charity said, pointing.

"Perfect, go right ahead."

Charity headed down the four little stairs separating the

lobby from the main restaurant and maneuvered in her heels around tables full of people in suits and dresses having lunch. When her father spotted her, he stood and kissed her cheek.

"Hi, Dad."

"I thought you were going to stand me up."

Charity looked down at her smartwatch, confused. "I'm right on time."

"How long have you been my daughter?" He spoke lightly, almost teasing, but the rebuke was still there. "Early is on time. On time is late. And if you're late, don't bother to show."

"I apologize. I was finishing up an order that needed time to cool before I frosted it."

Her father didn't bother to ask about what was being frosted or how business was going, which was typical. Instead, he curtly said, "Well, I'm ready to order, so let's stow the chitchat until after you've decided."

Charity opened the menu with a sharp snap of irritation and perused it, her gaze flicking over the prices. He would be insulted if she tried to pay for herself, so she'd look on the bright side and try to enjoy a free meal.

When she folded her menu, her father held his hand up, signaling the waiter. The thin young man hurried over with a nervous smile. "Yes, what can I get for you?"

"I'll take a Coke and a Cobb salad, house dressing on the side," she said, handing him her menu.

"And you, sir?"

"I'll have an iced tea with lemon and a steak baguette with side salad."

"Very good. I'll put in that order now."

"Thank you."

Once the waiter had hurried away, her father unfolded his napkin and laid it across his lap. "Will seems like a fine young man. Your mother wasn't impressed upon first meeting him, but he explained having to run his mother to the store last minute. We can't be perfect all the time, which I relayed to your mother. Of course, she changed her tune anyway after he brought her flowers. Smart move."

Charity blinked at him, resentment bubbling up in her chest. Her whole life he'd preached about image, impressions, and always looking their best, but it's okay for Will to slip up?

"I'm glad you hit it off with Will," she said sweetly.

"I did, but he's not why I asked you to meet me."

Charity started racking her brain for anything she might have done, but she was drawing a blank. "I'm hanging on to the edge of my seat, Dad. Why did you invite me to lunch?"

"Because I've decided to run for governor."

Charity's jaw dropped. "You have? Don't you need to be a representative first?"

"Arnold had no political experience before becoming governor, while I'm a well-respected judge. I think I'll be fine."

The waiter came back with their drinks, and Charity reached for her glass, taking a large gulp of the carbonated beverage, buying herself time to come up with something to say. While she knew her father had political aspirations, she hadn't expected them to unfold quite so soon.

"Congratulations?" The word came out more like a

question because Charity hated politics and couldn't imagine the appeal of arguing and fighting all the time. She got enough of that visiting her parents.

"Thank you. I've been considering this for a while, and when my party approached me, I had to answer the call. We need change in this state."

"I'm very happy for you, Dad. You're following your calling, like me."

"Yes, well, I know I haven't always been as supportive of your career choices," he said, and Charity held back a derisive snort. "But my campaign manager thinks your altruistic endeavors will actually aid my chances. I have two children who chose a professional path and another who gives back to her community."

Charity's jaw tightened. "At least your campaign manager is proud of me."

Her father's expression clouded. "I didn't come to fight with you today, Charity. I wanted to have an adult conversation and bury all this friction between us. Your mother told me the reason she'd insisted we leave Saturday was because you threw her out." She opened her mouth to protest, and he held up his hand, continuing, "I know what she said about Kara, and I understand your frustration, but she is your mother. Even when she puts her foot in her mouth, it's out of love and concern for you."

"Funny, it felt more about her concern for the size of my butt."

He looked around the room, probably to check if anyone had heard her. "Don't be coarse. We're in a restaurant."

"Fine, I'll reach out to Mom and clear the air."

"Good." The waiter came back with their food and set it in front of them. While Charity drizzled on the salad dressing, she noticed a few limp and soggy pieces of spinach and removed them from the salad and onto the table.

"Would you like me to ask for an extra plate?" he asked.

"No, I'll just put it back on when I finish eating."

She ignored her father's disapproval and took a bite, humming to herself. The house dressing was all right but a little too vinegary. When she finished chewing, she smiled. "The café salad is better. You should come by sometime. You've never seen it, and we're working on expanding into the space next door to accommodate our catering orders, which have doubled since before the holidays."

"You know I don't like cats," he said, using his fork and knife to cut smaller bites of his salad.

"You don't have to go into the social room to see what I've been working on."

"I'll try to make a stop to see it. My campaign manager says he's going to have me booked solid from now until November." He took a drink of his iced tea and switched the subject. "Elena is pregnant."

Charity grinned, genuinely happy for her brother and sister-in-law. "Really? When did you find out?"

"Anton let it slip Monday when we were having lunch. She

wants to do some big gender reveal online, which I think is on the tacky side, but Anton is supportive of it."

"I'm happy for them. Does he know you're running?" she asked.

"Yes, I told him and Billie over lunch yesterday."

Charity wasn't surprised she was the last to know. It just reinforced her place within the hierarchy. "What did Billie say?"

"That she would do her best to behave."

Charity rolled her eyes at the joke. "Yes, because she is such a troublemaker."

"More like her husband is the troublemaker. He's been putting pressure on her to slow down so they can try for a baby."

She paused with her fork poised a few inches from her face and set it down. While Jean-Luc wasn't her favorite in-law, she'd seen the way he looked at her sister with so much love in his eyes. Unfortunately, her sister had their father's ambition.

"What does she say about it?"

"That she can't slow down her momentum and be out of the game for nine months."

"Well, I'm sure they'll figure it out."

"This is why you have to be so careful when choosing your spouse," her father said, as if she hadn't spoken. "Your mother and I discussed all of our needs and what we wanted for our futures on our third date, and I knew she'd be the perfect wife for me." He shook his head. "I told Billie that Jean-Luc was too much of a man to support a powerful wife and look at where we are."

"It's just a disagreement. They love each other."

"Don't be naïve, Charity. People with different priorities don't stay together. All I asked of her was not to divorce him before the election."

Charity's stomach dropped out. How could her father be so cold? Billie had always been his pet, but she wasn't made of stone. If she was considering ending her marriage, Billie would be devastated.

"I'm just happy to have my family's support in this endeavor," he said, as if nothing he'd said was wrong on any level, and it wouldn't do her any good pointing it out. While her father was sharing career advancement opportunities, Charity might as well do the same.

"I'm happy you're pursuing your dream, Dad." She cleared her throat, gathering her nerve. "I have some news, too."

"What's that?" he asked distractedly.

"I applied a few months ago to be a contestant on *Bake That*, and I was selected. We start filming next month."

Her father stopped eating, his brown eyes narrowing. "Isn't that one of those reality baking shows?"

"Yes, it is. And if I win, I'll be able to afford to finish the industrial kitchen I've been working on and fix up our delivery van, which will expand the café's ordering capabilities."

Royce wiped his mouth slowly with his napkin, lowering his voice. "You're willing to make a fool of yourself on the slim chance you might win?"

Charity reeled back as if he'd slapped her. "I'm not going to make a fool of myself. I'm good, Dad. I know I can win this thing, but even if I don't, the finalists get money. And it's great exposure for the café."

"Yes, people will line up to get a look at the governor's daughter willing to pimp herself out to the masses for seedy entertainment."

"What are you talking about? It's not like I'm going to be an adult film star! I'm showing the world what I can do in a kitchen."

"If you need money that badly, I'll give it to you." He took a harsh bite of his sandwich, ripping through the meat and bread.

"I didn't ask you for money."

"And why not? I'm your father, and it is my job to support you. Consider it a charitable donation."

How could he be so completely shortsighted? "Dad, out of all the people who applied for this show, I was chosen. Me."

"Because you'll draw attention. You are a beautiful woman, who comes from a good family and runs a nonprofit. Those shows are all scripted dramas made to show people at their worst."

"I promise it won't be like that. You'll see. They're coming out next week to film me at the café and interview me. If you want—"

"Cancel. I'm sure they can find someone else to take your place."

Charity wiped her mouth with her napkin and set it

alongside her salad plate on the table. "I don't want them to. I want to do this."

"Do you really think so little of us that you would do this? To your parents? To your siblings and their families?"

"Do what? Take every opportunity I'm offered?" It was amazing how he could take a conversation about something amazing that had happened to her and make it about him. "This is for my life, my career. I support you and congratulate you on your accomplishments. Why is it so hard for you to praise me for mine?"

"I am sorry if I don't think my daughter making a spectacle of herself for money is a brilliant life choice."

"You didn't think running a nonprofit was, either, until your campaign manager told you so." She stood up and grabbed her coat and purse off the back of the chair. "Maybe you should ask him what he thinks before you make up your mind."

"You do not walk out in the middle of a meal, young lady."

"Actually, I do when I'm done. See you later, Dad."

Charity knew he wouldn't call after her and make a scene, so she climbed the steps and headed straight for the door, holding back the tears until she got into her catering van. Charity released a sob, wet streaks rolling down her cheeks as she put the key in the ignition and turned it. It sputtered a little and nothing. She tried it again to the same result.

Her van was dead in the parking lot. "Oh God, this cannot be happening to me."

She couldn't sit here for hours waiting for a tow. Her father was going to see her sitting here in a broken-down van, and it would be one more thing to add to his list of disappointments. Thank God she hadn't put the name on the side yet.

Crawling into the back, she called the tow company, wondering how her day could get any worse.

CHAPTER TWENTY-ONE

Cool Cat Tea

Looking for something refreshing? Our tea will quench your thirst and cool you down when you're working up a sweat. Or have too many warm kitties snuggling you.

"When I got your email, Roy, I thought I was going absolutely insane. Never in my life have I had a marketing firm tell me they can't take me on because of conflict but then come up with a solution for the conflict. You either really wanted to keep my business or you were bored out of your mind that day."

Will smiled from across the table at Edwina Powell, the owner of Cat's Meow Coffee, who was taking a sip from her iced tea. When Roy told Will they were meeting her for lunch today at a little bistro near the Galleria, Will had imagined every reaction under the sun to his email but not laughter or appreciation. The woman's blue eyes sparkled behind her cat-eyed glasses, and he responded with a humble shrug.

"I can't take credit for it, Eddie," Roy said, slapping him on the back. "It was all Will. I just proofed the email and endorsed it."

"Well, I'm glad you did," she said, holding his mock-ups in front of her. "These designs are outstanding, and I appreciate integrity. Although the coffee business can be cutthroat, I don't want bad karma for being ruthless. I want to make my mark on the world because people love my product, not because I stepped on everyone else to get where I am."

"I can appreciate that, Ms. Powell," Will said.

"Eddie, please. Now, I'm curious." She slipped the mock-ups back into the portfolio he'd handed her at the start of lunch and leaned forward. "Tell me about this café you didn't want me competing with."

Will cleared his throat. "It's a nonprofit cat rescue. The owners run it as a cat café and sell coffee, pastries, and other great food. They're currently turning the back of the café into a low-cost veterinary clinic for the area."

"That is an outstanding setup. I'd love to see it. If you couldn't tell by my company's name, I've always been a cat person."

"It's actually a few doors down from our office, if you would like to follow Will back," Roy said. "I have to take off straight from here or I would accompany you."

"Unfortunately, I need to take care of a few things this afternoon, but I will definitely stop by before I head back home." She held up the portfolio. "And give you my final thoughts on this. Really great stuff." She pointed to Will, but her attention was on Roy. "Don't let too many people find out about him or they might swoop in and steal him away."

Roy clapped Will on the back. "Will's been with me since he graduated. Loyal to the bone, this one. He's not going anywhere."

Will laughed weakly, and while Roy picked up the check, he contemplated what working this account meant for his future. He wanted to create art for clients, not schmooze them at lunches and sweat through his best shirt presenting them with all the reasons they should choose Kilburn, but that was the job. And after today, how was he going to get up the nerve to tell Roy he didn't want to do it anymore?

They shook hands and said their goodbyes, but Will headed to the bathroom instead of following them out the door. Too much iced tea had become a pressing issue, and when he finished, he washed his hands, wondering why Eddie was so curious about Meow and Furever. She'd successfully expanded her shops from one to eighteen in five years. You didn't get that kind of movement by playing nice.

Will turned the corner toward the front of the bistro, and he pulled up short, surprised to find Charity at the hostess podium, her eyes puffy and red as if she'd been crying.

"I'm sorry, I just need to use your phone for a few minutes. Mine died—"

"Charity?" Will called. She turned his way, and he hated the expression on her face, as if seeing him somehow added to her troubles. "What's wrong?"

"I—" She swallowed, and when he saw her eyes shimmering

with tears, he reached out and wrapped an arm around her shoulders, leading her outside.

"Thank you," he called to the baffled hostess. Once they hit the parking lot, he squeezed her shoulders. "I heard you say your phone was dead. Want to borrow mine?"

"Yes, please," she sniffled. "I was having lunch with my dad, and when I came out, the van I just paid to have fixed wouldn't start. So I called a tow, and then my deliveries to let them know why I was running behind, which was a lot of fun. Then I ran out of juice in my phone with no charger, and I didn't want to run into my dad as he was leaving, so I waited until he was gone to go back inside. I was just hoping the bistro would let me call the café so I could get Kara to come grab these orders, and that's when you walked up." Her entire explanation had come out in a rapid, emotional jumble, but he understood the highlights. There was a problem; he was a fixer.

"Where are the orders going?" he asked.

Charity pulled away from him, wiping her eyes. "One is a few miles that way, and the other is out toward Lincoln."

"Okay, well, how long did the tow truck say?"

"Forty-five minutes to an hour."

"Here's what we're going to do. Let's swap phones," he said, holding his Samsung out to her. "I'll charge yours in my car and go deliver the order a few miles away while you stay here and wait for the tow. If he shows up, just wait for me outside the bistro doors, and we'll take the order out to Lincoln when I get back."

Charity took the phone, passing hers over to him. "Don't you have to be at work?"

Will shrugged. "My boss left for a long weekend with his wife, and I can do everything I need to from home tonight."

"Yeah, but why? I know we're technically fake dating, but this is above and beyond the pretend-boyfriend job description."

"I don't know, I guess I thought we were friends," he said, horrified when she burst into tears again. "Why did that make you cry harder?"

"Because it's so nice," she wailed.

Will had no idea what else to say to that. "Okay, well, I told you I was nice. So, how about you get me the address and the package, and I'll get this show on the road?"

Charity led him out to the van and opened the back, revealing a double-door refrigerator. She opened the doors and grabbed a white pastry box from one of the shelves inside. She leaned out of the back and held it out to him. "The address is on the top."

Will took the box and shot her what he hoped was a reassuring grin. "I spent several years delivering pizzas in college. I got this."

Charity let out a chuckle, and he took that as affirmation that she did indeed trust him.

The delivery really wasn't far, and by the time Will returned, Charity's phone was charged to 38 percent. She was standing on the sidewalk in front of the bistro next to five large pastry boxes, her gaze focused on her van. He saw the tow truck was still in the process of hooking up the van as he parked in the curbside pickup space closest to her.

Will got out of the car and waved. "All right, you good to go?"

"Yeah, he's taking it to the clinic. Kara is going to meet him out back."

"He isn't going to take it back to the mechanic shop? Because if you just had it repaired and they didn't do their job—"

"I called them, and they said whatever this is, it's a separate issue, and it will cost me another eighty bucks just for them to look at it. No thanks, I'll take it somewhere else."

"A second opinion is always valid, especially if they missed something." Will bent over and grabbed the first stack of three boxes. "Ready to head out?"

"Yes." She picked up the second set of boxes and followed him to the car. "If I'd known I was going to get stranded, I wouldn't have worn a dress. Every time the wind picks up, I'm afraid my skirt is going to fly, and everyone will get a look at my chonies."

"So you're saying I should have been the caboose of this delivery train," he said, shooting her a wink over his shoulder.

"No, perv. Unless you want to walk so close you block the view for the tow guy."

"I can do that," Will said, swinging around and falling into step behind her. "Sorry for being flippant."

"You're making up for it now."

He opened the door and turned his back when she loaded

her stack of boxes in case she had a wardrobe malfunction. Suddenly, he felt warm lips on the side of his neck and a whispered, "Thank you."

Will's skin burned where she'd kissed him, but by the time he turned around, Charity was already climbing into the car. Will put his boxes onto the back seat safely and went around to the front, his mind reeling. He'd been collecting quite a few thank-you kisses from Charity over the last week, and he didn't mind it one bit.

He slid into the front seat and buckled up, noticing that she'd put his phone on the charger and had grabbed her own.

"Where are we headed to, boss?"

"Highway 80."

Will backed out of his parking space and got onto the main road headed to the freeway. "So, I know it's none of my business, but was it just the van that had you upset? Or did something happen with your dad?"

"How did you guess?" she asked, releasing a bitter laugh.

"Because your parents seem to be your trigger."

"Trigger is a good word for it. It's nothing new. Can we talk about something else? How did your mom take dinner being canceled Sunday?"

"She wasn't feeling great anyway. I was going to tell you that my family couldn't make it, but then I saw your text."

"Is she better now?" Charity asked.

"No. There's something going on with her, and the doctors haven't figured it out yet. Hopefully we'll know by next week."

"That is tough. She seems like a very nice woman."

Will smiled. "She is. She's a teacher. Loves kids. Can't wait for grandkids."

"Which you've mentioned," she said. "You can't help it if you're not ready."

"Exactly."

"Have you spoken to your mom since Saturday?" he asked, merging onto the freeway. "Or was she there, too?"

"No, it was just my dad. I told him I'd call her, but it's so frustrating. I know she canceled my birthday dinner because of what happened Saturday, but she was in the wrong. Why do I always need to be the one to take the first step?"

"Because you're an adult?" He saw her swing his way out of the corner of his eye and laughed, "Don't hurt me."

"My point is, she's adultier."

"That's not a word, is it?"

"I don't know, grammar police!"

Will lifted his fingers up off the wheel in a surrendering gesture. "I'm just saying that sometimes parents struggle to make the first move. Maybe she thinks you'll reject her, too."

"Maybe."

After several moments of silence, he glanced over to catch her staring at him. "What, do I have something on my face?"

"No, you're just not what I expected when we first met. You were so goofy and exuberant, like a labradoodle."

"Your compliments are very confusing and insulting," he deadpanned.

Charity laughed. "I'm sorry, but then you sit there and lay

out these incredibly mature insights, and everything I thought I knew goes right out the window."

"Just accept that I'm mysterious and amazing."

"I'm getting there," she whispered.

Will's heart kicked up speed, and he looked her way again, his gaze homed in on those lush, glossy lips—

"Look out!" she screamed.

Will's eyes returned to the road with enough time to slam on his brakes as a car from the left lane whipped into the car-length space in front of him. Will laid on his horn as the guy continued to the right onto the exit. Will gripped the steering wheel, his breaths coming in rapid bursts.

A warm hand landed just above his knee. "Are you all right?"

"Yeah, just—I should keep my eyes on the road."

"Probably," she said breathlessly. "At least we're okay, and the boxes didn't go flying."

Before she could remove her hand, he covered it with his own, lacing his fingers with hers. "Is this okay? I'm still a little shaken up."

"Sure." Charity adjusted their hands until they were interlocked and leaned back into the seat. "It's the next exit."

If Will thought looking at Charity was distracting, feeling her skin pressed against his was maddening.

"Thanks for being a friend, Will."

Although he normally considered the *f* word the kiss of death, Will realized he liked being Charity's friend.

"Anytime."

CHAPTER TWENTY-TWO

Lemeownade

Freshly made daily, our Lemeownade can be flavored to your tastes with one of our fruity options. Order it by the pitcher to share with human friends.

"So, how long do these go in for and how long do we let them cool?"

Marcela flipped through the pretty pink notebook she'd started carrying around after her first day at Meow and Furever and stopped on a page, smiling broadly, "Twenty to bake and fifteen to cool."

"Perfect!"

After two weeks, the very sweet woman finally seemed to be getting the hang of the recipes, which took a huge weight off Charity's shoulders. That didn't completely obliterate the stress wearing her down, but it was a start. With the TV crew coming next week and the missed call from her mother this morning, she needed a win.

"Do you have any questions on the morning prep?" Charity asked.

"No, I think I've got it. I've written everything down and will have it ready before we open."

"Thank you." Charity released a breath as she walked out of the back door of the small shop. While the renovation of the veterinary clinic was a priority, Charity hoped to build up the adjacent space into a production bakery as soon as possible.

Of course, endeavors like this took money, and while they'd managed to secure the funding for the veterinary clinic, everything she was doing for the bakery side, including the fixer-upper delivery van she'd bought and paid to have *"fixed,"* had come out of her pocket. Although the tow had been paid through insurance, she didn't have the money to blow another thousand dollars on the van right now. She was overextended and couldn't tell Kara, not after they'd just gotten out of one financial hole before Christmas.

Of course, if she even made it to the final round of *Bake That*, she'd win more than enough to get her out of debt, but she couldn't rely on that money. Accepting a loan from her parents was an option, but not a good one, especially after her dad's reaction to her news on Wednesday. Even if she dropped out of the show and took his money, her dad would lord it over her, and she would owe him. That was definitely not a position she wanted to find herself in.

Will's fears of getting involved with someone financially irresponsible popped into her head, especially after he'd saved her neck the other day. They'd held hands until they reached the delivery and discussed an array of subjects on the way back to the café, but she hadn't taken his hand again. Not because his palm hadn't felt wonderful against hers, but she'd set boundaries, and she didn't want to confuse things between them.

Plus it had been on the tip of her tongue to joke that she was exactly the type of woman he wanted to avoid. And vice versa if she wanted to have kids someday.

Charity stopped with her hand on the back door handle, floored by the direction her thoughts had gone. Three weeks ago, she'd been avoiding Will like the plague, and now she actually felt a twinge of disappointment that they didn't want the same things.

Charity unlocked the door and walked through the clinic to get to the café.

The place was empty except for the cats, who ran along the glass wall of the social room when they saw her. It was seven in the morning, and Kara should be along shortly to feed them, but when their newest additions to the social room, Bacon and Sausage, started springing from the cat tree to a tabletop and launching themselves against the glass, she stopped.

"Hey, uh-uh! You two need to chill out."

Sausage, the gray tabby with folded ears, seemed to shake his head at her while his darker, straight-eared brother scaled the nearest cat tree so he could be eye level with her. Without warning, he flew off the tree, and the normally sturdy structure wobbled until it fell completely over. The other five cats in the social room scurried out of their previous spots and ran, rudely awakened by the six-month-old's antics.

"Now look at what you've done. You need a home with someone who will play that energy right out of you." She turned the knob and stepped into the social room to right the cat tree and was immediately greeted by all the current residents. Bacon tried climbing up her leg to get closer, but she pulled him off in time for Sausage to launch himself into her arms. Sir Whisker-Lots weaved between her legs, his white-tipped tail twitching happily, and Viola and Duke sat next to each other, watching her with nearly identical yellow eyes in their black faces. Homer, the tubby yellow tabby, ambled away from her to the food dish and released a pitiful meow at her when he found it empty.

"I feed the people, not you. Your servant will be here soon to scoop your poop and fill your bowls."

She set Sausage down on the cat tree and pulled her phone out to snap a picture. The young brothers had been rescued from a breeding situation after spending the holidays with one of the café's foster families and were at a healthy weight and energy level. Charity sent the picture to Will with the caption Still looking for a cat? She took another picture of Bacon and added, Or two?

She left the social room against meowing protests and washed her hands. While she cleaned out the bakery case from the day before, her phone beeped, and she checked Will's message.

Do I get a discount if I take both?

Charity rolled her eyes. We're not running a charity here. Well, not for humans, anyway. Are you interested or not?

Someone hasn't had their coffee yet! Charity isn't running a charity? Ironic.

She was about to respond with something sarcastic, but a second message came in before she finished.

Will you be there in thirty minutes or so? I'll stop by.

Charity grinned down at her phone. I'll be here. Text me and I'll let you in through the back.

As she backed out of her messages, she saw the message from her mom this morning.

Please call me.

She slipped her phone into her pocket, finishing with the display case and relining the shelves. All the pastries from yesterday were bagged up and put in a standing basket on the edge of the counter with a sign that said "day-old pastries" on the front. She took the two bags that didn't sell and pulled a bottle of the lemeownade she'd made yesterday before she walked out the back door. The Roseville Helping Hands Kitchen had been the recipient of her day-old baked goods since they opened last year, and Dillon, the guy who ran it, was always really sweet when she dropped by.

Charity took a deep breath and dialed her mom because at least this way, if the conversation took a nosedive, she could hang up before finishing the five-minute walk to Helping Hands.

Her mom picked up on the second ring. "Good morning, Charity."

"Hi, Mom. How are you feeling?"

"Better, thank you. I know that we had to cancel your birthday dinner, but I thought we could do it tomorrow night."

"Honestly, Mom, it's not a big deal."

"You don't want to celebrate with your family?"

Charity rolled her eyes to the sky and thought, *Lord give me strength.*

"I was only saying that I'm fine not celebrating."

"If that's what you want," Iris said, her tone cool. "I know some things were said between us last weekend, and I would like to apologize. I know I was harsh about Kara, and I shouldn't have been."

"Thank you." Charity didn't want to apologize for throwing her mom out, especially when she deserved it, but she thought about what Will said about parents struggling with rejection, too, and she relented. "I could have handled it better than I did, too. I'm sorry."

"I'm glad we got that unpleasantness out of the way. Will your boyfriend be joining us?"

"I'll ask Will if he's available. I know his mom's having some health issues."

"Well, let me know as soon as possible so I can get a head count. Is there anything else you'd like to share?"

Charity almost laughed at the subtle probe. "I'm sure Dad already told you about *Bake That.*"

"He did, but I thought you would like to tell me about it."

"You know, now is probably not the best time," she said, rounding the corner. "Can we talk about it tomorrow before dinner?"

"Absolutely. Have a good day, darling."

Darling? Even that was a little over the top for her mom. "You too."

Charity ended the call and slipped the phone into her pocket. Her mother hadn't been quite her opinionated, snarky self, and it was a bit unnerving. Especially since Iris had to be chomping at the bit to tell Charity how asinine going on *Bake That* was. Would Will be okay acting as a human shield tomorrow?

"Hey!" Charity called out when she caught sight of Dillon and a couple other men unloading food from the back of a van.

He turned and waved before jogging to meet her. "Good morning," he said, flashing a brilliant white smile, his eyes crinkling deeply at the corners. His wild gray hair stood up on all ends, and his rough hands reached out toward her. "You've got some more sweet treats for us?"

"A couple of bags and some lemonade. I'm sorry it's not much."

"Don't be sorry. It just means you're selling out and doing well." He took the bags and bottle from her and opened a pastry bag to peek inside. "Hmm, I was hoping it would be your muffins. They're a favorite with the staff."

"Well, if you and your staff ever want to come by for a batch, they're on the house."

"I appreciate that." Dillon grinned at her, his eyes sparkling. "You wouldn't happen to know a Chris Varton?"

Charity almost groaned aloud. "He works with my dad. Why?"

"Because he started volunteering a little over a month ago on weekends, and he mentioned what a fascinating woman you were to me a couple of weeks ago." Dillon set the bags and bottle down on one of the ancient picnic tables nearby. "I told him you were a good egg who brought us day-old goodies every now and again. Oh, and that I was pretty sure you were single."

"Dillon, if you don't stop teasing, there will be no more baked goods for you. Just you."

He held up his hands. "All right, I'm just saying, he's an assistant DA. One of the good guys. The next time all the crew goes out to get a drink, maybe you'd like to join us?"

Charity startled. "Did he ask you to ask me that?"

"Actually, he wanted to know if he could get your number because he has some questions about his new cat? A little hinky, I know, making me the messenger, but he didn't want to come on too strong."

"That is an unusual request. He should be getting Kara's number. She's the veterinarian."

"Yes, but I'm pretty sure the cat questions are a cover."

"You don't say?" Charity chuckled. "I guess I should give him credit for thinking outside the box. You got a pen?"

Dillon pulled his phone out of his pocket. "I'll text it to him, if you don't mind me having it."

"I don't mind. That way I can let you know when I've got goodies for you. Save me a trip down here."

"Sounds like a plan. Number?"

Charity rattled off her number, and while Dillon was adding it, her phone buzzed. She checked the screen and saw it was Will asking to be let in. "I better go."

Dillon slipped his phone back into his pocket and nodded. "No worries. I went ahead and texted him. Chris is coming by tonight to help us fill sack lunches, so don't leave him hanging, all right? Otherwise, we'll be the ones listening to how disappointed he is about not getting advice on his cat."

"Oh, nice guilt trip." Her phone buzzed again, and she backed up. "I'll see you later, Dillon."

"See you, Charity. Thank you for the treats!"

"You're welcome." Although she hadn't felt an immediate spark with Chris, maybe they could build something on a solid foundation. And despite Will being in the picture, Chris was willing to throw his hat in the ring. Maybe he wasn't just a suit.

Charity came around the corner to find Will trying the front door.

"Breaking and entering, Schwartz?"

He spun her way, one eyebrow arched. "Well, where the heck did you go?"

"I was dropping off some of the day-old pastries from yesterday at the homeless kitchen. And besides, I said I'd let you in the back door."

"Sorry." Will chuckled. "I guess I can't be irritated with you when you're off doing kind things, huh?"

Charity ignored the twinge of guilt because, despite how much she might like Will, they weren't really dating, and if another man asked for her number, she wasn't wrong to give it.

"You shouldn't be irritated anyway. You had to wait two minutes, and you're fifteen minutes early."

"Hey, I said in the next thirty minutes, which means I could show up any time within that frame."

"Whatever, whiner." She opened the door, and he followed her inside and into the front lobby where he stopped and stared at Sausage, who was back on top of the cat tree.

"He looked a little different through the cage bars, but that is definitely the weirdest cat I have ever seen."

"Wow, he can hear you."

"Are you sure? The way his ear flaps are covering his ear holes, I bet I'm at least muffled."

"If you aren't interested—"

"I didn't say that." He studied her as he shrugged out of his jacket, hanging it onto the hook by the door. "Why are you so on edge today? I'm just teasing about the cat."

Charity didn't have a good reason for why his comments had hit wrong this morning and shrugged. "Sorry, my mom and I talked. Family dinner is back on tomorrow. If you can't come—"

"I can come. That just means you're joining us for brunch on Sunday."

"Sounds fair," she muttered. "If you want to go on in, I'll finish up what I was doing and join you after I check on Marcela."

"Who is Marcela?"

"My assistant, remember?"

"Oh right! So she's working out?"

"She hasn't burned down the kitchen," Charity joked, before adding, "No, she's doing really well, actually, and has been a big help."

"That's good. I'll go in there and say hi, let you get some work done."

Will ducked inside the social room, leaving Charity on her own. While she finished cleaning up the shelves, Charity kept stealing glances at him as Will said hello to all the cats. When she heard a muffled scream, she jerked up in time to see Bacon climbing his leg. Will picked the kitten off his thigh and set him against his chest, and Bacon flopped over his shoulder like a rag doll. Charity watched him place Sausage on the other shoulder and smiled when he turned and caught her staring at him, the kittens molded to his body as if they were made for him.

It was one of the top five cutest things she'd ever seen, and she hated the way she melted when Bacon leaned over and rubbed against Will's chin.

Charity's phone buzzed, and to her surprise, it was a text from an unknown number. Are you free tomorrow night for drinks? This is Chris, by the way.

She was still staring at her phone when Will came out of the social room, sans kittens.

"Can I pick them up after work?"

"You want both?" she asked, putting her phone away.

"Yeah, my mom always said that kittens are best in twos, plus I've seen what Chaos is like for Ben. With my hours, I'd rather they have each other." Will stopped talking, studying her face. "Are you okay? You look stressed."

"I'm good. I'll get you an application, and you can fill that out while I move them to the back."

"Hey," Michelle's voice called out. "Charity? Marcela is calling for you next door."

"Oh no," Charity squeaked.

"You better go," Will said. "I'm sure Michelle can finish me up."

"I can do what?" Michelle asked, coming through the doors from the back. Her chin-length black hair was sleek and shiny, and the long-sleeved colorful dress she wore fell just below her knees.

"He's adopting Bacon and Sausage. Where is Kara?"

"She asked if I could come in for her this morning, and I said yes," Michelle said, transferring her smile from Charity to Will. "I could use the extra hours."

"And I'm guessing my dear friend Ben is the reason Kara is playing hooky from work."

Charity rolled her eyes. "Probably. Can you get him the paperwork?"

"Yeah, of course—"

Marcela's shout traveled through the door faintly. "Charity, help!"

Charity gave Will a hurried wave before she rushed through the back and next door to find Marcela near tears, standing in front of a rack of cookies with an icing bag in one hand and a cat paw cookie in the other that was smeared beyond recognition.

"They look like blobs, not paws." She set the icing bag down on the counter and started untying her apron. "You should fire me right now, because if I can't do something as simple as frost a cookie—"

"Marcela, stop." Charity took a deep breath, pushing Chris, Will, and her mom from her mind for the time being and taking the frosting bag from her. "I'm not going to fire you after you've come so far. There is a trick to these cookies, and I failed as your boss because I didn't tell you. Let me show you now, all right?"

"Okay."

This was something Charity could handle. The rest she'd figure out later.

CHAPTER TWENTY-THREE

Kit-Tea

Over a dozen flavors for any time of day. Whether you like it piping hot in the morning or with a dash of cream and sugar in the afternoon, unwind with a cup in hand and a cat on your lap.

"DUDE! I'VE TOLD YOU a dozen times, stop sucking on my blanket! You make it all wet and nasty!"

Bacon proceeded to ignore Will's outburst, and, if anything, his sucking noises grew louder as he made biscuits on Will's bedspread, which was covering his lower half as he reclined on the couch.

"You know he doesn't understand a word you say, right?" Ben said, staring at the video game they were playing while Sausage lay comfortably across his lap asleep.

"He should understand my tone," Will said, setting his controller aside and lifting the kitten up until they were eye level. "Stop sucking."

Bacon reached for his face with a paw, and Will put him back on his lap, where he went right back to kneading the cozy Sherpa throw his sister had given him for a housewarming present.

"I give up."

"This guy is so chill; do you think he's okay?"

Will glanced over at the sleeping kitten and nodded. "Yeah, he's exhausted from tearing up a roll of my toilet paper this afternoon."

Ben chuckled. "Hey, if you'd asked me, I would have told you one kitten was crazy, but two?"

"My mom said they're always better in pairs."

"Nothing is better in pairs!"

Will grinned. "Are you sure about that?"

Ben shook his head, but Will saw his mouth twitch like he was trying not to smile. "Uh-uh, I'm not going to be pulled into these sordid conversations with you anymore."

"Wow, I was thinking about wheels on a bike. Get your mind out of the gutter."

"You're a pain in my—whoo-hoo! I won!"

Will tossed his remote down toward his feet. "Crap."

Ben pointed at Will. "I got to say, you looked wicked cozy with Charity at the party Saturday. Are you still sticking with the whole made-up dating thing?"

"I'm sticking with it because it's true. She asked me to pose as her boyfriend, and I did."

"And driving her around, making deliveries?" Ben asked.

"How'd you hear about that?"

"Kara told me."

"I thought women were supposed to keep each other's secrets," Will grumbled.

Ben's eyebrows lifted. "Whoa, what happened on these deliveries that can't be shared?"

"Nothing, I just don't know why it has to be a big deal. She needed help, and I was there. Besides, you're the one who reminded me we're friends. It's nothing I wouldn't do for you."

"I think it's weird. You see this kind of thing in movies, and it always works out where the two people pretending to like each other end up realizing they were meant to be together all along."

"Unfortunately, that isn't Charity and me. We already know that, even if we have feelings for each other, it will end in disaster. She wants a traditional life with marriage and kids, and I want to enjoy my perpetually single life until well into my fifties. Like George Clooney."

Ben laughed. "Except old George ages like fine wine and is rich to boot. He can afford to take his time."

"Which was exactly my point," Will said, waving his hand over his face. "This will only get better."

"Whatever you say, pal."

Will sighed. "Look, I like Charity. I even considered asking her out for real when we first met, but her impression of me wasn't good, which explains the hostility she'd had toward me. Now that we are on the same wavelength and understand each other a little better, I don't want or need that getting mucked up by pushing for something that shouldn't happen in the first place."

"All right, I'll back off." Ben set his controller on the back of the other couch and scratched Sausage under the chin. "I should probably head out anyway.. It's getting late, and we've got a lot of work to do on the Choco Vino campaign."

"I know," Will groaned. "I had tunnel vision about getting the account, and it's been sitting on the back burner ever since."

"Yeah, but whatever you come up with will be amazing. You're an artist, man. I might be a smooth-talking idea man, but you're the talent."

"I appreciate you saying so," Will said softly.

"I speak the truth. Honestly, when you leave and strike out on your own, I don't know what I'll do without you."

"Do you think I'm crazy to even consider going out on my own? Leaving a six-figure gig to start from the ground up?"

Ben shrugged. "I think you've got to be true to yourself. It's not about money for you. It's about doing what you love. I know you hate the presentations and just want to stay behind your computer making awesomeness. Going out on your own will do that. Or you could talk to Roy about revamping your position?"

"I already called in my one favor from Roy. I ask for anything else and he'll chuck me out the door."

"You never know until you do." Ben got up and stretched. "I better go feed Chaos his dinner. Every time I'm late getting home, he meets me at the door pacing back and forth with this high-pitched meow, like he's reading me the riot act."

"At least it's not Kara flipping out on you."

Ben smiled warmly. "Not my girl. Honestly, I hate spending nights away from her, but we agreed to take things slow. Plus, I think Charity gets sick of seeing me and my cat hanging around every other day."

"I'm sure that's not true, unless you're a cruddy house guest."

"No, I'm good, but the other morning, she came bursting into the room and jumped right on top of me like she didn't know I was there, screaming about getting onto a reality baking show. It was the strangest experience of my life." Ben rubbed his shin absently. "And she bruised my shin with her knees."

"Charity got onto a baking show?" Will asked.

"Did you miss the part where she injured me?"

"Oh, I'm so sorry," Will said insincerely. "Now, what baking show?"

"She didn't tell you?"

"No, she didn't."

"Makes sense. It's not like you're her *real* boyfriend," Ben said, dragging out the word *real*.

"Ha, you're funny. Now get out of my house."

"Whew, touchy."

"You're gonna think touchy when I smack the palm of my hand against the back of your head," he said, not meaning a word of it, especially since Ben was a good four inches taller and fifty pounds heavier.

"Thanks for having me, Schwartz."

"No problem. Anytime." Will opened the door, accepting Ben's one-armed hug as he left. After he locked the door, Will considered texting Charity and asking about the show, but that looked a little needy, right? Ben was right about her not owing him a thing, but it still seemed weird that she wouldn't share something exciting with everyone in her life.

Are you really in her life though? Or will she stop talking to you the minute this little farce is over?

He hated that he'd grown so accustomed to hearing from Charity and spending time with her that the thought of it ending made him ache in the pit of his stomach. He'd grown attached to Charity as a friend and didn't want things to go back to before.

Will flopped onto the couch and shot Charity a text. We need to talk about Saturday night and Sunday morning, when you get a chance.

He saw the text below his message go from delivered to read, but those three little dots didn't appear.

Dude, she's probably in the middle of something. Don't read too much into it.

His phone blared in his hand, and his mom's smiling face flashed across the screen. He tapped the green telephone and put it to his ear. "Hey, Mom. How are you feeling?"

"Not great, honey."

Will sat up, frowning. "What's up?"

"My doctor got back to me today and said they suspect rheumatoid arthritis. They ordered some medications that your sister is picking up for me, but my doctor told me that it might be time to think about retiring."

"Wow, Mom. What are you going to do?"

"I'm not sure. I could sell the house and get a small apartment. Use the money to live on."

Will's chest tightened, thinking of his mom moving into a rental and being at the mercy of a landlord who might not be on top of things, when there was no monthly mortgage payment if she stayed in her house. Her problem was that the money coming in to cover the power and other monthly bills wasn't enough to keep her afloat. She'd need some way to supplement, and although a selfish part of him hesitated, Will knew what had to be done.

"Will, are you there?"

"Don't sell your house."

"What? But Will—"

"I'm serious. Don't worry about anything. I'll take care of it." He swallowed hard, knowing his dreams would have to wait a little longer. "I promise."

"Will, whatever you're thinking, I don't want you using your money on me. You already did too much Sunday going through my bills and getting things current."

"Mom, it's obvious that you've got things going on, but I can help you get through this. I want to." Even as he said the words, a lump rose and lodged in his throat. He'd created an estimate on the home repairs, too. Getting everything up to code would take a chunk of his savings, and keeping his mom afloat if she retired early would chip away at the rest until her retirement kicked in. While he was happy to be there when she needed him, he still mourned his chance to do what he loved.

"You're a good son," Anna sobbed.

He cleared his throat, dislodging the lump. "Because I had a good mom."

There was no other way around it, though. Quitting Kilburn and striking out on his own would have to wait.

CHAPTER TWENTY-FOUR

Café au Lay-On-Your-Keyboard

This café au lait is the perfect excuse to take a break from work and enjoy it iced or hot. Made with half coffee and half milk, it's a delectable treat for even the busiest workaholics.

"I'M GLAD WE'RE DOING this," Kara said, carrying two cups of café au lait into the social room on Friday morning. They took the table closest to the exit since they only had about fifteen minutes before they had to open the doors. The weather outside was dreary and cool, but Charity was just happy they were taking the time to resume their morning breakfast and coffee together. She'd missed this.

"I know what you mean. I feel like our routine has been thrown off with training Marcela and Ben sleeping over."

"Is that bothering you? Ben being at the house so much?" Kara asked, reaching for a scone from the plate Charity had set in the middle of the table.

"No, of course not. I love Ben. When he makes food, he always includes me."

"The way to making my best friend love you is through her stomach."

"It's not just a guy thing."

"All right, well, speaking of boyfriends—"

"No, nope," Charity blurted, her face on fire.

"Oh come on, we aren't going to talk about Schwartz making deliveries with you?"

"Why would we need to?" Charity asked, frustrated that Kara still seemed hung up on this. The minute she'd told her about Will rescuing her, there had been this little twinkle in her eyes whenever Will was mentioned, and it was becoming annoying. "He was just helping me out, like he did with the flour and at my birthday."

"Charity, Schwartz has been into you since the first time he saw you."

"Kara, it wouldn't work even if I wanted it to."

"Why?"

"For many reasons, the most pressing being that Will doesn't want to get married. Ever."

"Char," Kara scoffed. "Every guy says that."

"Maybe, but if that's how he truly feels, why would I go into a relationship hoping he'll change his mind?"

Kara held up her hands. "Okay. I'm sorry. I just want you to find a nice guy and be happy."

"Honestly, Kara, I've got bigger stuff to worry about than a man."

"Like what? We're in the black, you are a contestant on a major baking show, and now that we've got the permits in order, construction is going to start on the clinic mid-February... We're doing great."

Charity swallowed, setting down her coffee cup. "We are, but I want the café to do better. With the oven on the fritz constantly, I am struggling to keep up with orders. I bought the van thinking it would be an easy solution to transport, but it turns out that it's a money pit, so now I'm out what I put into that. I just feel like I'm drowning, and the way my dad reacted to the show, our relationship is more of a hot mess than usual."

"Why don't we take some of the clinic money and use it to repair the van?"

"No, absolutely not. That is what we raised the money for, and that is what it's being spent on."

Kara reached across the table, taking Charity's hand. "Hey, everything that happens in this place is a you-and-me problem. I don't ever want you holding stuff in because you think I can't handle it. Look at what we were able to do in less than a year here."

"With the help of Ben and Will," Charity said, squeezing Kara's hand.

"And Michelle." Kara chuckled. "We are a team. Don't forget it, no matter how many times we fall down, as long as we stick together, we'll climb back up."

"Aren't you usually the one panicking when I bring up financial issues?" Charity teased.

"Yes, but if the last few months have taught me anything, it's to have faith in the people you love."

Charity's heart squeezed, knowing how much Kara had been hurt, and the fact that she was allowing herself to trust again was inspirational to say the least.

"I think Ben's amazing for you, Kar."

"I agree." Kara stood up with a sigh. "Should we clean up and open those doors?"

"Yeah. I should go check on Marcela, anyway."

"No, you shouldn't. This is her first morning coming in and doing all the prep herself. If you check in on her, you're going to destroy her confidence."

"I'm showing my support, and if she needs me—"

"She knows. Besides," Kara said, giving Charity a hug, "I need your smiling face up front with me until Michelle gets here."

Charity huffed before extracting herself from the hug and picking up the plate in one hand and her cup in the other. "Fine. But it's still my kitchen."

"I know. Speaking of, do we want to change over to the Valentine's décor before the TV crew gets here next Friday? It will be a few days early, but I think it will be cuter than the snowflakes. Really give the interview a vibe."

"Whatever you think." Honestly, decorating for the most romantic holiday of the year sounded like torture, and she'd rather skip it, but it was their first February at the café. Plus everything they'd ordered was pretty adorable. "I'm just hoping my dad's not right and this is all a mistake."

Kara wrinkled her nose. "No offense to your dad, but he can be a selfish tool sometimes."

Charity burst out laughing. "Kara Ingalls!"

"What?" Kara smiled sheepishly. "You're my bestie. I love your family, but I don't have to like them. Especially when they hurt you."

Tears blurred Charity's vision as they left the social room, and after Charity set the plate in the sink, she dabbed at her wet eyes with a clean towel from under the counter. She finished drying her tears and put their coffees under the counter before climbing to her feet. "I love you, but why are you trying to make me cry?"

"Oh, stop!" Kara said, wiping at her own eyes.

"Why are you crying?" Charity asked.

"Because if you cry, I cry! We're a package deal!" Kara waved her hand toward the door. "Hurry up and open the door. You can't bawl if you're taking orders."

"Truer words," Charity said, crossing the room to unlock the front door. She held it open when she realized there was a woman on the other side. "Good morning. Welcome to Meow and Furever."

"Hello there," the woman said, adjusting her cat-eyed glasses. "This place is fantastic."

"Thank you." Charity closed the door and rounded the counter to stand behind the computer. "What can I get you?"

The woman studied the menu for several beats before nodding. "I'll take a caramel meowcchiato and a pawp-tart. Strawberry Nutella."

"Good choices. Do you want them to-go or would you like to spend some time getting to know a few of our adoptable kitties?"

"I'd love to do that, but I'm also interested in getting to know the owner. Would that be you?"

"Actually, we co-own it," Charity said, gesturing to herself and then Kara. "I'm Charity Simmons, and this is my partner, Dr. Kara Ingalls."

"Oh, delightful." The woman brought out her wallet and handed Charity her business card and a twenty-dollar bill. "I'm Eddie Powell. I own the Cat's Meow Coffee shops in the Bay Area."

"Oh, uh... nice to meet you." Charity cashed out the transaction and handed her the change. "How can we help?"

"Actually, I have an interesting proposition for you both. I went on your website and read all about you, but it was Will Schwartz at Kilburn Marketing who turned me onto you ladies. You see, I was going to buy a space on the next street, but he was concerned my company might eat into your business. He went above and beyond, even brought me a stack of alternative properties miles away from your café."

Charity shared a wide-eyed exchange with Kara, her chest squeezing with emotion. "That... that was incredibly kind."

"It was, and part of the reason I decided not to open a new store in the area at all. Instead, I'd like to come to a business arrangement with you."

"What's that?" Kara asked.

Eddie pulled a bag of coffee out of her tote and tossed it to

Charity. "I'm going to try this meowcchiato, but I want you to brew a cup of mine. I guarantee you'll agree it's better than what you've been using."

Kara finished off the drink and held it out to Eddie. "And you want to sell it to us?"

"I want to enter into a partnership with you. You use my coffee in your café, and you keep cards advertising Cat's Meow Coffee. I'll supply the coffee free of charge for six months. Like a sponsorship."

"But why?" Charity asked. "You don't even know us!"

"Like I said, I like what I see and hear. If you're willing, I can have a contract drawn up for you to look over next week?"

Kara and Charity glanced over at each other and nodded.

"We'll take a look at it, of course," Kara said.

"It just sounds a little too good to be true."

The front door jingled, and three regulars came into the café. Eddie stepped to the side, taking one of their cards with her. "You try the coffee, and I'll shoot you the proposal next week. If it doesn't suit, you can come back at me or just delete it and move on. Deal?"

Charity shook the other woman's hand while Kara took orders behind her. "Sounds like a plan."

CHAPTER TWENTY-FIVE

Fur Real Fruit Salad

A sweet, refreshing side any time of day. Disclaimer: No fur was included in the making of this tasty treat.

Will slipped the strap of his laptop bag over his shoulder and followed Ben out of work. They'd stayed late finishing up several of the placement ads for Choco Vino, and Will was ready to be home and kick his feet up. He didn't feel like cooking tonight, so maybe he'd pick up dinner or order something for delivery.

"How is your mom?" Ben asked, breaking the silence between them as they climbed onto the elevator.

"She wants to finish out the school year, but her doctor told her that with the new medications, it's better if she takes a leave at least to see how they affect her. She's stubborn, though, and doesn't want a long-term sub to come in and 'mess with her students' progress.'"

Ben chuckled. "I'd have a hard time leaving my job high and dry, too, so I get it."

"Yeah, but she needs to take care of herself first." Saying the words out loud sounded hollow to him, maybe because Will knew most of his savings would be going to supplement his mom's income for the next several years at least. Not that he resented caring for her—he loved his mother with all of his heart—but the fact that here she was in her midfifties with no safety net made him all the more convinced that staying single would provide him with a better future.

"I think it's great of you to take care of her." They hopped off the elevator and exited the building. When they stepped onto the sidewalk, Ben clapped him on the back. "You're a good son. See you Monday?"

"I'll be here," Will said, hoping Ben wouldn't pick up on his dispassionate response.

"Later." Ben jogged toward the parking garage, probably in a hurry to see Kara. Will had invited him to go out for a beer tonight, but he'd already had plans with his girlfriend.

Will headed the opposite way past the café, admiring the big display window where frosty snowflakes had been painted on the edge of the glass. Inside, two black cats were lounging in a large, fluffy white bed, cuddling each other. A couple coming from farther down the street caught his attention and a flicker of envy settled in his stomach as he watched the woman snuggle closer under the man's arm.

It would be nice to find someone who wanted to keep their

financial freedom but was also willing to be in a mature, committed relationship without expectations of marriage.

Will rounded the building, suddenly not as eager to go home to his empty house. Yes, Bacon and Sausage were waiting for him, and they were excellent snugglers, but they weren't great conversationalists.

This morning he'd managed to find a spot two streets over from Kilburn and close to the main road, so rather than parking in the garage and having to weave through town to get home, he'd taken it. The sound of cursing and clanging interrupted his musings, and when he followed the sound around the corner to the alley behind Meow and Furever, he saw a feminine figure in coveralls bent over the engine of Charity's catering van, a large spotlight clipped to the open hood. As he drew closer, he saw it was Charity with a wrench in one hand and another light in the other.

"I didn't know you were a car mechanic in another life," Will called out.

Charity jumped, hitting her head on the top of the open car hood, and he rushed forward, catching her as she slipped off the stool she'd been on.

"Ow," she muttered, dropping the wrench on the ground to rub her head. "Don't you have the sense not to holler at someone like that?"

"Apparently not." Will slowly released her and pointed to the van. "What were you trying to do?"

She continued to rub her head, disturbing the topknot of

dark curls adorably arranged there. "I'm trying to figure out why the stupid thing won't start."

"Have you consulted another mechanic?"

"No, because I've put everything I have into renting the space next door and purchasing this hunk of crap"—she kicked the tire of the van for emphasis before continuing—"and the extremely expensive professional oven I had installed."

"Why would you do it now if you couldn't afford to expand?"

Charity shot him an exasperated look. "Because we needed it. Between stocking the café and the catering orders, the oven barely supports that, and three deliveries will fill my car up to the brim. This van would be a smoking-good deal if I could just figure out why it died on me."

Will felt like a heel for piling on to her stress with his question and wanted to make amends. "Do you mind if I take a look?"

"What do you know about engines?" she asked.

"Probably a cup more than you."

"Why, because you're a guy?"

"Nope," he said, taking her flashlight and climbing up onto her stool. "Because my dad and I used to rebuild car engines on the weekends for fun."

"Oh."

Will bit back a grin at her obvious chagrin. "Do you mind if I take a peek at this and then on the inside?"

"No, be my guest."

Will checked over the engine for several minutes, looking for any cracks or missing pieces.

"So, a woman named Eddie Powell from Cat's Meow Coffee stopped by to see us today."

Will paused in his perusal and met her gaze. "Oh yeah? What about?"

"She made us an offer. Kind of a sponsorship where she supplies us coffee and we advertise for her. It's great tasting stuff, but we want to read the fine print first." Charity leaned over the other side of the van. "She said you were concerned her shop might eat into our profits, and you brought her a list of alternative properties. That you convinced her not to move next to us."

"I did, but to be honest, Ben convinced me that, as a friend, it was the right thing to do."

"So I should thank Ben then?" Charity asked.

Will shrugged. "I'll take most of the credit."

Charity laughed. "Well, no matter why you did it, I want to thank you. I can offer to make you a tasty lunch including a sandwich of your choice and some fruit salad."

"That's not necessary. I was happy to do it," he said, holding her gaze for several moments before clearing his throat. "Do you know when they changed the battery last?"

"I don't."

"All right," he said, stepping down off the stool. "I'm going to check one more thing. Are the keys in it?"

"Yes."

He went around to the driver side and hopped in, turning the key. It clicked a few times and nothing.

"Okay, so I want to get a new battery first and see if that

fixes the problem, but if that isn't it, I'm worried about your starter."

"How much is all that going to cost?"

"Couple hundred, but I'll install them, so at least you won't have to pay for labor."

"I can't ask you to do that."

"What's a fake boyfriend for if not getting your van running? Speaking of fake boyfriends, we need to discuss tomorrow night."

"Yeah, I meant to text you. I'm probably going to skip dinner, but you should definitely go. My parents adore you."

"What do you mean you're going to skip it?" Charity didn't answer, and Will reached out, gently clasping her arm and pulling her closer. When she didn't meet his gaze, he placed his hand below her chin and lifted it. "Hey, talk to me. Is this about your lunch with him? Or the fight with your mom?"

Charity let out a heavy sigh and met his gaze. "My dad let me know he's running for governor. Exciting, right?"

"I guess..."

"So I told him I was picked to be on *Bake That*, and he lost it. Told me that being on reality TV was trashy and that he'd pay for everything I needed if I wouldn't do it." Tears filled her eyes, and she dashed at them jerkily. "It was humiliating."

"And what did you say?"

"I told him to kick rocks," she said, stepping away from his touch, and he let her go. "I'd rather go on that show and possibly lose than give him the satisfaction of owing him money."

"Did he say you'd have to pay him back?" Will asked.

"No, but he has never supported me or the café, and this would just be something for him to throw in my face later. This show could be huge for promoting the café. It's not just about the money, it's longevity. And I can't trust him not to use any money I borrow against me."

"How come you didn't tell me all this while we were out delivering?" He hadn't intended it to come off as accusatory, so he switched tactics. "Being on *Bake That* is huge."

"Because I know how you feel about financial stability, and this is sort of a Hail Mary for us. I didn't want you to judge me."

"No judgment here."

"Really?" she asked, skeptically.

"That depends. Do you have a smile for television, or are you an awkward goofball?"

Charity flashed him a grin. "How's this?"

"Pretty decent. Can I ask you one question though?"

"Maybe..."

"I heard yes, so I'm going to go for it. Playing devil's advocate, your dad is pretty much alleviating all your stress. This is a guaranteed get-out-of-debt card, but you're refusing it because he hasn't always been supportive of your business and life choices, and he *might* use it against you?"

"Yes, exactly."

"All right, just wanted to clarify."

"You think I should accept the money and skip the show?"

"I'm a safe-bet kind of guy. I don't gamble or play the lottery for a reason. I keep my spending on budget because I don't like being stressed financially. I couldn't gamble my life on the possibility of winning."

"Hang on. I believe in my abilities, and I know I'm amazing. I look at this as an opportunity, not a gamble." Waving her hand, she headed to the back of the building next door. "Come here."

"Charity—"

"No, I need to show you that I am absolutely capable of kicking some serious tail and winning this thing."

"It's your life. It doesn't matter what I think," he said, following her inside.

"It matters to me." She opened up the fridge and pointed at the cake inside. "You really don't think I have the skills to kill this competition?"

Will stared at the round cake that looked like water on the surface with the rippling reflection of trees surrounding the icing lake. On the shore by the trees was a red tent with two sets of legs poking out and a fire going beside it. *Happy Anniversary* was written across the top of the lake in forest-green icing.

"Here, taste it," she said, pulling out a covered cake pan and setting it on the counter. She popped the lid, revealing a frosted cake with several slices removed. Taking a fork from a nearby drawer, she scooped some onto the fork and held it out to him.

Will took the offered bite and licked his lips. "It's excellent."

"I know!" She gleamed triumphantly.

Will didn't tell her that there were probably a host of other candidates in the competition who were also excellent, because it would do nothing but tick her off.

"If you're still doing the competition and pretty much telling your family you don't care what they think, does this mean I'm off the hook for Saturday?"

Charity sighed. "No, I still need you. Specifically to run interference between my dad and me."

"Great, just what I wanted to do with my weekend, referee family drama. I'll pick you up?"

"That's fine. Is your mom coming?"

"No, she got some bad health news yesterday, so I think she's going to skip this one."

"Oh, that's terrible," Charity said, frowning. "Is she going to be all right?"

"I'm sure she will be. We're still doing brunch at my place on Sunday at eleven. My sister is going to bring my mom and the groceries over if you just want to meet at my place."

"I'll be there. Oh, dinner is at six thirty tomorrow, so we need to be there at six."

"Why would we get there a half hour early?" he asked.

"Because if we're on time, my dad will say we're late. Don't ask."

"Then I'll come by here tomorrow morning and work on the van. It'll give me time to get cleaned up."

"Look at us, coming up with a plan of action. High five for fake relationships," she said, holding her hand up.

Will clapped his hand against hers. "Go Team Chill!"

"Team Chill?"

"Your name and mine shipped together is—"

"No, we aren't doing that."

"Spoilsport."

CHAPTER TWENTY-SIX

Snowshoe Cookies

Our signature cookies are a delightful mix of white and dark chocolate chips and a chewy dome, perfect for dunking when you're having a bad day.

"Do you know where Michelle is?"

Charity finished plating a grilled panini and glanced toward the closed door leading to the back. "I thought she went outside for a break?"

"That was over fifteen minutes ago. Maybe I should go check on her," Kara said.

"Why don't I check on her?" Charity asked, washing her hands in the sink. "I want to follow up with Will's progress on the van, anyway."

"Sure, but don't be gone long. I must make a few calls to our contractor about the clinic. We're just trying to get everything ordered so there are no holdups."

Charity dried her hands and shot her a thumbs-up before

pushing through the door and into the clinic. When she rounded the corner by the bathroom, she saw the back door was open a small crack and frowned. She opened it all the way and found Michelle and Marcela sharing a bag of snow-shoe cookies, and two of the girls from the toy store across the street standing against the wall, watching...

Will, in a white T-shirt, arms streaked with grease, working on her van.

"Um, what's going on back here?" she asked, knowing full well what was happening.

Michelle's cheeks flushed. "We were—it's not—" She cleared her throat, her head bent. "I got distracted."

"I better go check the brownies," Marcela piped in, taking the long way around the van to the entrance of the kitchen space. Charity's eyes narrowed when her assistant's gaze dipped in the direction of Will's butt.

"We're on break, so don't mind us," one of the toy store girls said, tossing her long, braided hair over her shoulder.

Charity didn't like the woman's obviousness. "Did you ever think that maybe he minds being ogled like a sexual object?"

"He's the one putting it out there. We're just appreciating it."

"Funny, I'm sure that's exactly what men have said about women for hundreds of years, and we fought to make them stop. But it's okay for you two to stand out here and do the same thing to him?"

"You know you're uptight, right?" the taller woman said. "We're just living our best lives, and you come out here all high and mighty just because we appreciate what a fine man he is."

"Ladies!" Will called loudly, and all three of them whipped his way. "While your appreciation doesn't bother me as long as you're quiet, you're upsetting my girlfriend, who is too classy to tell you to take a hike." He stood up straight, rubbing his hands on a white towel, leaving streaks of black from the grease all over them. "So I'll do it for her." He approached Charity, leaning in to give her a long, lingering kiss that set her head spinning.

Charity's eyes closed of their own volition, melting into the warm press of his mouth while her heartbeat raced. She was vaguely aware of retreating footsteps before Will ended the kiss, giving her a wide, smug smile. "I appreciate you defending my honor. Chivalrous of you."

She glanced toward where the women had stood moments ago before meeting Will's blue eyes, swallowing hard. "Anytime. A man should be able to bend over a van engine without having a gaggle of women stare at his backside."

"Which is something you'd never do, right?" he asked, putting a hand on the wall behind her and hovering above her, his eyes drifting to her lips.

Her face burned, and from the way his grin broadened, she knew he'd noticed. "Charity Simmons, such a naughty girl."

"Okay, that's enough," she said, turning to head back inside, but his other arm came up, blocking her path.

"Don't you want to know how your van is doing?"

"I do, but I also want you to stop teasing me."

"Not a chance," he said, hopping down off the step and making his way to the driver's side. After he climbed in, it was only a few seconds before the van roared to life, and Charity forgot about her annoyance with him, jumping up and down with glee.

"Oh, my goodness, you did it!"

Will climbed out of the van, letting it run. "Lucky for you, it was just the battery. When you get some extra cash, you might want to have it looked at by an actual mechanic, but it should get you from A to B for a while."

Charity climbed down the stairs and threw her arms around him. "Thank you so much."

She stood on her tiptoes, hugging him, and the scent of grease and cologne tickled her senses in a way she shouldn't have found delicious, but did. Maybe it was just gratitude that made her want to hang on to Will a little longer, but the sound of Kara clearing her throat forced her to take a step back.

"I was just letting you know that there is someone up front to see you," Kara said, her gaze flicking between her and Will.

"Thanks, I'll be right there."

Kara nodded, giving Charity a pointed look before disappearing inside. Charity turned back to Will, her hands in the pockets of her dress. "Are you going to be here awhile longer?"

"Just long enough to clean up my mess, why?"

"Because I was going to send you off with lunch, if you're hungry."

"I'm always hungry, but I don't want to go inside like this."

"I'll bring it out to you. You like roast beef?"

"I love it."

"I'm on it, then."

Charity hurried up the stairs inside, a bubble of giddiness climbing up her throat. When she pushed open the door between the clinic and the café, she found it empty except for Kara, Michelle, and Chris standing by the door in a formfitting T-shirt. Seeing him reminded her she'd never responded to his message, and guilt shot through her.

"Chris. Hi. How is Lucifer?"

"He's completely taken over my bed, but I don't mind."

Charity cleared her throat. "I'm glad you two are working out."

"So am I, but I have to admit, I'm disappointed I haven't heard back from you about drinks tonight."

Charity caught Kara's raised eyebrow and ignored her bestie. "I'm sorry. It's been a crazy week, but I can't tonight anyway. Will and I are having dinner with my parents."

"What about after? There's this little bar I go to with the crew from Helping Hands called Beerbury. Maybe you'd both like to join us around nine?"

"I'm not sure—" Charity started to decline, but he cut in.

"Listen, no pressure. I'll probably be there until closing time if you change your mind."

"All right."

Chris winked at her and backed out of the café, turning right, and disappearing out of sight.

When she turned around, Michelle and Kara were watching her, one with clear disappproval on her face.

"Don't start, Kar," Charity said, joining them around the counter and gathering ingredients for Will's sandwich.

"Um, no, that isn't how this friendship works. Did I not see you hugging Will out back less than five minutes ago?"

"Oh, we were hugging!" Charity gasped dramatically. "Call the cops."

"It was more than a perfunctory hug. You were squishing him."

"There was squishage?" Michelle asked, pretending to be serious. "Wow."

"It was a grateful hug full of grateful feelings," Charity said, glaring at Kara. "There was no squish, and I've already explained there is no future there. Believe me, Will Schwartz is not interested in me. He thinks I'm an irresponsible dreamer."

"Are those your words or his?" Kara asked.

"I'm done with you," Charity said, slapping the bread down on the prep bar.

"You can't be done with me because I'm your person."

"Right now, you're about to be the woman I squirt with spicy mustard if you don't stop giving me guff," Charity said, holding the open bottle toward Kara like a weapon.

The front door opened, and Kara pointed at her as she backed toward the register. "This ain't over."

Charity would have laughed if she didn't think the rest of her situation was just plain sad. Chris was a nice enough guy, but she wanted Will, and it was time to be honest with herself.

She'd completely lost her mind.

CHAPTER TWENTY-SEVEN

Catfè Mocha

Calling all chocolate lovers, this mocha has two extra shots for those early birds or night owls that need a little extra energy.

Charity climbed out of the car and reached under her peacoat to straighten the bodice of her red dress. When Will came around the back and held out his hand, she hesitated. After her revelation this afternoon, it was hard to cross the line with Will knowing she'd only fall deeper into the pit of unrequited feelings.

Dang, her life was beginning to feel like one of those bad, soapy dramas, and she was done with it. She'd settle for boring if it meant her body didn't come to life every time Will came within a foot of her. Even hearing his name or thinking about him conjured up all kinds of nonplatonic feelings, and Charity didn't know what to do. She was too deep to end the fake relationship, and if she was being honest, she wasn't sure she wanted to. Charity liked spending time with Will, and when he was gone, she'd started to miss him.

"Remember, hand-holding was included in our fake-dating acceptable touches," Will said, holding out his palm to her with a grin. "Besides, those steps look slick."

Charity pursed her lips but took his hand, her skin immediately tingling. *I'm a goner.*

"Just say you wanna hold my hand, because I know my parents salt their walkways. The last thing my dad wants is for the FedEx guy to sue him."

Will brought her hand to his mouth and kissed the back of it. "I want to hold your hand."

Charity's heart lodged in her throat until he started singing, rather loudly and off-key, "I Want to Hold Your Hand" by the Beatles.

"Stop it," she laughed, shaking off his hold and preceding him up to the porch.

"I think you'll understaaaaand—" Will continued, right on her heels until he wrapped his arms around her waist, his singing softer as he danced her in a circle. Charity's laughter subsided, her hands hanging on to his shoulders as he shuffled with her, his vocalizations a low humming.

"You have lost your dang mind," she murmured, loving that he actually had rhythm.

"If it means getting to hear that great laugh of yours, I'll be absolutely ridiculous every minute of the day."

His tone was like hot maple syrup pouring over her, and she melted into him, putting her head on his chest.

The door flew open, breaking the spell as her sister Billie frowned at them. "What are you two doing out here?"

"Enjoying a moment of peace?" Charity said, her tone saccharine sweet.

"Well, we need to talk, because the poo has hit the fan. Come on." Billie reached for Charity, dragging her away from Will and inside the house. When he stepped over the threshold after them, Billie gave him a tense smile. "Will, it's nice to meet you. I'm Billie. Now, go into the family room and just tell them I needed my sister's help with something...private."

"Um, okay."

Charity let her sister pull her up the stairs and into what used to be Charity's bedroom, rubbing her wrist when Billie finally dropped it. "Ouch. What is wrong with you?"

Billie planted her hands on her curvaceous hips, scowling at her with their mom's gorgeous green eyes. Her skin was a shade lighter than Charity's, and her hair flew around her like a curtain as Billie snapped, "This entire family is falling apart, that's what is wrong, and you and Dad want to take this hot mess public!"

"I have no clue—"

"The reality show?" Billie cut her off. "Dad wanting to run for governor? This is not the time to shine a spotlight on this family."

"Why? Are you and Jean-Luc getting a divorce?"

"What are you talking about?" she asked.

"Dad said you and Jean-Luc were fighting because he wants to start trying and you don't."

Billie released a frustrated groan. "Once again, he is deflecting! Jean-Luc and I are fine. When I spoke to Dad, yes, I had reservations about becoming a mom, but the one thing I can guarantee is we are not going to raise our kids like our parents did."

"What? You worship Dad."

"Are you seriously this dense?" Billie asked, releasing a laugh tinged with bitterness. "Being the daughter of Judge Royce Simmons opens doors for me and my clients. I can't afford to alienate him, but the man lives with his head in the sand, and it's all going to sift out from under him if he makes these moves."

"Okay, can we stop with the metaphors and just tell me what you're talking about?"

Billie's eyes bored into hers as she said flatly, "Mom's leaving Dad."

Charity froze. "When?"

"Before he announces his run for office."

"But why? I thought they were the perfect couple?"

"Charity..." Billie shook her head. "I know you keep your distance for self-preservation, but you miss a lot when you stay away. He's been cheating on her for years. Mom found out a couple of years ago and showed up at my door, losing her mind. I told her to leave him then, but she loved her life and didn't want to mess up things with any of us."

"Why are you telling me this?" *Why didn't Mom tell me this?*

"Of all of us, you're the only one who can't seem to lie with a straight face. But it doesn't matter because she met someone a few months ago at…I wanna say Whole Foods, but I can't remember for sure. They're in love, and she was waiting until after the holidays to ask Dad for a divorce, but he dumped this political run on her, and it's now or never."

While she was still reeling that her strong, opinionated mother stayed with a cheater, Charity still couldn't fathom what was so dire. "What does it matter if they get divorced? We've all moved out. They can split their assets, and Dad will pay Mom alimony. It's not the end of the world and has no bearing on whether I'm on *Bake That*."

"Charity, she's about to disappoint him. You more than anyone should know what that's like."

"Thanks a lot," Charity snapped.

"I'm not saying that to be a jerk. I'm showing you what Mom's facing, so maybe you can drum up a little sympathy."

Charity didn't even respond to that ridiculousness. There was no comparison between her mom deciding to leave her cheating husband and Charity being continuously mocked and ridiculed for not doing what's expected of her.

"If she's going to tell him, why did they invite all of us here?"

"Because he already set this dinner in motion. He told all of us that you're going to be a contestant on a reality baking show, and we all have to convince you not to do it."

"So that's what you're doing?" Charity asked. "Telling me not to do the show?"

"Listen—" Billie took her hands and pulled her onto the bed next to her. "I know I can be a crappy sister to you, but

I've always admired the way you bucked their expectations and did what you wanted. I applaud your independent streak and the fact that you're obviously amazing at what you do, but this is bigger than all of us. Just accept Dad's money and don't do the show. At least, not now."

Charity's thoughts were swirling around like a Tilt-A-Whirl, and she couldn't seem to make them stop. "I'll think about it."

Billie released her hands and stood. "That's all we can ask."

"Is Mom telling Dad tonight?"

"I think after everyone leaves, yes."

Charity let the fact fully sink in that her parents, who she always thought were in sync, weren't actually perfect, but a fragile bomb waiting to explode. For years, she'd hated herself because she couldn't make them happy until she'd accepted that it wouldn't happen and loved herself anyway. Finding out they were fake, imperfect beings that used an image to manipulate others, including their children, lit a fire in her belly, and she wanted to watch this house of cards burn.

Charity followed Billie out of her room and down the stairs, making a beeline for Will as soon as she saw him. Anton was with him, and when she reached Will's side, he stopped talking and glanced at her. "Everything okay?"

"Yeah, it's fine. Hey, Ant."

"Hi, Squirt," he said, using his childhood nickname for her. She made a face, and he laughed. "So, I hear you got accepted on *Bake That*?"

"I did, although some people think it's a bad idea," Charity said, shooting Billie a pointed look as she joined their mother by the bar.

"I never said that," Will said, defensively.

"I actually wasn't talking about you."

"Who, Dad?" Anton laughed. "If I were you, I'd do whatever the heck I wanted. Lord knows, everyone else in this family does."

Charity frowned at the bitter edge in her brother's voice. What the heck was going on? "Where's Elena?"

"She wasn't feeling well today and decided to stay home with Isabelle."

Suddenly, an arm slipped through hers, and her mother said, "I'm going to steal her away for a minute."

Charity released Will's arm reluctantly and let her mom lead her into the kitchen, where their cook was busy pulling a roast from the oven.

"Hi, Ellen," Charity said warmly. She loved Ellen with her whole heart and credited her for instilling a love of baking in Charity.

Ellen smiled at her over the steaming pan, her plump cheeks pink. "Hello, Charity. How are you doing?"

"I'm surviving."

"Ellen," Charity's mother said brusquely, releasing Charity's arm. "Would you please take dinner out to the table, and after you're done, you may go home for the night. I'll clean up."

"But Mrs. Simmons, I have two hours left—"

"You'll still be paid for your time, but I need to be alone with my family."

"Yes, ma'am." Ellen shot Charity a curious look but disappeared into the other room with the roast.

"I thought we could take a few minutes before dinner to talk," her mother said. "Even though I apologized, I know you're still upset with me about what I said the other night about Kara."

Charity waited for her to finish her sentence until several moments passed. "Yes, I am still quite upset."

Her mother sighed. "I thought so. I love Kara. And I am so glad that she found a man to love her, all of her."

"Do you even hear yourself?" Charity asked in a voice heavy with exasperation. "You're not making it any better, Mom."

"I'm sorry, it's just... when you start off beautiful and your body changes, you can't expect the person you're with to still feel the same. That's all I was trying to explain."

"I'm sorry that's been your experience, but when you marry someone and love them, it should be about more than their appearance."

"For some people, yes, but not all of them."

Charity shook her head, thinking about what Billie had said about her father no longer being attracted to her mother, and for the first time, Charity took a good look at her tonight. There was something different...

Her mother wasn't wearing makeup. She wore a simple sheath dress, and her usually shiny, blown-out hair was pulled back in a low ponytail.

Her mother cupped her face, green eyes boring into hers.

"I'm sorry, Charity. I'm sorry I pushed my own insecurities onto you."

Ellen came back into the room for the rest of the meal, and her mother released her.

"Thanks, Mom. I appreciate that you—" Her mother's eyes were shimmering with tears, something she hadn't seen often in her thirty-three years. "Are you all right?"

"Yes, everything is going to be fine after tonight." The steely tone in her mother's voice hit Charity like a ton of bricks and suddenly, Billie's worries truly sank in. Her mother had been pushed to the limits, and this was the night of her retribution, her breaking point. She was the wrecking ball, and Charity's father? The wall.

Oh, holy hockey sticks, this is going to be bad.

CHAPTER TWENTY-EIGHT

Tortoiseshell Brownie

This chocolatey dessert isn't just pretty to look at with swirls of caramel and marshmallow fluff but is a decadent dessert you won't want to share.

THE TENSION WAS THICKER than the slices of beef that Royce was cutting for the table. Will sat between Charity and her brother and listened to Billie and her husband talk about their upcoming schedules at work.

When he couldn't take it anymore, he leaned over to whisper in Charity's ear, "What's going on?"

"Will, would you like to say grace?" Royce asked.

"Um, I'm actually Jewish, so I'd rather not."

"Oh, my apologies. Charity didn't mention that. She must have been preoccupied with her reality show debut," Royce said, an edge of bitterness in his tone.

"Actually, I believe she did mention it. You just never pay attention," Iris called from the other end of the table, taking a spoonful of green beans and passing them to Anton. Will couldn't miss the arch look Iris sent her husband.

"When did she tell us that Will was Jewish?" Royce snapped.

"Two weeks ago, when we were asking her questions about Mexico, but you were two scotches into the night."

Royce's expression darkened. "What is wrong with you?"

Charity leaned over and whispered, "It's about to go down."

"You, Royce," Iris said, picking up her wineglass and taking a long, slow sip. "You are what has been wrong with me for thirty-seven years."

Charity started to get up from the table along with Anton, Jean-Luc, and Billie, but by the time Will got on board, Iris said, "No, you all need to stay for this. I'm sorry, Will and Jean-Luc, but it's about time we cleared the air. And we're a family, right?"

Royce set the knife and serving fork down, placing his hands flat on the table. "Stop making a scene, Iris."

"I should have made a scene years ago when Anton wanted to go to film school," Iris said, her tone saccharine sweet and heavy with sarcasm. "But oh no, I followed your lead and convinced him that going to law school was what was best for him. Did you know he has a cosplay channel on TikTok with ten million followers? He records the videos with Elena, who, by the way, cannot stand your sorry behind but shows up for family dinners because she loves our son."

"What is TikTok?" Royce asked.

"It's a social media app with short videos—" Will stopped explaining when Charity squeezed his thigh.

"And let's talk about Billie, who has wanted to quit her job for five years but is too afraid of disappointing you to be honest about it."

"Mom!" Billie hollered.

"You can be mad at me, baby, but he needs to hear this."

Royce's scowl shifted from Billie to Iris and, lastly, to Anton. "I need to hear that my family has been lying and going behind my back for years?"

"Oh, please don't play the victim," Iris laughed. "Did you think I didn't know what all those late-night work dinners really were?"

The entire table burst into the conversation except for Will and Jean-Luc, who shared a glance as if silently asking if they should leave.

"Mom, I thought you were going to do this later?" Billie asked.

Anton gaped at his mother. "He was cheating, and you stayed?"

Charity didn't say a word but drained her wineglass and poured another finger.

It was chaos, and Will had no idea what to do except to sit there quietly and soak it all in.

"Enough!" Royce boomed, his large chest rising and falling rapidly as he glared at his wife. "Is this what you wanted? To pit our children against me?"

"You're giving her too much credit, Dad. You did that all on your own," Charity said, getting out of her seat.

Will couldn't stop his fist from going over his mouth to cover his jaw dropping. He was equally mesmerized and terrified of what was coming next.

"Excuse me?" Royce turned the full weight of his fury on his daughter.

"It's funny. I've been stressing all day, and I came here tonight intending to cave and accept your offer to pay for my bakery expansion because it would be a sure thing. Even knowing that it would be an ax hanging over my head forever, I thought it would be the right move for everyone. But now? There is no way I'd accept money from a hypocrite. My whole life you"—she turned her attention to her mother—"and you"—a quick flick to her brother and sister—"you all made me feel like I was the weird one in this family. The defective one. I even convinced Will to pretend to be my boyfriend and come with me to these awful dinners just to make them bearable."

Everyone turned his way, and he smiled in what he could only imagine was a mix of awkward and sheepish.

"Turns out, I'm the only person in this family who owned the fact I wasn't perfect, and you know what? I'm okay with it. Because as broken as this family is, I built my real family. I live with my best friend in the whole world who is my sister in all ways but blood. I had a house full of people who showed up for my birthday and told me how much they loved and accepted me. And this guy?" Charity held her hand down to Will, who took it. "He's a part of that, too, because he's been through the trenches with me, and I feel awful I brought him here to have dinner with you people."

"Charity," her mother started, but Charity held up her hand.

"No, Mom, enough is enough. You're my family, and I love you. However, I don't like any of you right now. We're going to let the rest of you enjoy your dinner, and I won't be back, not until there is a major overhaul on the way we treat each other."

Will cleared his throat as he climbed to his feet. "Good night."

"If you walk out that door, young lady," Royce hollered, his voice echoing through the room like thunder, "you are out of this family. Do you understand?"

She turned in the doorway and said, "Dad, catch up. I literally just said I'm voluntarily exiting stage left."

Will let Charity practically drag him out the door and down the steps when she stopped suddenly, screaming at the top of her lungs. An echo of dogs barking throughout the neighborhood responded, and Will bit his cheek to avoid releasing the tense laughter building in his chest.

"Are you okay?" he asked.

"Are you kidding? I'm amazing. I'm free." She suddenly threw herself against him with a laugh. "We should go celebrate."

"Sure, where do you want to go?"

"There's a bar called Beerbury. The team at the homeless kitchen is meeting there. Want to go?"

Will pushed a loose curl away from her face and smiled. "Sounds good. Find me an address."

Charity let him go with another breathless laugh, and they raced to his car. As he followed the directions, he kept glancing over at her, searching for the right thing to say.

"You know, it took a lot of guts to be honest with them tonight. Although I think you were a little hard on Anton. He seems like a good guy."

"He's better now, but before Elena, he would be right in there with Mom, Dad, and Billie, tearing me down. And I don't know if it was guts as much as repressed rage. Once I found out my family was a bunch of liars and hypocrites, everything kind of exploded from me."

"Including the fact that we weren't really dating?"

"Which, I guess, makes me a liar, too," she said with an unabashed grin. "But at least now you're off the hook for awkward family dinners."

Will chuckled. "They're more interesting than mine. We mostly sneak champagne from the bottle during family brunch and pray that none of my mom's coworkers have new grandchildren."

"Is your sister married?"

"No, she likes being alone."

"Like you?"

"Eh, my sister doesn't have that drive to be with anyone, whereas I get lonely and enjoy having someone in my life."

"You just don't want to get married. Wait, no, you don't want to get married to anyone who will spend all your money and put you into debt." Charity giggled, giving Will the indication that she might be a little bit tipsy.

"You make it sound trivial. It doesn't matter anyway. I have no money."

"Um, did you have money and lose it? That's a pretty cryptic way to say that."

"No, I—my mom has rheumatoid arthritis, and her doctor wanted her to quit her job while they get her pain under control. But my mom's too young to withdraw from her retirement or Social Security, and she has no savings left. I'm using mine to supplement her income."

"Of course you are. You're a good son."

Will shifted uncomfortably at the praise. "So I've been told."

"What were you saving up for?" she asked.

"I was going to leave marketing and do freelance graphic design."

Will saw Charity spin in her seat to face him out of the corner of his eye. "That's amazing. Why can't you do that still?"

"Because with everything happening, I don't want to give up a steady income for something that might not pan out."

"Why do you think it wouldn't happen for you? Aren't you talented? I mean, you designed our cat café logo, and it rocks."

"Yes."

"Then why are you doubting yourself? You have a degree in marketing, so having your own business should be a breeze, because you know how to get yourself in front of the right people. If you're scared, just say that, but don't act like you can't do it."

Will glanced at her out of the corner of his eye. "Are your pep talks always so combative?"

"It's part of my charm."

CHAPTER TWENTY-NINE

Frap-Purr-Ccino

Blended cold brew with your choice of syrup is guaranteed to leave you purring with every sip. Try our fan-favorite flavors Snow Leopard or Bengal Tiger.

It had become clear to Will in a matter of minutes that the person who'd recommended this particular bar was Chris Varton, who was watching Charity take a shot with a smug smile on his face. While she'd introduced Will as her friend instead of her boyfriend, the irrational, un-friendlike feeling rumbling inside him shook Will with the urge to knock Chris off his barstool and carry Charity out of there as fast as he could.

Instead, he sat on her other side, nursing a beer, and trying to figure out the best exit strategy before he made a jerk of himself.

"Hi," a woman in her late twenties said, leaning against the bar next to him. "I like your shirt. It really makes your eyes look blue."

It was on the tip of his tongue to tell her that's because they are blue, but there was no reason to be rude to a stranger. "Thanks, that's what I was going for."

"I am such a sucker for blue eyes and black hair. Like Damon Salvatore."

"Who?" Will asked.

"She's talking about Ian Somerhalder from *The Vampire Diaries* show," Charity offered, and he grinned, realizing she'd been listening the entire time. Did that mean she cared that he'd been approached by another woman or was she so bored with her conversation with Chris she was looking for a way out?

"Got it." Will spun back to the woman with a shrug. "I've never seen the show."

"It's so good. Damon is such a jerk, but with a heart of gold."

It was obvious the girl was on the dangerous edge of drunk, and he reached out to steady her. "It sounds like a good show. Do you want me to call you a ride to take you home?"

"Are you going to come with me?" she asked sweetly.

"No, but I'm happy to make sure you get there safely."

The woman pouted. "You're no fun."

Before Will could respond, she'd grabbed his beer and taken off to talk to a group of guys on the edge of the room.

"Wow," Charity laughed, drawing his attention back to

her. "Can we get another beer for my friend? Some drunk girl ran off with his."

There was that word again. *Friend.* He'd realized that she'd used it quite a few times since she'd told her parents they weren't together. Was she doing it on purpose to assure him there weren't any more expectations? Or was it to convince Chris that she was completely available?

The bartender handed him the beer, and Will put five bucks on the counter. "Thanks."

Charity bumped his shoulder with hers. "Don't be so glum. There are plenty of women where that one came from."

Will looked around the bar, and she was right. There were lots of women, beautiful women, but he didn't have any interest in talking to one of them. The only person in this bar he wanted to spend time with was sitting next to him, putting him in his place.

The *friend* place.

Dude, what did you expect? You've been browbeating her with your lack of interest in her or any kind of future, so why would she waste her time?

"Actually, you can have this," Will said, setting the beer down in front of her and gathering his coat off the back of the stool. "I'm going to head out. Can you get a ride, or do you want me to call Kara?"

"I can get a ride." Charity's brow furrowed. "Are you sure about leaving? I can finish up, and we can go."

"No, I'm good. You're having fun, and I'm really tired."

"All right. Thanks, Will."

"Hey, nice to see you again, man," Chris said, reaching out to offer his hand.

Will took it, giving his palm a squeeze and releasing it. "Sure, you too. I'll see you later."

"Am I still coming over for brunch tomorrow?" she asked.

"What for? Cat's out of the bag now, right?"

Charity's eyes flared, but he didn't know what else to say. He was mad at himself for feeling like this, for wanting her but knowing he'd pushed her so far away that there was no getting her back. As friends, with no pressure for anything more, she'd revealed a side of herself beyond the slightly spoiled, snarky girl he'd met over two months ago. Instead, there was this fierce risk-taker determined to love and be loved, to find her fulfillment while possibly losing it all. Putting herself out into the world in front of the camera, just to get her shot.

Will envied her bravery and her strength. If he pushed aside his fears and told her she'd gotten under his skin, that he wanted her, all of her, would she reject him? Would she take a chance on him? Or would he be just another disappointment to her?

Will hadn't reached his car yet when his phone started ringing, revealing his sister's smiling face on his screen. He tapped the answer button, leaning against the car.

"Hey."

"Hi, what are you doing?"

"Standing outside of a bar, contemplating my life choices."

"Well, a bar seems like the perfect place to do that. Have you talked to Mom about brunch tomorrow?"

"No, but I thought maybe you could pick her up and bring her to my house. If you'll buy the fixings, I'll handle all the food prep, and you two can relax."

"Wow, this sounds like my brother, but I can't remember the last time you offered to cook."

"It's been a while, but I figure, with everything Mom's going through, the least we can do is take a little bit of the stress off her."

"She told me that you're paying her bills while she takes a leave of absence."

Will sighed, wishing she'd kept that between the two of them. "Like I said, she's our mom. It's the least I can do."

"I can help, too, you know," Sarah said gently. "It doesn't always have to be you."

Will swallowed past the lump suddenly blocking his throat. While they may tease and torment each other, Will knew his sister loved him and would always have his back. And he would have hers. "It kind of does, though. That's my job as the eldest, to take care of you both."

"Please, I make bank. I don't need you to do squat for me, and I can help with Mom."

"Sarah, if you want to help, no one is stopping you," Will said.

"Mom is. I offered to end my lease and move in with her, pay her rent to help, and she turned me down. Said a single woman needed her own place."

"So why don't you tell her the truth?" he asked.

"Please, you barely understand, and you're a few years

older. If I tell Mom I have no desire for either sex or want to just live out my life in peace, maybe get a pet, she'll have a stroke."

"You'll never know until you say something."

"All right, oh, wise, advice-giving brother, if you know everything, then why are you confused about your life choices?"

"Because I'm struggling with whether I behave selfishly or walk away before I hurt someone I care about."

"I heard somewhere it was better to have loved and lost than never to have loved at all?"

"Really? You believe that?"

"The question is, if you walk away, are you going to be able to live with not knowing what could have been?"

Will stood there, gripping the phone to his ear for several seconds before he cursed out loud and strode back toward the bar.

His sister's laughter rang in his ear. "Go get her, Tiger."

Charity sat on the edge of her stool, listening to Chris and the bartender talk about football while her mind wandered to the empty seat next to her. Why had she suggested they come here? Chris was a nice enough guy, but no matter how much she tried to talk herself into him, there was no spark. She didn't gravitate toward him when he smiled, and it had taken her walking through that door to realize what a mistake she'd made, but Will wasn't exactly giving her clear signals. Dancing with her. Kissing her in front of those rude women and then acting like it was all part of their act.

Only, the things he made her feel? They weren't fake anymore.

While she no longer thought of him as a player, he had some reservations about relationships, and how could you change someone's core beliefs?

"Everything okay?" Chris asked.

"Actually, it's not," Charity said, getting up from the stool. "I'm going to try to catch up to Will and apologize."

"Apologize for what?" Chris asked, his brow knit in obvious confusion. "I thought you two were just friends now?"

"No, we're...it's complicated, but we're definitely more than that."

Chris shrugged; his full lips spread in a sheepish smile. "Oh well. Can't blame a guy for trying."

"I'm sorry I led you on. I think you're great."

"Thanks. And hey, if I hadn't met you, I wouldn't have Lucifer, so no worries. We're good."

Charity kissed his cheek. "I'll see you around."

She turned toward the door and saw Will's back before it shut behind him. Had he returned to talk to her? Did he think kissing Chris's cheek meant something?

Cursing her high heels, Charity weaved her way around the other bar patrons and out the door, yelling Will's name. To her frustration, he ignored her, briskly marching across the asphalt toward his car.

"Will, I can't run in these shoes! Wait up!"

He turned around, and in the parking lot lights, his expression was a stony mask. "Why? What do you want now? Do you need me to come back inside and make that guy jealous?"

"No, of course not," she said, hope spreading through her chest as she watched him pace. "What are you so angry about?"

"I'm not. I'm frustrated because you wanted to stay, but now you're out here chasing me down for—what?"

"Why did you come back in?" she asked.

"What difference does it make?" he muttered, coming to a stop.

When Will started to turn away again, she grabbed his arm, keeping him from leaving. "It makes all the difference to me."

Will released a heavy, bitter laugh. "Fine, you wanna know why I came back? To tell you that I didn't want to leave you alone with that guy. That we came together, and we were going to leave together, and that after everything, I didn't deserve to get chucked as soon as you didn't need me anymore."

Charity threw herself against him, her arms circling his neck. "I'm so sorry. I am a jerk. I didn't want to make you feel that way, but I thought... I didn't think you wanted me."

Will scoffed. "Then you're oblivious, because I've shown you over and over that I wanted you."

"When? You've helped me, but always as a friend. You've kissed me, but I thought it was all in fun, part of the agreement."

He dropped his head, his lips covering hers softly, nudging

them open, and she returned his kiss, her fingers gripping the back of his neck. Will pulled back enough to brush his lips along her jaw, whispering against her skin, "I agreed to be your fake boyfriend to be close to you, Charity. How did you miss that?"

"Because you kept telling me why we wouldn't work."

"Maybe I was wrong. Being with you, spending time with you, it feels too good to stop."

"Then don't stop," she whispered, catching his gaze. "Take me home."

"You mean..."

"Yes."

Will's smile lit up his face like the sun. "Your place or mine?"

CHAPTER THIRTY

Catprese Salad

Fresh mozzarella cheese and tomatoes sprinkled with basil leaves and doused with olive oil and vinegar make a classic Italian dish.

CHARITY DIDN'T WANT TO get out of bed. Between Will's warmth radiating beneath his comforter and his kittens pinning her legs down, she could stay like this forever, cozy and cocooned with his arm around her waist.

If only her other arm wasn't dead asleep.

As slowly as possible so she didn't disturb him, Charity tried rolling onto her back, scooting first one leg around the kittens and then the other. Sausage lifted his head, watching her through sleepy eyes as she slid from under the covers and onto the floor with a less-than-graceful thump.

"Are you trying to sneak out on me?" Will mumbled.

Charity peeked over the bed, hyperaware of her nudity.

"No. My arm was asleep, and my bladder is causing me a bit of discomfort."

"You should definitely take care of that and come back to bed. I'm cold without you."

Charity snatched his shirt off the floor and slipped it over her head before she climbed to her feet. "I don't know how you're cold. Your body is practically radioactive. I swear you run a hundred and twenty degrees!"

"Is that a bad thing?" Will asked, rolling to his side and cradling his head in one hand.

"No, I'm just saying."

He grinned. "Then how about hurry up because I miss you next to me. Is that better?"

Charity couldn't suppress the giddy smile on her face as she headed into the master bath. When she came back into the room, Will was standing by the side of the bed in a pair of boxers with his phone in hand.

"What time is it?" she asked.

"Ten eighteen. My mom and sister are going to be here in twelve minutes."

Charity's eyes widened. "Oh my gosh!"

"I know. No more snuggle time."

"Seriously, that's your first thought? I don't have a change of clothes, and my dress is wrinkled on your bedroom floor!"

"I'll iron it while you take a shower. Just let me pee."

That pulled Charity up short. "You're offering to iron my dress for me?"

"Yeah, why not? I iron my shirts and suits. You're my guest.

Plus what would your mother say about you entertaining in such a state?" he asked in a high, snooty voice.

Charity hiked a brow. "Are you making fun of my mother?"

"No," Will said.

"I mean, it's okay, but you're not doing the voice right. It's more like—" She put her hand on her hip and continued, "Charity, you cannot go around looking like you slept in your clothes! March right back into that bedroom and get changed."

Will pretended to tremble. "Oof, you sound just like her. Is this what my future holds?"

"Are you seriously asking if I'm going to turn out like my mother?"

"Hey, I'll probably end up balding with a small cookie pouch like my dad—" He gathered his hands at his flat stomach and pinched his skin, making it move while he said, "Hello, Charity. Enjoy this while it lasts."

"I'm getting in the shower," she said, her voice shaking with laughter. Before she could fully escape, he seized her hand and drew her against his body.

"I'm glad you're here," he murmured before his lips pressed against hers. She kissed him back without opening her mouth, hyperaware of the morning breath she had going on. When he finally broke the kiss, he placed a chaste one on her nose. "There's towels in the linen cabinet and washcloths in the basket next to it."

"Thanks."

Charity didn't linger in the shower and had barely wrapped the towel around herself before Will knocked on the door.

"Hey, are you almost done? Your dress is hanging up out here."

"I'll be right out."

Charity put some toothpaste on her finger and used it to brush her teeth, her gaze drifting around the clutter-free bathroom. She kept her bathroom straightened in case they had guests over, but she'd expected Will's place to look like a stereotypical bachelor pad.

When she was dry, Charity opened the door and stepped out to find Will standing outside with a bundle of clothes in his arms.

"It's all yours," she said.

"I won't be long. If you hear the doorbell, go ahead and answer it but be prepared. My sister and mom are very friendly."

Charity laughed and grabbed her dress off the hanger. It was wrinkle free and looked like it hadn't been worn at all. Charity got dressed and realized she didn't have another pair of underwear. She peeked her head into the bathroom and hollered through the steam, "So, I don't know about going without panties in a dress at breakfast with your mom and sister here."

His deep laughter echoed along with the pounding water, bringing a smile to her face.

"You can get into my top drawer and steal a pair of mine."

"Isn't that weird?" she asked.

"Not for me. Maybe next time I spend the night at your house, I can wear your underwear."

Charity heaved with laughter at the imagery. "Now you're just getting freaky."

She closed the door on Will's guffaws and snatched a pair of his boxers out of his top drawer, slipping them on under her dress.

The doorbell rang as she descended the stairs, and she paused. She was playing with the messy bun on top of her head, wishing she'd had her leave-in conditioner and a comb.

Charity opened the front door to find Will's mom and a tall, dark-haired woman standing on the front stoop.

"Hi," she said. "Will's in the shower, but he will be down soon."

"Hello again, Charity," his mom said, smiling. "You beat us here."

Charity's cheeks burned. "Yes, I did. Please come on inside."

"I don't know if you remember from the grocery store, but I'm Anna," Will's mom said.

"Yes, of course I remember."

"I'm going to use the little girls' room and then head into the kitchen. If you'll excuse me."

Charity stepped aside to let Anna pass.

"And I'm Sarah. I'm Will's younger, funnier sister." Will's sister carried two sacks of groceries but somehow managed to extend a hand to her.

"It's very nice to meet you. I've heard a lot about you."

Sarah made a face. "Oh, I just bet you have. My brother likes to tell tall tales about me. Don't believe a word he says."

The sound of a door opening above and feet falling on the

stairs preceded Will calling out, "Funny, I was about to tell her the very same thing about you."

Charity turned and watched Will jog down the stairs in a blue T-shirt and jeans, his bare feet slapping against the wood. Bacon and Sausage raced along beside him and around the corner.

"When did you get cats?" Sarah squealed.

"A few days ago," he said. His hair was wet and tousled and her fingers curled, resisting the urge to brush it back off his forehead when he stopped next to her.

"Why? Cats hate you!"

"Not those two," Will said.

"What do you mean, cats hate him?" Charity asked.

"We had several cats growing up, and the majority of the time, they wanted nothing to do with Will," Sarah said, smirking. "It's like they could sense evil in him."

"Oh, like Lucifer giving you side-eye with his ears pinned back. And didn't Chaos used to scream at you?" Charity laughed at Will's disgruntled expression.

"First off, those are two difficult and aptly named cats, and Chaos adores me now. Where is Mom?"

"She was going to use the bathroom and head into the kitchen," Sarah said, holding out the grocery sacks to him.

Will took the groceries and squeezed past them. "I told her I was gonna make breakfast."

"Apparently, she doesn't trust you," Sarah called after him, grinning at Charity. "Have you had Will's cooking?"

"No, I haven't yet."

"That's because he can't cook."

Charity smiled. "Well, I guess that's why he invited me over."

"That's right. You own a café?"

"Yes, I do."

"Well, thanks for saving us!"

"Happy to help," Charity said, waving her hand. "After you."

Charity followed Sarah down the hallway that led into an open floor plan that included the living room and dining room. Off to the right was the kitchen, where Will was arguing with his mom.

"No, you need to go sit down and rest. I got this."

Charity stood in the doorway watching Anna hold on to the container of eggs Will was trying to take with a glare. Bacon weaved in and out of her legs, but she didn't pay the kitten any attention. "You do not have this. You can barely make scrambled eggs, let alone frittatas!"

"Can I help?" Charity asked, holding out her hand to his mom. "I promise, if you hand over the eggs, I'll be the one in charge of the kitchen, Mrs. Schwartz."

"Betrayer!" Will gasped, pushing Sausage gently off the counter when he tried to jump up.

His mom set the eggs on the counter and wagged her finger at her son. "Will, you let her do her thing. You don't even know how to cook an egg."

"You taught me how to cook! I just choose not to."

"You heard it from his own mouth. I tried. It didn't take."

His mom headed out of the kitchen, her tone changing as she talked directly to Bacon. "You're a pretty baby, aren't you?"

"Mom, come sit down with me and let the two of them duke it out," Sarah said, pulling out a bottle of champagne and orange juice from one of the sacks.

"You're not going to fight me, are you?" Charity asked sweetly.

"Not when you use that tone of voice."

"What tone?"

"The pretend nice one. It's creepy."

Charity threw the bag of green onions at him, and he caught it against his chest. "I guess I should be happy it wasn't the eggs."

"Get to prepping the veggies, sous chef."

"Oh, good call, Charity," Sarah called from the doorway. "That will keep him busy and out of your way."

"That's what I was thinking."

"I'm standing right here," Will grumbled.

Charity leaned up on her toes and kissed his cheek. "I know, hon."

"Oof, that's gross. Do you want a mimosa to disinfect your mouth?" Sarah asked.

"Can I throw her out?" Will asked.

"Hey, it's your home. I'm just cooking in it."

While Charity and Will prepared breakfast, Sarah pulled a chair from the dining room table over so her mom could join the conversation, and Bacon immediately made himself at home in Will's mom's lap. Listening to their loving, effortless teasing got Charity thinking about her own family. How much she wished they knew how to relax and have fun.

"You don't have to worry about making mine," Will said, interrupting her musings. "I'll show all of you I can make a kick-butt frittata."

"Are you really not going to let your girlfriend make one for you?" his mom asked.

Will glanced at Charity, as if silently asking what he should say, but telepathy wasn't in her skill set. Finally, he set down his knife and said, "She's not my girlfriend. At least, not yet."

"What do you mean? I thought..." Anna trailed off, her gaze shifting between Will and Charity.

Charity cleared her throat. "The thing is, Mrs. Schwartz—"

"Anna, please."

"Anna. Will was pretending to be my boyfriend because I asked him to."

Several beats passed before Anna asked, "But why?"

"Because my family likes to set me up on awkward blind dates and I needed a break." Charity leaned against the counter, smiling at Will. "But I didn't expect him to grow on me."

"Like a fungus?" Sarah laughed.

Will glared at his sister while her mother pinched her arm. "Be nice. Continue, Charity."

"I was just saying that I think Will and I are going to try this for real and see where things lead."

The tender expression on his face sent shock waves through her body.

His mother clapped her hands in obvious delight. "Oh, I'm so happy. Out of curiosity, what religion do you practice?"

Will groaned. "Why does that matter?"

"I guess I'm Christian but we didn't go to church unless my dad had business there. So I'm open to other beliefs."

"Excellent. And how many children do you want to have?"

"Mom!" Sarah and Will shouted together.

Charity laughed. "That should be a question for your son, not me."

"Oh, and why is that?"

"Because he's the one who told me that he's never getting married and he's not sure if he wants children."

Anna frowned. "I don't know what my son told you but I want two grandchildren at least, and in quick succession."

Will opened the oven and pretended to stick his head in.

All the women burst out laughing.

"Come on, Will," Sarah said. "Charity is taking Mom's demands in stride."

Will stood back up with a glare. "You're having way too much fun with this."

"That's what little sisters are for," she said, taking a gulp of her drink.

"Hey, Sarah, what's your relationship status?" he asked pointedly.

"My relationship status is none of your business."

"See, Mom, she should be the one you're worried about."

"I worry about both my children, but at the moment, I'm more concerned with my son scaring away a wonderful girl like this because of some misguided notion about being a confirmed bachelor."

"I think this was a mistake getting the three of you in a room."

Charity laughed. "You're the one who has hang-ups about marriage, not me. Afraid your future wife is going to tank your credit score and—"

She paused when Will made a strangled sound, and she noticed all the color had drained from his face, staring down at a long cut along his finger.

"Will!" She grabbed a handful of paper towels and rushed to his side. "Are you okay?"

"Yeah, I'm good," he said, his voice strained. Wrapping his other hand around his paper towel–covered fingers, he continued, "I'm going to clean this up."

"What happened?" Anna asked.

"Nothing, Mom, I just cut myself. I'll be back."

Charity followed him up the stairs to his bathroom, her stomach twisting into knots. "I'm sorry. I didn't mean to overstep or say something to upset you. I figured your family knew how you felt."

"They don't," he said, uncovering his wound. "I didn't want my mom to hear why I have an aversion to marriage, because then she'll know."

"Know what?"

"That she and my dad are the reason I don't want to get married," he said in a rush. Charity's stomach dropped out as she leaned against the bathroom counter, watching the warring emotions on his face. "The way they lived their lives? My mom is still catching up on debt that she had with my dad three years ago. I must help my mom pay her bills because my dad never started a retirement fund or could afford enough life insurance to keep her going if he died unexpectedly. Growing up, we lived paycheck to paycheck. If I have kids, I never want them to experience that."

Charity waited several beats before she spoke, reaching for his injured hand. "I understand why you feel that way, but were your parents happy?"

"I—Yes." He let her examine his finger, wincing as she blotted the oozing slice.

"Did they love each other?"

"Charity..."

She leaned up and kissed his mouth, stopping his protests. "Go with me on this."

"Without a doubt, they loved each other very much," he said.

"Then the other stuff didn't matter to them." When he opened his mouth to argue, Charity covered it with her hand. "I understand it was stressful for you, but your parents had two beautiful children, and from the way you and your sister behave, it's obvious you never wanted for anything, especially love. It's okay to learn from their mistakes so you don't struggle, but that doesn't mean you have to miss a chance at happiness because you're afraid of ending up like them."

Will covered her hand with his, kissing her palm before pulling it away from his lips. "Is that really how you feel?"

"Yes. My parents got married because it made logical sense. They wanted the same things out of life, only that changed over time because there was nothing else keeping them together. There was no love. No friendship. It was a marriage of convenience." She wrapped her arms around his shoulders and leaned into him. "I don't want that. I want more."

Will cradled the back of her head with his good hand before giving her a soft, sweet kiss. "I like you."

"I like you, too," she mumbled against his mouth.

CHAPTER THIRTY-ONE

Meowty Tasty BLT

With hunks of savory bacon cooked to perfection, this classic sandwich brings a new meaning to the word "satisfaction." Turkey bacon available upon request.

"DON'T BE NERVOUS. WE want this to be as stress free and natural as possible."

Although Donna Ren, the show's interviewer, had a delightfully soothing voice, her words didn't have the calming effect on Charity's nerves the interviewer was probably hoping for. It had been a long, nerve-racking week getting ready for the crew to arrive. On Wednesday morning, she'd come in at five with Kara to scrub off the snowflakes on the glass and take down all the winter décor so they could switch over to Valentine's Day. The lobby now had red and pink hearts hanging from the ceiling and cats and hearts painted along the glass between the café and social room. Sparkling red garland rested along the top of the bookshelf and hung in loose loops from the front of the counter. Cartoon cats in love were taped onto any open wall space, and on the front door was a large, pink heart wreath. It was a little much, but Kara was right; it did create a vibe.

The actual crew itself was creating a knot of anxiety in the pit of her stomach, and she didn't have issues with public speaking. Maybe it was because they'd closed the café on a Friday afternoon for this interview, and with a half a dozen people holding lights, microphones, and makeup brushes in her face, Charity felt a bit like she was back doing beauty pageants. All she needed was her mother barking at her to stand up straight and she'd be right back there.

"All right, where do we start?" Charity asked, giving her what she hoped was a friendly smile. Being in the spotlight should be old hat for her, but with everything riding on her success on the show, she couldn't seem to sit still.

"Let's start with what got you interested in baking?"

"It was actually our family cook, Ellen. I'd come home from school, and she'd have made a pan of fresh brownies or cookies for my siblings and me. When I was in middle school, I stayed home a couple days because I was having problems with the bullies at school, and Ellen taught me how to make some of my favorite treats. I still make them when I need a pick-me-up."

"Your cook taught you? Not your mom?"

Charity laughed. "My mom can't cook or bake."

"What can she do?" Donna asked.

Charity drew a blank for a moment, panic seizing up the

back of her throat, and then a memory flashed through her mind. "My mom has a talent for voices."

"Voices? What do you mean?"

"When she'd read a book to us, she could do all the characters' voices and make them distinctively different. Her accents and the way she could completely alter her voice—I remember wishing she'd never say good night because I could listen to her forever."

"It sounds like you had a wonderful childhood. What about your father? He's a judge?"

"Yes. He works a lot, but we get together every weekend for dinner."

"But during the week we can find you here?" Donna asked.

"And Saturdays, too."

Donna went on to ask about how the café got started, what people can expect when they come in, and finally, the sixty-four-thousand-dollar question.

"Why do you want to be a contestant on *Bake That*?"

"To win. I want to show the world and my family what I can do, but I also want to expand the café and be able to do more with the catering side of the business, which means more money for equipment. The recognition is great, but I'm doing this because I believe I'm good enough to go all the way."

There was a moment of silence before Donna cried, "Perfect!" The crew around them clapped, and Donna waved her finger. "I think we got it. Now the crew will go around getting some shots of the café, the outside entrance, and then we can head out to your home."

"My home?"

"Yes, this is a background interview. We want to see where you work. Where you live. We need the audience to fall in love with you, to care about whether you succeed or fail."

"Oh, well, I guess I'll run home really quick and clean up," Charity laughed, and Donna joined her.

"Perfect." Donna climbed to her feet. "We need some time to talk to your business partner. We'll head out that way in an hour or so after we grab a bite to eat on the way."

"If you're hungry, we can put together some soup and sandwiches for your crew. Just let Michelle know up front I okayed it."

"You're very sweet, but we'll pay for it. Don't want anyone to get the wrong idea that you're bribing us."

"I wasn't—"

Donna laughed, her brown hair falling back in a glistening waterfall. "My goodness, you are wound up! I'm just teasing you, darling. Take a breather."

Charity laughed nervously. "All right then, I'll leave you with Kara and Michelle. You have the address?"

"We do."

Charity left the lobby and headed back into Kara's office, where her friend was sitting behind her computer. She looked up when Charity walked in.

"Are they gone yet?" Kara asked.

"Not yet." Charity flopped down in the chair across from her, fighting the nervous fluttering in her stomach that wouldn't subside. "They want to talk to you, do some shots of the café, and then they're going to order lunch to go. I'm going to head over to the house to clean up."

"Why do they need to do all that?" Kara asked.

"Something about making the audience fall in love with me."

Kara shook her head. "And why do they want to talk to me?"

"Because I told them you know me better than anyone."

"Charity," Kara said, her voice tight. "You know how I feel about interviews."

Once upon a time, the thought of any kind of social media or interview would send Kara into a full-blown panic attack, but she'd been working hard to find ways to cope. Still, she knew that her friend still struggled to maintain her composure when put in the spotlight.

"I know you do, but you're not the focus here. I am." Charity reached across the desk and took Kara's hand, giving it a squeeze. "I promise, it will be painless."

"I hope so. I should warn you; your mom called me."

Charity clenched her jaw. "When?"

"A few minutes ago. I told her you were doing an interview and would call her when it was done."

"Or I could not."

Kara patted Charity's hand before releasing it. "I think you'll feel better if you hear her out. Maybe she's ready to really listen and mend what's broken between you."

"Maybe. Or she wants me on her side during her divorce from my dad. Either way, I'm going to deal with the pressing issue of our messy house."

"Oh, can you grab tampons on your way home? I started yesterday, and it is not fun."

Charity froze. "You did?"

"Yeah, didn't you?"

She should have. She'd been on birth control for so long that it was just something that happened at the same time every month. She never had to worry about being surprised, until now.

I'm never late.

"You know, it's probably just the stress. Even with birth control, it can mess up your cycles."

"Yeah, I've heard that," Kara said slowly, her forehead knit with concern. "Do you think you're—"

"Nope, no. No, I'm not." Several moments ticked by and panic set in, making her voice squeak. "I'm so sure, I'm not going to even say it out loud. I am going to leave, grab the tampons and some cleaning supplies, and get the house ready for company."

"Are you sure you're okay?" Kara asked, getting up from her chair, but Charity waved her back down.

"Seriously, I'm good. See you at home." Charity backed out of Kara's office, the air around her stifling. She rushed toward the back of the clinic in a fog, her mind racing. As she pushed out the back door and took a deep, gulping breath, she heard her name called as if from a distance. Charity looked up to find her mom leaning against her car in a pair of—

Yoga pants?

That explained everything. This was a nightmare, and she just needed to wake up.

"Are you all right?" her mom asked, making her way up the stairs toward her.

"I'm fine," Charity said, her voice breaking. "What are you doing here?"

"I wanted to talk to you and couldn't get ahold of you. I thought if I waited by your car long enough, you were bound to come out sometime."

"Well, you caught me," Charity said, her voice high and tight. "What can I do for you?"

"Straight to the point." Iris cleared her throat. "I know I've disappointed you numerous times over the years, but I was hoping we could move forward with a clean slate. We can rebuild our relationship slowly, and I'll be here. No matter how long it takes."

"Is this about you and Dad getting divorced and whose side I'm choosing? Because you don't have to worry. He wins the major-jerk award."

Her mom shook her head. "I'm not asking anyone to take sides. The two of us will work this out between us or the lawyers can duke it out. This is about you and me."

Charity had lost count of the times she'd wished her mom would reach out to her and ask her to go do something fun, not because it would boost their confidence or detox their skin or give her an edge on a beauty competition. She just wanted her mom to spend time with her.

"I'm up for starting over," Charity whispered.

Iris reached out her hand to take Charity's. "I know it won't mean much now, but I love you, honey. And I'm so very proud of you."

Charity swallowed hard, wondering if her mom would still feel that way if Charity ended up being a single mother.

"I have to go home and clean up before the camera crews get there. Maybe we can talk later?"

"Can I call you tonight?" Iris asked.

"I'd like that."

Iris squeezed her hand again before she released it and walked back to her car, leaving Charity contemplating the biggest, scariest decision of her life. If she wasn't just stressed and she was pregnant, did she want to keep it? And how would she break the news to an already relationship-shy Will?

There's no point obsessing before you know for sure. Take a test and go from there.

CHAPTER THIRTY-TWO

Fruit and Granola Pawfait

Thick and creamy Greek yogurt with fresh berries and granola, this sweet breakfast treat is a healthy and satisfying way to start your day.

Will waited until the camera crew left before he headed up the driveway to Charity and Kara's place with a bag of tacos and a six-pack of Corona. He figured after a full day of smiling for the camera and being on her best behavior, Charity deserved to relax.

He parked next to her car and got out, a definite spring in his step. Since they'd admitted their feelings for each other, Will had noticed the world looked a little brighter in the mornings. He'd even gone into work without the failure to strike out on his own hanging over his head. All the fears of getting serious with someone had faded, and he looked forward to seeing how his relationship with Charity progressed.

Will knocked on the door, the six-pack pinned to his side

with his elbow. When Charity opened the door, she wore an oversize sweatshirt and baggy sweatpants.

"Did you wear that for the TV show?"

"No, I just changed. Why?"

"Because you look cozy enough to snuggle and eat tacos with," he said, stepping into the house and giving her a hard, fast kiss. When her response was less than enthusiastic, he pulled away, studying her face. "What's wrong?"

"Nothing. It's just been a long day."

"I thought you might say that, so I brought you tacos, beer, and two of my favorite movies of all time."

"That sounds great," she said, her tired smile finally reaching her eyes.

"Good. Wanna set everything up in the living room while I hit the head?"

"I can do that," she said, taking the beer and bag of tacos from him, lifting herself up for another kiss. This time, her lips softened under his, and his heartbeat kicked into high gear.

She finally broke the kiss with a breathless laugh. "Go pee. You can kiss me after tacos, unless you ordered extra onions and spicy sauce."

Will clutched his chest. "You would deny me kisses for stinky breath?"

"Until you use the bottle of mouthwash under my bathroom sink, absolutely."

"I bought you a toothbrush to keep at my place, and I only get a bottle of mouthwash?" he asked.

"Because it gets a little crowded over here, and if we're staying anywhere, it's going to be at your place."

"Sound logic."

As Charity turned and disappeared into the living room with her cat, Robin Hood, hot on her heels, he called out, "Don't let that feline pig get my tacos!"

"No promises if you don't hurry up!"

Will grinned, heading down the hallway to her restroom and closing the door. As he stood in front of the toilet, a pink box in the waste basket caught his eye. On the front was a white stick that looked a lot like a—

"What the heck?"

Will finished his business and tilted the box by the corner, making sure it was exactly what he thought. His throat tightened, making it hard to catch his breath as he washed his trembling hands.

There was a pregnancy test in Charity's bathroom. The chances of it being Kara's were slim since she had her own bathroom, and he doubted one of the TV crewmembers would take a pregnancy test at someone's house and leave it there.

Is that why she was so tired? He thought she'd seemed stressed, but why wouldn't she have told him about this?

Maybe because she's afraid you'll panic and bail?

Will knew that would be a realistic expectation given how he felt about marriage and kids, but he'd be there for her.

He dried his hands and exited the bathroom, where he found Charity with a napkin tucked into her sweatshirt like a bib. In one hand, she had a taco still in its wrapper, and in the other, a bottle of water.

"You didn't want a beer?" he asked cautiously.

"Not right now. I put *Willow* on."

"Good choice. Have you seen it?"

"No, I had to google what it was about."

Will pulled a taco out of the bag but didn't unwrap it, his stomach turning too forcefully to eat. "Charity?"

"Yeah?" she asked, taking a bite of her taco and chewing slowly.

"Do you have something you want to tell me?"

She paused, her gaze locking with his. "I spoke to my mom today."

"You did? How did that go?"

"Pretty good, actually. She wants to get together and make a fresh start. I'm actually excited about it, although deep in my heart I'm afraid that there's a shoe somewhere just waiting to drop on my head."

"I'm glad you saw your mom and you're trying to work things out, but I'm talking about the pink box in the bathroom garbage can."

Charity's gaze darted away. "It was a false alarm."

"Meaning?"

"I'm on the pill, but realized I was late. I took the test as a precaution, but I'm not pregnant."

Will released a sigh of relief, sagging back against the couch cushions. "That's great."

"You're probably right," she said, her tone crisp and angry.

He lifted his head off the back of the couch and frowned at her. "You don't think so?"

"It doesn't matter what I think."

"You sound like you're angry with me for being relieved."

"I'm not angry," she said softly, setting her taco down on the coffee table. Robin Hood wasted no time jumping up and snatching what he could before she shooed him away.

"Then what?"

"I just had an array of different reactions to the possibility, and then, when I realized I wasn't, one of them was disappointment. I wouldn't have been heartbroken if it had been positive, and I can tell by looking at your face you would have been devastated."

Will had no idea what to say to that at first, and it took him a second or two to collect his thoughts. Calmly, he reached for her, his hands resting on her shoulders. "Charity, I want to enjoy what we have. It's new and exciting, and I want you all to myself, so of course I panicked when I thought you might be..."

"So it had nothing to do with being stuck with me, then?"

"No, I mean..." He trailed off, trying to come up with the right thing to say, and she must have taken his silence for affirmation because she climbed to her feet.

"I'd never ask you to give up your life, Will, even if I were pregnant. If you didn't want to be involved, I would have wished you well as you walked away."

Will got up from the couch and faced her. "Why is this becoming a thing?"

"Because I'm scared of falling in love with you, hoping you're going to change your mind about marriage and kids and how our future looks, only to be disappointed when you don't."

"Charity, there's no guarantee what's going to happen in the future, but I think we can both agree neither one of us is ready for kids. I'm taking care of my mom and you run a non-profit and don't make enough money to put back into it." Will knew it was the wrong thing to say the minute the words left his lips, but there was no taking them back. "Charity," he said, reaching for her, but she shied away from him, eyes glistening with unshed tears.

"No, you're right. I'm in a tough spot right now, but I believe things will go my way because I'm a hard worker. I know I've got talent, and I'm going to show it to the world."

"And that's my point," Will said, throwing his hands up in the air. "This is our time to be selfish and enjoy ourselves. We have enough responsibilities without adding kids into the mix."

"But I want to add kids to my life eventually, sooner rather than later. I know you've got plenty of time to decide whether or not kids are in your future, but I don't. No matter how much I care for you, I can't waste my time with someone... someone who doesn't share the same vision for their life as me."

"Are you kidding me?" he said, his voice rising with emotion. "I've been second-guessing myself for weeks about my ideas on marriage and what I want, but you're ready to throw in the towel after a week? Because I wasn't over the moon about an unplanned pregnancy?"

"Listen to what I'm saying," Charity pleaded. "Spending time with you the last month made me realize how happy we could be, how happy I am just being with you. When I sat in that bathroom, waiting for the results, I imagined my life with you, and it was amazing. Brunch with your family on Sundays and trips to the park and buying a house big enough for Bacon, Sausage, and Robin Hood to have their own space away from each other if they want. I could see me with you for the rest of my life, but... you only see me for now."

Every word out of her mouth was like a slap in the face. "That's not what I said. I just want to be together."

"I know," she said softly. "But if you can't imagine us together forever, I'd rather you break my heart now than two years in the future."

Will's stomach dropped out as he tried to imagine his life, their life together, but he couldn't think past his dwindling savings. Never accomplishing all he wanted in his career. Never being able to give Charity what she truly wanted and make her happy.

"I can't promise you anything but how I feel about you right now."

Charity nodded. "I understand. I just wish it was enough."

CHAPTER THIRTY-THREE

Kitty Tail on a Stick

Enjoy one of our rich, chewy cake pops in Calico (Neapolitan), Tuxedo (chocolate-vanilla swirl), and Orange Tabby (orange creamsicle).

"ARE YOU ALL RIGHT?"

Will looked up from his avocado toast and fruit salad to meet his mother's gaze. "What?"

"She's been trying to talk to you, but you've been out of it since you got here," his sister said.

"I'm fine," he grumbled. "Just a lot going on at work."

"I'm sorry it's stressful for you," Anna said, making him feel about an inch tall, which wasn't helping his mood. His mom was being so kind and understanding. Even his sister hadn't tried to pry his troubles out of him, and he wished he hadn't come to her house today. He'd wanted to stay in bed with his cats watching *Supernatural* for the thousandth time.

Dean's a rolling stone who can't commit, and women still fall for him.

Except Will didn't travel around the country fighting demons. The demons were all inside him.

That's a little dramatic, even for you.

The truth of the matter was that Will wanted his life a certain way, and if that wasn't enough for Charity, then that was all she wrote. He wasn't going to pine for someone who wasn't willing to accept him, warts and all.

"I made a decision about my job," his mom said abruptly.

"What's that?" Sarah asked.

"I spoke to the school, and they are bringing in a long-term sub until they hire someone who will be a good fit to take over my classroom."

"That's good, Mom," Sarah said.

"You need to rest," Will agreed.

"But my principal put me in touch with a local online school, and I have an interview with them next week. I'll be able to prerecord classes online when I'm not feeling great and answer emails and take video calls with students who are struggling. It could be a great alternative fit for me."

Will nodded. "And you'll save on gas and other expenses you incur when leaving the house."

"But you don't get as much social interactions at home, so you'll need to practice self-care," Sarah said enthusiastically. "Having friends over for a meal or we can do a walk around the neighborhood when you're feeling good."

"That sounds nice, honey." Anna took a bite of her fruit salad and turned her attention to Will, chewing thoughtfully. "I was a little disappointed that Charity didn't come with you today."

Will's stomach turned. "We aren't seeing each other anymore."

"I knew it," Sarah said, thumping the table with her hand.

"Sarah, stop—" his mom started, but Will spoke over her.

"What does that mean?" Will glared at his sister.

"Just that your commitment issues are becoming pathological. It was obvious you're crazy about her, but you probably self-sabotaged the relationship because that is what you do."

"Sarah," Anna scolded.

"Oh, that's rich coming from the woman who dumped her last boyfriend because he salted her popcorn without asking."

"Oh, so wanting a little consideration from your significant other is unreasonable?"

"Is that the real reason? Or was it that he just didn't do it for you?" Will taunted.

Sarah paled. "You—"

"Stop it! Both of you!" Anna shot Will a solemn expression. "What happened between you and Charity?"

He stabbed at his fruit and mumbled, "We just wanted different things. She asked me to guarantee her that we had a future that included marriage and kids, but I couldn't do that."

His mother shook her head. "I swear, William, I don't

understand you sometimes. Your father and I met in college and were in love until his death. I still love him and miss him every day, and I want that for you and your sister."

"Which is why I'm holding out. I want what you and Dad had, not a guy who won't share his French fries with me," Sarah said, still giving Will side-eye.

Will's jaw clenched as he set his fork down, the silent voice inside screaming, but he was hurting. "Stop lying to her."

"Will, don't," Sarah said.

"Lying to me about what?" Anna asked.

Will's body coursed with a frustration and rage so intense that his sister's pleading expression barely registered. "Are you going to tell her?"

"Will someone tell me what's going on?" Anna asked.

Sarah's jaw clenched, and she focused her attention on her mom. "I'm not really interested in anyone romantically. I don't look at Ryan Reynolds or Blake Lively and think, 'Oh my gosh, they are so hot.' I've never had those supercharged feelings about anyone. I am perfectly fine on my own and I'm not looking for anyone to share my life with. If something changes, great, but I don't think it's in the cards for me." Sarah took a moment to glare at Will as she added, "That's what Will wanted me to tell you, because he has to deflect his own issues and throw someone else under the bus."

His mother paused, as if mulling over Sarah's words carefully, and finally reached for her hand. "I don't really understand, Sarah, but I'm sorry. I'll stop pestering you about relationships. I shouldn't have made you feel pressured."

"You're apologizing to her and not me?" Will asked, incredulously. His mom was being supportive and understanding of Sarah but chiding him over decisions he'd made about a relationship doomed to fail? What about her terrible decisions?

"What does she need to apologize to you for?" Sarah asked angrily, standing up from the table.

"How about borrowing money from me when I was sixteen because they didn't have enough to keep the power on?"

His mother's face drained of color. "That was one time, and we paid you back, plus interest."

"That's not the point. You both were so irresponsible with money, and whether you meant to or not, it skewed my views on relationships. The thought of sharing financial responsibility with anyone, especially someone who is self-employed like Dad was? Like Charity? Scares the heck out of me."

"Stop it, Will," his sister snapped, but he kept going.

"No, she wanted to know why I'm this way; I'm explaining it to her. Sarah and I never went without, but you and Dad made us hyperaware that we were always worried about money. Counting down the days until the next check would arrive. It's why I started taking odd jobs at twelve because I hated asking for anything, knowing how stressed you were every month. If it was exhausting for you, imagine what it was like for us!"

His mother swallowed hard before she responded, softly, "Your father and I did our best to always get you everything you wanted and needed."

"But you never let me forget it. Either of you."

"Will!" Sarah hollered, and he scowled at her.

"What? You know it's true. It's why you buy all those designer clothes, because she wouldn't take you shopping at the mall. It was a waste of money to spend eighty dollars on a pair of jeans when you could get them for five bucks at the thrift store. And now you buy twelve-hundred-dollar purses!"

"I have one purse, and that isn't about Mom. I am a single, successful adult, and if I want to splurge on my wardrobe, I will!"

"I—I think I need to lie down," Anna said weakly, climbing to her feet. She didn't look at Will but simply disappeared down the hallway of his sister's apartment, and he heard the door open and shut.

"What is wrong with you?" Sarah started in. "You are an adult, but you're sitting here blaming Mom and Dad for your shortcomings?"

"It's how I feel, Sarah."

"So what? Everyone feels like their parents jacked them around in one way or another, but you are responsible for your own choices now! Our parents did their best and taking it out on Mom or me isn't going to make your life better. You made the decision to let an amazing woman go, and I know you're kicking yourself for it, but instead of owning that loss and frustration, you're pushing us away!"

Will got up from the table. "I don't need this. She was going off on me about my life choices, and I was just telling her that she doesn't get to sit in judgment of me. Not when my core belief system came from their relationship."

"That is such crap, Will," Sarah snapped. "We grew up in the same house and were raised by the same people. The difference is, I don't pass the buck when I make a mistake."

"I didn't make a mistake. We had no future!" he said, running a hand through his hair and tugging it in frustration. "Nothing I would have said short of lying to her or compromising my beliefs would have changed that."

"You can keep telling yourself that and live a sad, lonely life where you will eventually become the bitter man on the street yelling at kids and calling the cops on couples kissing. Or you can get a therapist like me, start working through your warped relationship fears, and chase after her. Get yourself a whole lot of happiness."

"How about you get into a functioning relationship before giving me advice?"

"Just because I'm asexual doesn't mean I can't have an opinion on your love life. I'm your sister, and I love you, even when you make dumb decisions. And letting Charity get away because you are scared is going to be the biggest regret of your life."

"You telling me what I should do isn't going to change that Charity and I aren't compatible." Will pushed in his chair and grumbled, "Tell Mom I said goodbye."

"Tell her yourself and add an apology onto it, you jerk."

Will did neither and walked past the spare bedroom door on his way out of the apartment, regret twisting in his chest like someone turning a knife slowly. But despite knowing that he'd brought this down on all of them, he couldn't bring himself to stop and make it right.

CHAPTER THIRTY-FOUR

Maine Coon Croissant

Our jumbo croissants may not be twenty pounds and furry, but they are definitely easy to fall in love with. Available in ham and cheese, chocolate, or plain.

THE DIM, ROMANTIC LIGHTING in the upscale French restaurant created the perfect atmosphere for Valentine's Day, which was slightly awkward considering it was the three of them. Their table was by the window, and they'd added a third place setting on the end for Charity, as if she needed to feel more like a third wheel. They'd landed at LAX a little after 3:00 p.m., and a driver named Gustav had been waiting to take Charity to her hotel in a fancy town car. They'd sat in the back, asking the driver about the best restaurants, and he'd suggested this one. She'd offered to stay back at the hotel, claiming she was tired after the flight to LA, but both Kara and Ben had insisted she come.

Charity scanned the restaurant as Kara and Ben talked

about the menu, wishing she were in bed watching the comic Gabriel "Fluffy" Iglesias. She needed a good laugh after the last two weeks of working as many hours as she could, perfecting several recipes she had up her sleeve for the competition. Anything to keep busy and not think about Will, and as much as she loved Kara and Ben, being out the week before Valentine's Day at a place like this, single and heartbroken, was like pouring salt in an open wound.

A gentle poke to the upper muscle of her arm made her turn toward Kara, who was sitting next to her with an expectant expression on her face. Charity tilted her head. "Yes?"

"We came down here to support you, and you haven't said more than two words to us."

I didn't ask you to come.

Charity hated the unkind thought the minute it passed through her mind. Kara had been trying to be there without pushing her about Will, and Charity was surprised her restraint had held on this long. When Kara told Charity that Kara and Ben had decided to fly down, too, and enjoy a short vacation, she knew it was a way to get her to open up. And she wasn't ready to do that.

"I'm just taking in the atmosphere. It's so intimate." Man, she didn't like herself right now. "I'm sorry. Can we start that over?"

"Of course, babes," Kara said kindly.

Charity closed the menu and set it aside, forcing a smile. "I was thinking I'd try the duck."

"Really?" Kara turned to Ben. "What about you?"

"I can't pronounce half the stuff on the menu, so I'm just going to say 'steak.'"

Charity almost laughed. The server came back, and sure enough, Ben told him "steak" after trying and failing to correctly pronounce the item's title. Luckily, the server was a young guy who took their menus and winked at Ben. "I can't pronounce it, either, and I've worked here for months."

When the server left the table, Ben pointed at his retreating back. "That dude earned his tip right there."

"You're so easy to please," Kara teased, running her palm over his forearm. When Ben covered her hand with his, Charity looked away, searching the restaurant for someone interesting to watch.

A server came by with a plate of crème brûlée, setting it on a table between an elderly couple. The two of them each reached for a spoon and proceeded to share the dessert, smiling at each other as they conversed between bites. It was a much sweeter scene than the couple at the next table who'd been scrolling through their phones and ignoring each other since they sat down.

"Why would you stay with someone you can't even have a dinner conversation with?" Charity asked abruptly, spinning away from the couple, and reaching for a piece of bread from the basket in the middle of the table.

"I'm not sure," Ben said.

"Maybe they're just comfortable with each other."

"There is comfort, and then there is taking the person in your life for granted. Creating unattainable expectations for them because you can't see past your own issues to compromise."

Kara leaned in, her eyes heavy with sympathy. "Are we talking about Will, Char?"

"No, of course not. You want to talk about Will, not me."

"I never said that. I'm just trying to figure out what that tirade was about because you're not usually so...grumpy. Especially given what an amazing opportunity you're here for!"

"Kar, I wasn't born yesterday. This place is for couples. Not couples and the miserable bestie. You brought me out here to get me to talk, in a public place where I can't make a scene and escape."

"Maybe I want to discuss what you're going to do in your downtime while filming, did you ever think about that?" Kara swung toward Ben. "Right, babe? I just wanted her to come eat some food and talk about her plans?"

Ben met Charity's gaze and smirked. "She wants to talk to you about Schwartz."

"Hey!" Kara said.

"See, even your boyfriend knows you didn't want to make sure I'm going to have fun when I'm not filming. You may be down here to partly have a romantic weekend with your man, but—" Charity pointed a finger at Kara, who tried to bite it, but she managed to move it swiftly. "You wanted to get me to talk, when there is nothing to say."

"Fine," Kara said in a stage whisper, throwing up her hands. "I thought you might want to vent about how much you're missing him."

"If I did, I would, but I don't, so I won't."

"Mature." Kara rolled her eyes. "Fine, but you're just prolonging the inevitable."

Ben leaned forward, speaking to Kara but looking at Charity. "Kara, she probably doesn't want to talk about it in public like this because she isn't into my guy."

Charity glared at Ben. "Actually, I am—was—into your guy, and he shot me down."

"What exactly did he say?" Kara asked.

Charity looked around at the full restaurant and shook her head. "Like Ben said, I'm not really interested in airing my dirty laundry in public."

"Fine," Kara said, settling back into her chair. "But I'm done watching you suffer alone. The moment we get back to the hotel, you and I are going to have a heart-to-heart."

Charity smirked. "I love it when you get bossy."

"If I'd known that, I would have pinned you down two weeks ago."

Ben shook his head. "You ladies are—"

"What?" they asked in unison.

"Never mind."

"Smart man," Charity said, grinning.

"What are you two going to do down here for the next three days?"

"I have a few things planned." Ben's evasive tone and Kara's side-eye directed at him gave Charity a jolt. Was this trip a next step to something big between them? They'd only been dating a few months, but Charity couldn't have handpicked a better guy for her best friend, so if they were making future plans together, Charity was all for it.

Ben changed the conversation to sights he wanted them to see, giving Charity plenty of time to think about what she would tell Kara later when they were alone. That maybe Charity had been overthinking and jumped the gun by demanding that Will promise marriage and kids in the future. They hadn't really been dating for real, and while she may have fallen for him before they were official, men moved slower toward realizing their feelings.

You made the right call. The end was going to come sooner or later.

When the server set down their dinner plates and walked away, Ben nodded at Charity. "Can you pull out your phone and start recording?"

Charity only had a moment's hesitation, wondering what he was up to, but did what he asked. Kara's eyes widened as Ben pulled a small, wooden box out of his pocket and Charity caught her breath. Ben had been planning a big, romantic gesture, like a proposal, and she'd almost ruined it by letting her moping get the better of her.

"Ben, what is this?" Kara asked.

He lifted the lid of the box, revealing a key inside. "Kara, when we first met, we agreed to take things slow because we'd been burned by moving too fast with the wrong people. The difference between then and now is I know that you're the one. We already spend most nights together, so why not make it official? Kara Ingalls"—he paused, placing the key in Kara's palm—"will you move in with me?"

Charity's chest squeezed when she saw tears spill down her best friend's cheeks, her smile widening. "Yes." She leaned into Ben, kissing him enthusiastically. "Yes!"

The tables around them broke into loud applause, and Charity laughed, realizing her own eyes were watering at her friend's happiness. "Congratulations," Charity said, ending the video and handing the phone off to Ben so she could hug Kara. She squeezed her bestie in a hard, tight hug. "I am so happy for you. I love you."

"I love you, too," Kara sobbed, wiping at her eyes as they pulled away from each other. "If I'd have known this was happening, I wouldn't have worn makeup."

"You're beautiful," Ben said softly, pulling her in for another kiss, and Charity pushed back the rush of envy. That is what she wanted in a relationship. Laughter. Playfulness. Love.

Suddenly, Charity's stomach plummeted. Not because she didn't want her best friend to find happiness, but because that meant never getting a break from Will. First, it would be helping Kara and Ben move and then, eventually, wedding planning and events with Will. Charity was never going to escape the fact that she wasn't enough for him. Eventually, Ben and Kara would trade off double dating with Will and his date and Charity and her date. Her friends would try not to mention him, but eventually one of them would slip about his new girlfriend, and things would be awkward, which is exactly what she'd been trying to avoid since the moment they met and she'd messed up. Charity didn't want to catch feelings for Will, and now that she had, she just hoped that these next few weeks in LA would give her some time to get over him.

"Hey, Char?" Kara said, breaking into her thoughts. "Are you okay with this?"

"Of course I am. I am ecstatic for you."

Kara released a rushing breath. "Oh good, because I know you just moved in with me, but the house is yours to stay in for as long as you want. You're my family, and my home will always be yours."

"I know, Kar."

Ben and Kara dug into their food, playfully arguing about what changes she was going to make as Charity tried to swallow past the lump in her throat. Will should be here with them, sharing this moment. He'd say something funny, and everyone would laugh, but then he'd follow it up with something sincere and heartfelt. Because that was who he was, and she loved him for it.

As much as Charity kept telling herself that this stint away from home was going to be just what she needed to kick her feelings for Will, she knew it wasn't going to be that easy. Not when Charity was deeply in love for the first time in her life. There'd been men before Will she'd dated longer, but never had the connection been so strong. How could she have been so naïve to think a little distance was going to change anything?

"Are you all right? You seem a little... off," Kara asked

carefully, as if afraid the wrong word was going to detonate Charity to explode.

Charity smiled ruefully. "I'm good. Just thinking about all the redecorating I'm going to do once you're moved out."

"That's the spirit." Kara laughed. "I knew we could find something to turn that frown upside down."

As hard as Charity might try not to put a damper on this special night, the only thing that could possibly make her happy was Will, and he was over five hundred miles away, getting on with his life.

If only Charity's heart would let her move on, too.

CHAPTER THIRTY-FIVE

Cup of Bombay

A cup of our steaming black coffee in light, medium, or dark blend.

WILL HEADED DOWN THE hallway toward Roy's office Tuesday afternoon, carrying the three mock-ups his boss had asked him to bring by. The office was decked out in red, pink, and white everywhere, thanks to several employees feeling festive about Valentine's Day coming up on Monday. Will looked around at the chubby cherubs, conversation-heart cutouts, and lip clings on their glass windows and resented the constant reminder of what he'd lost. Charity.

What made his single life more depressing was trying to distract himself by staying busy and witnessing the constant barrage of happy couples all around him like an upbeat rom-com. Seeing all this cupid vomit in every store, every bar, and even his place of work was a constant reminder that he didn't have anything to go home to except his cats.

Will knocked on the doorframe before stepping inside the office. "Hey, Roy, I have those files you asked for."

"Good. I have something for you, too."

Roy picked up an envelope from his desk and held it out to Will, taking the files with his free hand.

"You both did a good job on the Choco Vino account. Just another well-deserved reward for my best team."

Will opened the envelope to peek at the check inside and smiled. "Thanks for this."

"I'll get Ben his when he gets back tomorrow. I've got to get the heck out of here and home to my wife before she skins me alive."

"I hope you have a great time, Roy. Thanks again for this," Will said, taking a step backward toward the door.

"I may be a jerk, but I want my team to know I see the work you do and I appreciate you." Roy set the files on the side of his desk and picked up his jacket off the back of his chair. "Do you have any big plans tonight?"

"No, I don't."

"Really? What happened to Charity?" Roy asked. "I thought you were seeing her."

"I was, but we're not together anymore."

"That's too bad. I like her. She is a good egg, and she makes a mean sandwich."

Will feigned a chuckle, but the pain clawing up his throat made the sound raw and ugly. "Yes, she does."

"Well, the one thing I remember about being single is it'll

give you more time to put into building your career. Tomorrow, I'm going to give you the pick of upcoming pitches and let you work your magic. You're my dream team, after all."

Will paused in the doorway, Roy's words sinking in. While he had put aside the dream of going out on his own to help his mother, it didn't change the fact that he wasn't happy with his job and what he was doing. The money was great, but Will wanted more. He didn't want to stay here another ten years sweating through shirts before pitches or worrying that he was going to flub a word and lose a client. He wanted a job that highlighted what he did well and one that he loved.

Before he thought too hard about the consequences, Will turned around and shut the door to Roy's office. While there might not be very many people in the office, if he was about to get fired, he didn't want them to overhear.

"Roy, I've been with you for ten years, and while I think you are a fair boss, this isn't what I want to be doing."

Roy frowned, sitting back down in his chair. "I don't like the way this is going."

"The truth is, I hate pitching, and I hate schmoozing. I love art and creating designs that hook the client. I want to be the guy in the background, the graphic designer, not the partner on your best sales team. I've been saving ten years to strike out on my own so I can do what I love, but what I realized is, I actually love this company. I love working with Ben and appreciate you as a boss." Will smiled ruefully before adding, "Although, if you wanted to dole out a little more praise, I wouldn't be opposed to it."

"Get to the point, Schwartz?"

"The point is, I'm standing here, scared out of my mind because those savings are gone, and I'm asking you if you would be willing to create a position for a graphic designer. Only a graphic designer. No marketing rep. No pitching. Just the art side of things."

Roy stared at Will thoughtfully. "You're telling me you just want to be the graphics guy. No bonuses for signing new clients or finishing a job?"

"Yes, I wanna be that guy."

Roy placed his elbows on his chair and steepled his hands in front of him. "Before I decide, where is the money you were saving to go out on your own?"

Will swallowed. "My mom had to quit her job because of health issues but isn't old enough to collect Social Security or retirement. I am using my savings to support her and supplement her bills. She is more important to me than going out on my own."

"I see." He tapped his fingers to his mouth. "And how do I know that you won't just up and leave even after I make this concession for you?"

"Trust the guy who's spent a decade working for you, doing a job I hate, but was loyal enough to stay. This whole conversation might come off a little out of the blue, but I realize that my happiness should be more important than this job, and if I'm valuable to you, this is something that you should at least consider."

"Wow." Roy climbed to his feet and shrugged into his

jacket, the silence stretching painfully. He came around the desk and stood in front of Will. "That is a bold statement that...happens to be true."

Will's head jerked up to meet Roy's gaze.

"You're right. Loyalty is hard to find these days, and even if you hadn't put in hours of hard work, you're the most talented graphic designer in our area. I'd be a fool not to treat you as such. So here's what I'm gonna do." Roy turned away and headed back around his desk to pull out his large checkbook.

A moment of panic lanced through Will as he considered whether or not this could be an angry ploy from Roy and any second, he was going to laugh and give him a check that said, *You're fired, loser. Get out.*

When Roy filled out a check and held it out to Will, he took the paper rectangle tentatively.

"Enjoy your ten-year bonus. I usually give them on your anniversary but maybe this will be a little incentive for my best design guy to stay. Especially since I'm promoting him to director of our creative team."

Will's eyes widened. "Roy..."

"Man, I am giving you exactly what you wanted! What's wrong now?"

"This is too much."

"No, listen to me. I'm a guy who puts my money where my mouth is, and you are worth it." Roy stood up and held out his hand, waiting for Will to take it before he gave it two firm pumps.

"Thank you for this opportunity, Roy."

"I'll have a contract drawn up for your new position next week." Roy released his hand and nodded toward the door. "Now get out of my office. Or I'm going to tell my wife that you're the reason I was late for dinner."

Will chuckled. "Enjoy your night, sir."

Will started to leave, but Roy called his name and he turned back. "Yeah?"

"You're a good guy. I hope your mom appreciates it."

Will didn't know how to respond and simply nodded. If he was such a good guy, why had he lashed out at his mom and piled all his reservations about relationships at her feet? That was something he should have taken to the grave. If he were a good guy, he would have reached out to her before two weeks had gone by and apologized for upsetting her when she was already stressed and struggling.

It might be too little too late, but Will could at least make up his behavior to her, starting with flowers and an apology.

His phone dinged as he exited the building and walked onto the street. When he checked his screen, he saw a text message from Ben with an attached picture. He tapped it with his thumb and stopped in his tracks when it loaded.

It was a picture of Ben with a goofy grin on his face, holding on to Kara's hand and showing off a shiny silver key clutched between her fingers. Charity and Kara's faces were blurry in the background, but Charity had her arms wrapped around Kara and they were laughing.

I asked her and she said yes!

Will's forehead furrowed, and he texted back. Asked her what? To legally come into your house?

No idiot. Kara is going to move in with me.

What about Charity?

She's going to stay in Kara's house.

Wow, congratulations. I thought you guys weren't gonna rush into anything?

When it's with the right person, it doesn't feel like rushing. It feels like we can't get to the good parts fast enough.

Will leaned back in his chair, staring down at those words. His best friend was celebrating, moving to the next step in his relationship. Love had changed his mind about his future.

He scrolled up to study the picture of the three of them, wishing he could be there, celebrating, holding Charity, and thinking, *Someday, that could be us.*

Will's chest squeezed at the surprising thought, too scared of what it meant.

CHAPTER THIRTY-SIX

Minskin Doughnuts

These small, round doughnuts are melt-in-your-mouth buttery goodness and dipped in a sweet, sticky glaze. Another perfect example of how great things come in small sizes.

"YOU'RE GOING TO DO amazing," Kara said, squeezing Charity tightly on Thursday morning. They were standing on the sidewalk outside the hotel waiting for the Uber to pick up Ben and Kara and take them to the airport. Ben had run back in to use the restroom, giving them a moment of privacy.

"Are you sure you're okay with Ben asking me to move in?"

Charity rolled her eyes. Kara hadn't stopped asking Charity if it bothered her for the last two days, and she didn't know what else she could say to convince her bestie she was happy for her.

"I get to live in your house rent-free. I am good."

"I know, but you only moved in two months ago, and now I'm ditching you—"

"You're moving in with your boyfriend ten minutes away, so if I need to tell you something, I'll drive over and barge in," Charity interrupted with a laugh. "I will need a key, however. And we see each other every day for work. It's not as if you're moving to the moon."

"I know. I feel guilty, though."

Charity took her hands and squeezed. "Never feel bad for going after what makes you happy."

Kara eyed her suspiciously. "Did you see that on Instagram?"

"No, on the billboard behind your shoulder."

Kara turned to look over her shoulder and burst out laughing, just as Ben rejoined them.

"What did I miss?" he asked.

"Just saying goodbye." Charity would be heading to the studio shortly to get started on introductions and pretaping. They were going to start their first episode today and finish it tomorrow. The producer had already warned her that the days could be anywhere from ten to sixteen hours depending on what needed to be reshot, and she needed to get plenty of rest when she could.

"I love you," Kara said.

Charity hugged her hard. "I love you, too."

A black SUV pulled up and rolled down the window. "I'm here for Ben?"

"Babe, that's us." Kara gave Charity another hug and helped Ben load up their suitcases.

When Ben awkwardly held out his hand to Charity, she pushed it to the side and gave him a hug. "You're moving in with my bestie. We're practically family."

Ben laughed. "I'll remember that the next time Kara gets mad and you both come for me."

"As families do."

Charity waved to them as they drove away and went back upstairs to her hotel room to finish getting ready. Gustav the driver texted her to tell her that he would be there in fifteen minutes, so she finished off her makeup with a brush of gloss on her lips and headed out the door. As she waited outside the hotel for Gustav, she thought about how her life would look now that her best friend was moving out. They were in their thirties, and Kara had found someone she was head over heels for, and despite hating being alone, Charity could never begrudge her best friend happiness.

Gustav pulled up and opened the door for her. In the back seat was a bakery bag, a cup of coffee in the drink holder, and a bearded stranger in the other seat.

"Hello," Charity said pleasantly, shooting a puzzled glance at Gustav.

"This is Mr. Wyatt. I'll also be driving him to and from the studio."

Charity climbed inside and sat down before holding a hand out to him. "I'm Charity."

"Dayton Wyatt," he replied with a deep Southern accent without taking her hand.

"Nice to meet you," she muttered, moving the bakery bag

to buckle herself in. "Did the studio send the coffee and breakfast, Gustav?"

"Yes, because it was such an early morning, they had me pick you both up something, but Mr. Wyatt didn't want his and gave it to me."

"You don't like coffee?" Charity asked, horrified.

"Not particularly."

His cool, clipped tone was unarguably hostile. She took a sip of her coffee and said, "That's delicious, Gustav. Thank you."

"You're most welcome. They normally have a pretty good spread for you on set, but I thought you might need a pick-me-up before you arrive at the studio. You must keep up your strength with a competition show."

Charity laughed as she opened the bag and peeked in at the breakfast sandwich. "You make it sound so dire."

"Oh, I just know some of these shows can get a little hairy behind the scenes."

Charity took a bite of her sandwich and shrugged. "I'm not worried about it. I'm just here to do my best and try to win."

"Would the two of you please be quiet?" Dayton griped. "I'm trying to get another fifteen minutes of sleep, and you two yammering is cutting into that."

"I'm sorry, Mr. Wyatt," Gustav said quietly.

Charity bit back her scathing response to Dayton's self-absorption and stared out the window, watching the city lights flicker by in a blur as she ate her sandwich. Gustav pulled up to the studio gate and pressed a code into the keypad. When the gates opened, they pulled through and stopped in front of studio nineteen.

Gustav hadn't fully come to a stop before Dayton was climbing out the other side without so much as a thank you. When she opened the door, Gustav called out, "I hope you have a great first day, Charity."

"You too, Gustav. And thank you for the coffee. Do you want me to take the bag and throw it away?"

"No, that's okay, Charity. I'll take care of it."

"I appreciate you."

Charity opened up the door and climbed out with her coffee in one hand, approaching a small, skinny man with a headset and a tablet.

"Name?" he said curtly.

"Charity Simmons."

"Perfect. I got you down." He pressed a button on the earpiece and said, "All right, I've got Charity Simmons." He paused a moment and nodded. "Copy that." He released the button and pointed to the door behind him. "Go on inside, and Tim will take you to makeup."

Charity walked through the door and glanced around at the bustling crew. Gustav was right about the massive table of food. Dozens of trays with pastries, fresh fruit, and sandwiches in the shape of hearts covered the table surfaces, and several decanters of coffee were stationed at the back against the wall. The large warehouse-sized room had a brightly lit stage with several baking stations like she'd seen on the show and seating for the live audience to watch.

Another man with a headset approached her, an earnest expression on his face. "Are you Charity?"

"Yes," she said.

"Hi, I'm Tim." He took her latte before she could blink and threw it in the nearest trash can. "You're supposed to be in hair and makeup right now, so let's hustle."

"Oh, I'm sorry," Charity said, staring at the trash can forlornly before rushing to catch up. "I didn't know I was supposed to be anywhere."

He pulled up and swung around so fast that she almost ran into him. "Didn't you get a schedule?"

"No."

The PA sighed dramatically and snapped his fingers. "This way."

Charity followed him into an adjacent room where bright bulbs lined the mirrors. "When your stylist finishes with you, I'll lead you to the main stage, and we'll get some shots of the cast before we start shooting the first episode."

"All right." Charity sat in the first chair, and within minutes, a bubbly woman with pink curls bounced in. She spoke so fast that Charity didn't catch her name, but when she finished, Charity stared at her smoky eyes and glistening lips, her hair pinned back from her face.

"Ah, you're perfect! Let's get you changed into your smock." She helped Charity off the stool and led her into a room with racks of white jackets. She sifted through the jackets for several moments, finally releasing a joyous cry of, "Here it is."

Charity took the chef's coat with her name monogrammed

on the front. On the back they'd printed the show's logo. She slipped it on, placing the hanger back on the rack.

"You look perfect," the stylist said. "Let's get you out there."

Charity followed her to the main stage, where a group of about twenty-five people of various ages and races mingled. When Charity joined them, they greeted her excitedly, and she realized the cameras were already rolling.

To her surprise, Dayton popped up out of nowhere and gave her a hug, smiling down at her. "Glad you made it!"

"Do you two already know each other?" another contestant asked.

"We met prior to filming," he said coyly, and Charity had no idea what his game was. "It's just crazy that two people who are supposed to be in competition with each other can have so much chemistry."

Before Charity could ask what he was talking about, a loud, booming voice called out, "Hello, everyone! We're going to pair you up in small groups for the preproduction commentary and dive into the first episode. Is everyone ready for this?"

A chorus of screams and whoops erupted, and then the cameras shut off.

Dayton's demeanor changed, and he sneered. "Nice knowing you, sweetheart. After today, you're going home."

CHAPTER THIRTY-SEVEN

Catcao Treats

These nut-filled chocolatey balls are packed with wholesome energy.

WILL HAD STOPPED BY his mom's house on Tuesday to deliver flowers, but she wasn't home, and he didn't want to have their reconciliation conversation over the phone. He'd left the flowers on the front porch with a sappy, heartfelt card he knew she'd love and went home to feed his cats.

His mother had called him and left a message, thanking him for the gift, but they hadn't been able to connect since. On Friday morning, he'd received a text from his sister reminding him about Sunday brunch, as if he'd been blowing them off.

He jogged up the steps to his mother's home on Sunday, and after three weeks of not speaking, Will knocked on the door. A few moments passed before Sarah answered, her brow furrowed. "So we're knocking now?"

"Considering what went down between us, I have no idea

what the protocol is. I wasn't sure if just walking in was the appropriate move if this was a trap."

"If you think that, you might not want to eat the food," she said, grinning evilly.

Will stared at her for several moments before shrugging. "Eh, I'm hungry. I'll risk it."

"Famous last words." Sarah stepped back and let him in. "By the way, how come Mom gets flowers and a very nice card and you didn't apologize to me?"

He scoffed. "What am I apologizing to you for?"

"Making my Sunday very uncomfortable? Trying to out me to Mom?"

Will sobered. "I am sorry for ruining your Sunday brunch, but mostly, I apologize for taking my frustrations out on you. You didn't deserve it, and I shouldn't have tried to force you to talk to Mom."

"Eh, as it turns out you actually did me a favor. Mom is trying to understand and has promised to stop begging me for grandchildren, so I guess I won't stay mad at you." She flicked his ear as she passed him by. "But do it again, and I'll be expecting better than words. Think vacation. Expensive—"

"I get the picture."

"Good. Mom's in the kitchen. I'm going to use the bathroom and give you a minute to talk."

"Thanks, Sarah."

Will walked into the kitchen and spotted his mom at the table. His heart hammered in his chest when she turned to him, her eyes shiny with tears. She got to her feet and held out her arms. He went to her and hugged her tight, the knot in his chest easing as she patted his back.

"I'm so sorry, Mom," he murmured, his words muffled in her shoulder.

"I know, sweetheart." A few more comforting pats on his shoulder. "It's all right."

"I was a jerk."

Anna pulled away and gave him a trembling smile. "You were honest in a jerk way. There is a slight difference."

Will released a wet chuckle. "Thanks for going easy on me, even if I don't deserve it."

Anna cupped his face. "I will always love you, no matter what."

"I know. I love you, too."

"I know you do. Your struggle is that you keep too much inside, Will. You always have, and sometimes it erupts out of you all at once like a volcano. The problem with lava is, you can't put it back once it's out, and it can harden the world, or in this case, people around you. Do you understand what I'm saying?"

"Be careful with the things I say to others because they can't be unsaid," Will recited. "Dad used to say that to Sarah and me when we'd get into it."

"I know, I just wanted to put my own spin on it," she said.

"I know you and Dad did your best, and I'm sorry for putting all my issues on you. I shouldn't have lashed out the way I did. It wasn't fair or right."

"We could have been better with money, there is no doubt, but what we lacked in fiscal responsibility, we made up for in loving you and your sister." His mom gave him a trembling smile. "At least, I hope we did."

"You did."

"And I'm not taking any more of your money—"

"Mom!" he said.

"No." She held her hand up, and he shut his mouth to let her finish. "Listen, it is not because of what you said. This is not retaliation. That money is for you to go out on your own and live your dream. And I'm not taking that away from you. Your sister is going to move in with me—"

"Mom, she is a grown woman who needs her space." Will grinned and glanced toward the hallway, where his sister's shadow graced the floor.

"Hey!" Sarah called from her hiding place in the hallway. "I can make up my own mind where I want to live."

"It would only be temporary and give her a chance to save up to buy a house."

Will took his mom's hands and met her gaze, willing her to believe he was earnest. "My point is that my dream is to create, not be a sales guy, and I spoke to my boss about it. He is making me director of creative. No more pitches. Just doing what I love, and I don't have to worry about where I'm getting medical insurance."

"Will, are you sure?" she asked.

"Yes. What I said to you? I was just lashing out. I was upset about Charity—"

"I knew it!" Sarah crowed, peeking around the corner. "He loves her!"

"Will you get in here and stop hanging in the hallway like a creeper?"

"So rude," Sarah muttered, coming fully into the room with a shameless grin on her face. "You're just irritable because I totally called it."

"Like I was saying," Will said, scowling at his sister for a split second before returning his attention to his mom. "I was upset by what went wrong with Charity, and I wanted to put the blame somewhere. But I'm an adult. I need to face the fact that I've been using money as an excuse to not get close to anyone, and then she came along and everything changed. I just... I love her. She is funny and frustrating and—"

"Will you call her already? She's probably been waiting for you to make the first move, and you've been a stubborn—" His mom shot her a warning look, and Sarah added, "delightful man."

"She probably doesn't want to talk to me." Will sighed.

His mom put her hand on his shoulder and squeezed. "You'll never know unless you put yourself out there."

It was the same thing she'd told him in high school when he'd been struggling socially. Put himself out there, and people would be drawn to his authentic self.

And she was right. Charity liked you and wanted more from you.

"I'll be right back."

Will stepped outside and pulled his phone out of his pocket with trembling hands. He dialed Charity's number, holding his breath as he waited for the first ring, but it went straight to voice mail.

"Hi. It's Charity with Meow and Furever Cat Café and Catering. Please leave me a message after the tone."

Will cleared his throat, hating that he was doing this over the phone, but when it beeped in his ear, he started talking.

"Hi, Charity. It's Will. I have been thinking a lot about us. I hope you're having fun in LA. Kick all their butts. Oh, and happy early Valentine's Day. I miss you."

He ended the call before he did something unromantic, like tell her over voice mail how in love with her he was. That was probably worse than waiting three weeks to wake up and realize it.

The door behind him opened, and his sister stepped out onto the porch with him, frowning down at her phone screen. "Have you seen this?"

"What is it?"

Sarah held the phone out to him, and he took it, pressing play. It was a commercial for *Bake That*. They had a clip of all the contestants laughing and talking, and Will's gaze zeroed in on the man hanging on Charity. It cut to a woman telling the camera that the rest of the contestants should just head on home because she was going to win. Another called out Charity by name, wondering what a little rich girl was doing here. And then the guy with the beard, who'd been all over Charity in the first clip, cast a sinister grin at the audience. "I'm going to undermine her at every turn, and she won't even see me coming."

"What the heck? Why are they targeting Charity?"

"Prison-yard rules. You find the toughest inmate to beat, and you knock him out. That's what they're doing to her."

Will handed her phone back and shook his head. "They don't know who they're dealing with. Charity is unflappable, and she is going to walk away with the whole shebang."

"I hope you're right, because if I had twenty-four people looking to take me down, I don't know if I could take the heat."

CHAPTER THIRTY-EIGHT

Chartreux Fries

Smothered in three different cheeses and a spicy cream sauce, these fries are incredibly addicting. Like adopting cats. You definitely can't stop at one.

CHARITY SAT IN HER hotel room eating room-service French fries and questioning her life choices. It was after midnight, and she had a 5:00 a.m. call time, but she couldn't sleep. She'd been at the studio every day since Thursday for at least twelve hours, and she was mentally and emotionally exhausted. She'd seen reality TV. She knew that there were always the villains, but she'd thought it was all for show. Charity never expected so many people to be this mean when the cameras turned off.

When she'd seen the promo air, her stomach hit the floor. They'd made her look like she'd paid her way onto the show, talking about her dad and upbringing. The audience hadn't seen Charity wow the judges the first day with her fairy-tale crepe with clotted cream. Or the five bakers who were sent home the following day while she stayed to go head-to-head against the remaining nineteen participants.

They were down to ten bakers. Dayton, the snake, was one of them. In five more days, they'd know who the best was, but in the meantime, the audience would see her as weak. As a poser who had no business going up against professionals. They'd think the entire show was rigged in her favor if she won. Was the money worth the negative publicity and hit to her reputation?

Outside her hotel room window, the bright lights of the city twinkled, and the electronic sign of one of the banks flashed:

Happy Valentine's Day. Someone is thinking of you.

Yeah, everyone in the world is thinking I suck, including the one person I wish were here.

She'd stopped going downstairs to the hotel restaurant because it seemed as though everyone was there for a pre–Valentine's Day celebration, rubbing their happiness in her face. Now here she was on the most romantic holiday of the year, wide awake and miserable.

Charity climbed off the bed and picked up her phone from the nightstand, powering it on for the first time that day. The only person who might call her would be Kara, and she could imagine what her bestie would say about the promo.

When her screen saver lit up with a picture of Robin Hood, she smiled, missing her big, food-thieving sweetheart. She ran her thumb across to open it, and Will's smiling face, Bacon in his arms and Sausage on his shoulder, made her heart ache. Charity missed him so much that she hadn't found the strength to delete his picture.

Her phone started beeping rapidly, and she watched messages cross her screen, one after another, from family and friends.

Kara: Are you okay? Why aren't you responding? Hello?

Mom: I saw the promotion for the show. Did you know that was going to happen?

Billie: Call me! We will sue the pants off them!

Elena: I'm here if you want to talk.

Two new voice mail notifications popped up, one from her dad, and the other…

It was from Will.

She called her voice mail, but her phone blared to life before it could dial. Charity winced before pressing the green phone icon to accept the call.

"I'm surprised to hear from you this late. Are you calling to gloat?" she asked.

"I suppose I deserve that, but no. The truth is, I've been calling you every fifteen minutes since I saw that despicable promo."

"You have? Why?"

"I'm your father, and I thought you might be upset."

Charity walked over to the window, staring out at the lights, unsure of what to say. "And you were concerned about me enough to call all night?"

"Why wouldn't I be?" he asked.

"We haven't exactly been on good terms, and you've never worried about me being upset before."

Her father sighed. "It's one thing for me to be the one to hurt you, but someone else? That doesn't fly."

"Why not?"

"You're my daughter."

"You've said that already. Is that the only answer you can come up with? That you must check on me out of obligation?"

"There shouldn't need to be another reason, but I can understand why you're skeptical. I've been hearing from all my kids lately that I've been a terrible father and a worse husband, but that doesn't mean I don't love my family. I'm just lousy at showing it. It's not an excuse, but I want to be better. Losing everything has been a wake-up call to what's important." Her father laughed bitterly. "My dad was all about ambition and put his wife and kids on the back burner. I—I never realized I was doing the same thing. I thought I was teaching you to be strong, successful adults, but I ended up pushing you all away. I didn't listen to what you had to say, but I'm here now. I want to change."

Charity released a ragged breath. "It's a little late to turn over a new leaf, isn't it?"

"Maybe, but better late than never, wouldn't you say?" he asked.

"I suppose," she conceded, afraid to believe him. Could someone really change their entire character? "I'm fine, by the way. I've made it through to the top ten."

"I never doubted it."

"Not going to tell me doing the show was a bad idea?"

"Would it make any difference?" he asked.

"No, but it might end this conversation rather quickly."

"You don't need me to explain that there are awful people in the world. I'm wondering how you're going to deal with them. Are you going to quit?"

"Is that what the call is for? Trying to save your bid for governor?"

"No. I gave up on that the night your mother kicked me out."

"Then what do you want?"

"I want my daughter to do exactly what she told me she was going to do. Win."

Charity's lips twitched. While the conversation didn't make up for thirty-three years of her father neglecting their relationship, it was definitely a start.

"I will. Thanks for checking up on me, Dad."

"I'd like to have dinner when you get back. Maybe take the first step toward a fresh start."

"We could give it a chance," Charity said.

"I appreciate that. Give me a call when you get home or if

you need me to come down there and look over that television contract—"

"I've got this, Dad."

"All right, Charity. Thanks for taking my call. See you soon."

"See you."

Charity ended the call, releasing a rueful chuckle. Who would have thought it would take her father losing everything to finally turn into a halfway decent human being?

Finishing what she started before the phone call, she pressed one and waited for her voice mail to play.

"First voice mail. Hi, Charity. It's Will. I have been thinking a lot about us. I hope you're having fun in LA. Kick all their butts. Oh, and happy early Valentine's Day. I miss you."

Charity's eyes stung with tears. He missed her. The voice mail started off friendly, almost jovial, and then his voice deepened on those last three words and she knew. Being apart was killing him, too.

She went to her contacts and tapped his name, waiting for him to pick up. On the third ring, his voice came through as a husky rumble. "Hey."

"Hi."

"How are you doing?" he asked.

"I'm hanging in there. Trying to soak up the sun during the ten minutes I'm outside per day."

"Long days, huh?"

Charity released a bitter laugh. "Trust me, some days they feel endless."

"Looks like you're catching a lot of grief."

"All part of the glamorous life of a reality star."

"Are you sure that's how you feel?" he asked softly.

Charity laughed, wiping at her wet eyes. "No, but it doesn't do any good to whine about it."

"As a guy who grew up dealing with obnoxious jerks, sometimes it helps to vent about it at least."

"Honestly, I'd prefer a hug."

"Yeah? I could make that happen if you're talking about one of mine."

"I could be, if you want to elaborate on the *missing me* part of your voice mail."

Will chuckled. "We're going to do this over the phone?"

Charity flopped back onto the bed. "It will be another week before I'm home to hear it in person. Might as well get a jump start if there's something to talk about."

He cleared his throat. "I want there to be something."

"You do?" she whispered.

"I always did. Since the moment I met you. I just let my hang-ups get in my way."

"Not anymore?"

"No. Not if you'll still have me."

Charity smiled, happiness rushing through her for the first time in weeks. "I'll consider it."

"Oh yeah?" She could hear the smile in his voice, and her stomach fluttered. "What's going to tip the scales in my favor?"

"How fast can you get here?"

"How fast can you get down to the lobby?" he asked.

"What?" Charity sat up with a start. "You flew all the way here? How did you know where I was staying?"

"I asked Kara."

"What if I wouldn't talk to you?"

"I'd have camped down here until you did."

"Stalker," she teased.

"No. I'm just a guy who knows when he messed up and I'll do whatever it takes to make it right."

"You weren't the only one who made mistakes. I shouldn't have pushed you. We weren't dating long—"

"Charity, can we save the apologies and recriminations until I see you face-to-face?"

"I'm in room 545."

"I'll be there in a minute."

"I'll be waiting."

Only the minute they ended the call, she didn't wait. She rushed out the door and stood by the elevator, watching each round floor number light up as the elevator climbed at a snail's pace. The door finally opened to reveal Will hanging on to a small suitcase and a bouquet of flowers.

"Happy Valentine's Day," he said, his blue eyes sparkling.

Charity threw herself inside and into his arms. He dropped the suitcase and flowers to catch her, kissing her soundly.

"You're really here."

"I really am."

"We could have talked when I got back."

"This isn't something that could wait."

"The fact that you missed me?" she said, smiling, her fingers teasing the back of his neck.

Will reached back and held her hands against his skin, his eyes boring into hers. "The fact that I love you."

Charity's heart beat faster. "You do?"

"Yeah, I do."

A lump rose into her throat. "I love you, too."

Will grinned, his eyes twinkling. "I had a feeling."

"Oh yeah? You getting cocky?"

"No. I figured you wouldn't see a future with a guy you didn't have strong feelings for."

"You're probably right."

The doors opened as a family of four got onto the elevator with them, the parents giving Will and Charity disapproving looks while the youngest child whispered loudly, "Mom, that lady dropped her flowers."

Charity released Will and squatted down to retrieve them, taking Will's hand to pull herself back up. He leaned over, breathing softly into her ear. "Should we take this reconciliation back to your room?"

"I think that's an excellent idea."

CHAPTER THIRTY-NINE

Almond Hisscotti

Dip this long biscuit into your coffee and enjoy.

Charity took a deep breath as she made her way back onto the studio stage for the final taping, her nerves raw and ragged. It was down to her and Dayton, and the smug smile on his bearded face made Charity want to throw a metal mixing bowl at him.

Unfortunately, the judges might frown upon physical violence, no matter how repugnant a human being he may be.

They'd already done the preshow trash talk and commentary, and then after they finished the competition, they would have postshow commentary to film. Charity couldn't wait until all was said and done and she could go back to the hotel room with Will. Whether she won or lost, at least the man she loved supported her.

Charity took her place at her station and continued to take

deep, even breaths as the director called out, "And we're rolling in three, two, one..."

The host's jovial voice rang out like a merry melody. "Good evening and welcome back to *Bake That*! Tonight is the grand finale, and we're down to just two very talented bakers. Dayton, are you ready?"

"I was born ready, Gregory. I've got this in the bag."

"Big talk from our bearded baker. Charity? What say you?"

"I'm going to let my food do the talking for me," she said, smiling brightly.

"Then let's get to it. Your theme for tonight's final round will be *sentimental*. Think about a recipe that brought you joy as a child, or something your significant other makes you for your birthday. Like every other round, gather everything you need. And start!"

Charity raced over to the pantry shelves and grabbed a basket, filling it with everything she needed. When Dayton pressed his elbow into her side painfully, she ignored him.

"Hurry up."

She shot him a withering look, refusing to play his game. She was not going to come off as a petty Betty on TV, no matter how hard he pushed her. She'd gotten this far based on her talent and skill in the kitchen, so she wasn't going to be provoked by an ill-mannered little boy who happened to be able to grow facial hair.

Charity got her ingredients together and looked out at the audience for Will. He was a few rows back from the front of the stage, smiling proudly and nodding his head, as if silently telling her that she's got this. Having him at the hotel when she got done filming was a reward after the grueling hours and hostile competitors. Today, they'd opened the finale to a live audience, and she'd managed to get him in. Before she'd left him at the audience entrance, he'd leaned over and told her how proud he was of her.

Charity straightened her shoulders and went to work cracking eggs into her pan one after the other, whisking furiously with her eyes on the clock. She'd come too far, and while second prize wouldn't be a bad thing under normal circumstances, after all the hell he had put her through, there was no way she was letting Dayton win.

Charity finished loading all the dry ingredients into the mixer and flipped the switch, ready to pour the wet ingredients in, but nothing happened. The mixer was dead.

She looked under the table where the cord should have been plugged in, but it had been cut. She glanced over at Dayton to confirm her suspicions and caught the glee in his expression.

Fury shot through her, but what could she do? If she called attention to his sabotage, that would just create more drama for the show's audience, or worse, what if they didn't believe Dayton had sabotaged her? Thought that she'd cut the cord herself to create controversy?

Fighting against the urge to call him out, she grabbed a hand mixer off the shelf and beat her batter furiously, her arm muscles aching from the vibration of the device.

She overheard the judges and host questioning why she wasn't using her standing mixer but tuned out everything except pouring a quarter of her cake batter into a smaller bowl and dyeing the contents red.

The drone of the conversations around her and the ticking of the clock played like elevator music in the background as she worked. She finished frosting the cake with five minutes left to plate her dessert and have it ready to be presented to the judges. She drizzled strawberry syrup and a few candies over the dollop of homemade strawberry ice cream on all three plates, seconds before the timer went off.

"All right, back away from your plates so our servers can deliver them to our three celebrity judges."

Two young men went to Dayton's workstation first and picked up the plates, carrying them across the soundstage to a long table. In the first chair sat Bruce Callen, an award-winning chef from the Bay Area. Monique Kimani sat next to him, the most critical of the three professionals. And on the end was Yuki St. James, who'd been the winner of the very first season of *Bake That*.

"Dayton, please step into the circle," their host, Gregory Finn, called; although, after nearly two weeks, Dayton knew the drill.

"What have you prepared?" Yuki asked.

"I've made you my mother's famous German chocolate cake with a very special ingredient, and it's not love."

The judges took a bite, and Bruce chewed, his expression unreadable. When he swallowed, he waved his fork toward his plate. "I must tell you, coconut is not my favorite. The cake is dense and moist, but there is nothing special about the presentation. And to be honest, there is this aftertaste I can't quite place."

"I can," Monique said, wiping her mouth.

"What is it, Dayton?" Yuki asked.

"It's a dash of cinnamon."

Yuki made a face. "You put cinnamon in a German chocolate cake?"

"Yeah, that's the weird flavor I'm getting, but it doesn't taste like a dash," Monique said.

"I wouldn't say it's bad, because I have tried German chocolate with cinnamon," Bruce said, setting his fork down before he leaned forward, frowning, "but that was maybe an eighth of a teaspoon. It almost overwhelms the rest of the cake."

Charity watched the blood drain from Dayton's face, and based on the dropped jaws, he clearly shocked the judges when he took a step forward and picked up Bruce's fork, taking a bite of the cake. He frowned. "It tastes fantastic."

"Not to me," Monique said bluntly.

Before Dayton could argue, Bruce held up his hand. "You've done really well so far, but I think maybe, had you stuck with your mother's original recipe, this would've been a strong contender. Unfortunately, it's just not doing it for me."

Monique nodded. "It's a no for me, too. It's a shame because, up until this point, your plating and food have been superb."

"Unfortunately, I'm not a fan, either."

Charity listened to the judges' feedback with her heart in her throat. If they liked her cake, this could be it.

"You're excused, Dayton," the host said.

Dayton stomped to the back of the stage to give his reaction interview while Charity stepped into the circle in front of the judges. She waited anxiously for them to cleanse their palates as the servers placed her cake in front of them.

"Charity, what have you made for the judges today?"

"I've made a romantic twist on strawberry shortcake. You'll see in the center of your slice of cake is a perfect heart. When my brother asked my sister-in-law to marry him, our cook made this cake for him to give to her, and they've been together for seven years now."

"So, what you're saying is, if we want to fall in love, we should definitely eat this cake?" Yuki asked with a grin.

Bruce set his fork down. "I've been married four times. No thank you."

Monique gave his shoulder a bump. "Knock it off and try it."

All three judges took a bite, and Charity held her breath as they chewed slowly, time passing at a snail's pace until Bruce finally swallowed.

"Wow, that cake is buttery, melt-in-your-mouth perfection."

Charity released the breath she'd been holding until Monique chimed in. "While it's a little sweet for me, I agree that the tartness of the strawberry flavor and richness of the cake are a great blend."

Yuki held up both thumbs after taking another bite, making the other judges, the audience, and Charity laugh.

"Charity," Gregory asked, "why don't you step into the back and let the judges talk among themselves?"

Charity left the main stage, narrowly missing running into Dayton as he stormed past her to the greenroom. When she finished her interview, she was relieved that they didn't have to wait long before they called them both out to hear the results.

Monique was the first to speak. "You both had a stellar run during this competition, but unfortunately, there can only be one *Bake That* champion." She turned her gaze to Dayton. "Dayton, even if you hadn't bombed your final dessert, you would have been disqualified."

"What? But why?"

Gregory held up the cut cord of Charity's mixer. "You sabotaged Charity to give yourself an unfair advantage."

"And for that, you're not all that. You're"—the judges sounded off in unison—"done here!"

Dayton went into a tirade, cursing and screaming at the judges and Charity until security hauled him off the stage. When it was just the five of them left on stage, Bruce said, "Charity, you have shown a strength of character few practice in real life, let alone on reality TV. Because of that and your incredible talent, you are the newest *Bake That* champion."

Charity cried happily as the host presented her with a check and turned her toward the audience, who had climbed to their feet to cheer. Her gaze immediately went to Will, who was being escorted to the stage, but then more movement caught her eye and she saw her parents and siblings standing farther back, clapping and cheering.

When Will reached her side, she sobbed, "Did you do that?"

He followed the direction she was waving to and shrugged. "They wanted to be here, and your producer thought it would add dramatic effect."

Charity laughed. "Of course she did."

"I'm so proud of you." He pulled her in and kissed the side of her head. "You feel up to enjoying a little celebratory dinner with your family after this?"

A few weeks ago, Charity would have dreaded it, but after everything that had evolved and changed between all of them, she was ready to leave the past where it belonged.

"If you're with me, I'm up for anything."

CHAPTER FORTY

Meow and Furever Sweetheart Cake

This soft, sweet cake has a hole in the center for you to place a plastic heart, perfect for slipping in those small keepsakes that will make their heart sing. Have no fear, we'll cover the imperfection with our rich cream cheese frosting. We wouldn't want to ruin the surprise.

Will stood by Charity's side as they celebrated the grand opening of the low-cost clinic and café expansion. It had been six weeks since Charity won *Bake That*, and Will couldn't believe all that had changed in such a short amount of time. He'd officially started his new position when he got back from LA, and the arrangement seemed to be working out for Roy and Will, although Ben had been a little perturbed at losing Will as a partner. Every other day Ben seemed to gripe about his new partner, but no matter how much his friend pleaded with Will to change his mind, there was no way he was giving up his position. For the first time, his life seemed to be falling into place, and he was more than happy with the way things had turned out.

Did he still break into a cold sweat watching how fast the money for Charity's café and catering expansion flew out the door? Absolutely, but as she'd pointed out to him, she had a spreadsheet that showed how, even with all the equipment and vehicle work, she was still eight thousand dollars below budget.

Plus, she'd reiterated that it wasn't his money and he needed to chill out.

"What are you thinking about so hard?" she asked, squeezing his hand.

"How amazing this place looks." He leaned over and kissed her cheek. "You did good, babe."

Charity beamed up at him. "Thank you. Oh, there's Eddie! Wanna go say hi?"

"I'll be over in a minute. I'm going to check on my mom."

"All right," she said, heading across the room to greet Eddie, Meow and Furever's new coffee supplier. Will was still surprised he'd had the gumption to give Eddie an ultimatum, but it had all worked out in the end. Meow and Furever was thriving, and Eddie's coffee was being distributed in the Placer County area without needing to open a new storefront.

Will crossed the room to sit next to his mom at one of the small tables they'd set up for people to sit and try the delicious platters of food Charity and Marcela had prepared earlier in the day.

"How you feeling, Mom?"

"A little stiff, but I love watching Charity move around the room greeting everyone. She is definitely in her element."

Will followed her gaze to his smiling girlfriend and agreed. The closer the café expansion got to finishing, the more lighthearted and happy Charity became. All the stress that had been weighing on her seemed to lift, and he wanted to be a part of that for the rest of their lives.

"You look awfully serious, my son. Penny for your thoughts."

"Nothing, Mom. I was just thinking how, someday soon, I'm going to marry that woman."

His mom choked on a small sandwich, her eyes wide with surprise. "Does she know about this?"

"No, but when we get to that time, I don't think she'll object."

His mother beamed. "I should hope not. I've already got my heart set on her being my daughter-in-law, so don't do anything to mess up my plans."

Will chuckled. "I wouldn't dream of it, Mom."

"Wouldn't dream of what?" Charity asked, leaning over him and slipping her arms around his shoulders.

"Disappointing my mom."

"Ah, yes, that's probably wise." She squatted down in front of Anna. "How are you feeling?"

"A little sore. I think I'd like to head out soon."

"I've got to stay behind and clean up, but if you two want to go on ahead, it won't hurt my feelings."

"Charity, this is a huge accomplishment. You should be very proud."

"I am, Anna. Thank you."

"Are you sure you're okay with me leaving?" Will asked.

"Absolutely." She stood up and kissed him. "Will I see you after?"

"Yeah, just let me know when you are on your way home, and I'll head that direction."

"Sounds good." Charity gave his mom a gentle hug. "I'll see you tomorrow morning for brunch."

"Just promise me you won't let my son help anymore. He burnt the hash browns so badly that not even ketchup could save them."

"Hey, it's the thought that counts!"

"Not when we have to go out to eat because it's completely inedible."

Will scowled at his mom and transferred his dark look to Charity. "You should defend me."

"I can't do that. I want your mom to like me, and arguing with her about your culinary talents seems counterintuitive."

"Just for that, I'm bringing Bacon and Sausage with me tonight."

Charity gasped dramatically. "You would sic the little terrors on my defenseless tootsies?"

"Hey, if you didn't move them in the middle of the night, they wouldn't pounce."

"I'm going to give you a similar speech next time Robin Hood steals your unattended snack."

"Maybe we should get a hotel and get a good night of peaceful sleep."

Charity frowned. "And leave the kitties all alone? What kind of monster have I gotten involved with?"

Anna laughed, slipping her arm through Will's. "As delightful as this banter is, I would like to get home before my pain pill wears off. I am delighted for you, Charity. See you tomorrow."

"Get home safe."

Will led his mom out of the building and to his car. When they reached the passenger door of his car, she put a hand on his arm. "I have something for you."

Will opened her door, watching her rummage around in her purse. "Mom, if it's one of those peppermint candies that have been living at the bottom of your bag for thirty years, I'll pass."

"Don't be rude. Those candies stay good forever, like Twinkies."

"Whatever you say."

"Aha." She pulled out a small blue velvet box. "This is what I wanted you to have."

Will stared down at the ring box as she opened it and revealed a round-cut solitaire diamond ring. He waited for the familiar panic to claw up the back of his throat and shoot back down his spine, but instead, he calmly reached out and took the box from her. "Why are you giving this to me now?"

"Because when you are ready to take that step with Charity, I want you to be prepared. And based on the way you look at her, how happy she makes you, that time might be sooner than you think."

"Thanks, Mom."

"Do you think she'll like it?"

"I'm sure she'll love it."

CHAPTER FORTY-ONE

Purrfect Match Combo

Your choice of soup, salad, or half
a sandwich combo.
Any choice you make, you'll be
happy furever.
Or until the next time you're ready to order.

CHARITY PULLED UP TO the house almost two hours later, her feet aching with every step. One of the problems with being the other half of party hostess was the inevitable cleanup duty. Now all she wanted to do was take a hot shower and curl up with Will watching *Friends*. They'd started the series together three weeks ago when he told her he'd never seen it, and she'd been bound and determined to turn him into a superfan.

Will's car was already there, and when she opened the door, she expected to find Will kicking back on the couch watching TV, but the living room was empty.

"Will?"

"I'm in the kitchen!"

"You aren't cooking, are you?"

She heard his irritated huff. "Jeez, why can't the women in my life appreciate the efforts I make?"

Charity walked into the kitchen to find a trail of rose petals leading to the kitchen table, which was set with two mojitos and two plates of chicken Alfredo. Her silver dress from New Year's Eve was hanging off the side of the kitchen cabinet, and Will stood behind a chair in the suit he wore in Mexico.

"What's going on here?"

"I thought we could have a drink, unwind, and maybe dance a time or two?"

Charity arched a brow. "Babe? What's going on?"

"I organized a little do-over of our night in Mexico. I ordered the pasta from that Italian place you like, so if you want to go change, we can eat, drink, and be merry."

He waggled his brows and she laughed, unhooking the dress from the cabinet. "I was going to take a shower and see if you wanted to watch *Friends*, but this is so...cute, I can't say no. Plus, I probably owe you a do-over, especially of the morning after."

"Let's never speak of it again."

Charity took the gown and went into her room to change. When she came back into the kitchen, her heart started hammering when she saw Will on his knee and a velvet ring box resting on the palm of his hand.

She blinked at the box several times. Charity looked into Will's face, soft with tenderness, and swallowed hard. "I don't understand."

"Let me explain." Tears stung her eyes as he opened the box and revealed the gorgeous solitaire inside. "If I told you I wasn't terrified out of my gourd right now, that would be a lie. My hands are shaking, and I'm sweating out of every gland in my body."

Charity laughed. "Attractive."

"I know," he said with a cocky grin. "But I've found that I'm more terrified of waking up without you beside me. Of not being able to listen to you hum in the kitchen while you bake. Or missing out on the moment your voice gets unnaturally high when you see a cute cat or dog. I want all of you for the rest of my life. Will you marry me?"

"Yes," she whispered, her hands cupping his face, and then she was sliding to her knees in front of him. Her lips covered his, and the electricity that had always been between them surged, and he dropped the ring box to wrap his arms around her.

The ping of metal meeting something hard stalled his embrace, and Charity followed his gaze, watching in horror as the ring bounced across the floor and landed in front of Sausage. He stared down at the ring and then at them.

"Saucy..." Will growled. "Don't you dare—"

Out of nowhere, Bacon flew over his brother and landed on top of the ring, swatting it across the floor, and the chase was on. Charity and Will scrambled to get up off their knees as Sausage picked the ring up in his teeth and skittered out of the room.

"Don't let him choke on it!" Charity hollered behind Will

as they chased the gray tabby across the entryway and into the living room.

"If he swallows that ring, I'm buying a new one! I do not want to be digging through cat poop!"

"Why do you always make with the descriptive imagery?"

The ring dropped out of Sausage's mouth and rolled under the couch, both kittens pressing their noses beneath the gap. When Bacon tried reaching his paw in, Charity managed to scoop him up into her arms.

"No you don't, troublemaker."

Will got down on his hands and knees, pushing Sausage gently out of the way. When he came back up with the ring in his hand, he was disheveled and out of breath, and she'd never found him more attractive than in this moment.

"All right, let's try this again." He rose on one knee and held the ring out to her. "Do you want to put the cat down so I can put this on you?"

"Oh, yes," she said, dropping Bacon onto the couch and holding her hand out to him. "I'm ready."

Will slipped the ring onto her finger, keeping her hand in his. "I guess this means we're engaged."

"Getting cold feet yet?" she teased.

"No, you?"

"My only concern is our mothers battling to the death over who gets to throw us an engagement party."

"Do you think they can come to a compromise without bloodshed?"

Charity groaned. "My dad is going to insist on paying for the wedding."

"My mom's going to have strong opinions on the menu and who officiates."

"Should I convert to Judaism?" she asked.

He stilled, his gaze locked on hers. "Do you want to?"

"I want us to be happy."

Will wrapped his arms around her. "If you want to, I'd be incredibly happy."

Charity grinned. "Your mother would be ecstatic."

"You'd be her favorite daughter-in-law."

"I'd be her only daughter-in-law." She sighed, sinking into his embrace. "I worry that wedding planning is going to become one long, drawn-out ordeal filled with drama."

"Are you suggesting we skip a large wedding and go straight to the good part?"

Charity shook her head. "I would, but it would break your mom's heart."

"What if we did a small ceremony with just my mom and sister and your parents and siblings, with Ben and Kara being our best man and maid of honor? Then we host a party for all of our extended friends and family? Whoever wants to come can, but this is about us. Not anyone else."

"I'm in." She stood up on her tiptoes and kissed him before leaning back with a frown. "How are we going to have a honeymoon? We just expanded! I can't take time off."

"And I can't leave again anytime soon or Roy will fire me

for sure." He pressed his lips to her forehead. "Should we make plans over a few drinks and Italian food?"

Charity laughed. "I don't think drinking ever leads to good decision-making."

"I would argue with you there. Without mojitos, you might never have admitted your undying love for me."

"My undying—please! Maybe I had a tiny attraction to you—"

"I think we can both admit it was a big attraction," he said, grinning wolfishly.

Charity pushed him back onto the couch and straddled his lap. "I don't need to drink to tell you how happy I am because of how much I love you."

She kissed him, letting him roll her onto the couch, his strong arms caging her in from above. "I love you, too."

"Wanna watch *Friends* and cuddle?"

His jaw dropped. "We just got engaged, and instead of celebrating, you want to watch TV?"

"I want to watch TV with you. There is a distinction."

Will flopped onto his side, and she took that as a yes. "Old married couple, we are. Might as well skip the wedding."

"You tell your mother, and I'll tell mine."

"Deal."

Royce Simmons,
Iris Wilkinson, and Anna Schwartz
request the pleasure of your company
at the marriage of their children,
Charity Anne Simmons
and
William Martin Schwartz

SATURDAY, AUGUST 21 AT 5:30 P.M.

In lieu of a registry, the couple asks that you
donate to Meow and Furever Cat Café
and support the feeding and well-being of
homeless kitties in the Roseville area.

Dinner and dancing
to follow the ceremony.
Please RSVP by June 24.

Acknowledgments

So many fantastic people went into the making of this book, but first and foremost, thank you to my amazing husband and two wonderful children for giving me the time and space I needed to finish *Finding Mr. Purrfect*. I don't know what I would do without you!

To my awesome agent, Sarah, for believing in me and working so hard behind the scenes every day. I appreciate you.

To the team at Forever, especially my editor, Alex, who was so patient every step of the way. Thank you for all you did to make this book shine.

To my parents and extended family and friends, who buy and share my books and feed my need for words of affirmation, I love you.

Special thanks to affoGATO Cat Café in Cleveland, Ohio, for their adorable menu items. I stumbled across their café while googling feline-word foods and fell in love with their café! Thank you to the owners, Mandy, Eddie, and Lea, for being so kind to this weird author from Idaho and allowing me to use some of their creations in this book!

Erica, my dear friend, thank you for reading this book and for all your insights. They were truly invaluable, and I treasure you.

My sister from another mister, Tina, who is always there for me, even when her zoo is going crazy. I love you.

To my friend Stephanie, for making me smile.

A special shout-out to @BDylanHollis for your amazingly funny baking videos and the nasty and delicious recipes you share. The three-ingredient peanut butter cookies were a blessing and a curse while writing this book.

For readers, who are constantly tagging me in funny videos, telling others about my books, and helping me share all my news, thank you so much for your support. I know you are all busy, and it is an honor to have you as part of my team.

I need to thank my TikTok family of amazing authors, bloggers, and fantastic creators, who entertain and inspire me every day. Love you!

For my talented and enthusiastic Bookstagrammers, who have shown me so much love and kindness, thank you for sharing my books.

About the Author

Author photo © BG

Codi Gary is the author of thirty-two contemporary and paranormal romance titles, including bestselling books *Things Good Girls Don't Do* and *Hot Winter Nights* under the name Codi Gary and the laugh-out-loud Mistletoe series under the pen name Codi Hall. She loves writing about flawed characters finding their happily-ever-afters, because everyone, even imperfect people, deserves an HEA.

A Northern California native, she, her husband, and their two children now live in southern Idaho where she enjoys kayaking, unpredictable weather, and spending time with her family, including her array of adorable fur babies. When she isn't glued to her computer making characters smooch, you can find her posting sunsets and pet pics on Instagram, making incredibly cringy videos for TikTok, reading the next book on her never-ending TBR list, or knitting away while rewatching *Supernatural* for the thousandth time! Wanna get to know her better? You can learn more at:

codigarysbooks.com
Twitter @CodiGary
Facebook.com/CodiGarysBooks
Instagram @AuthorCodiHallGary